MARKHAM THORPE

Giles Waterfield

headline
review

First published in 2006 by
HEADLINE REVIEW
An imprint of HEADLINE PUBLISHING GROUP

First published in paperback in 2007 by
HEADLINE REVIEW
An imprint of HEADLINE PUBLISHING GROUP

1

Cataloguing in Publication Data is available from the British Library

ISBN 978 0 7553 2970 0

Typeset in Perpetua by Palimpsest Book Production Limited,
Grangemouth, Stirlingshire

Printed and bound in Great Britain by
Clays Ltd, St Ives plc

Headline's policy is to use papers that are natural, renewable and recyclable
products and made from wood grown in sustainable forests. The logging
and manufacturing processes are expected to conform to the
environmental regulations of the country of origin.

HEADLINE PUBLISHING GROUP
A division of Hachette Livre UK Ltd
338 Euston Road
London NW1 3BH

www.reviewbooks.co.uk
www.hodderheadline.com

For Peter

I am grateful to Charlotte Gere and Pamela Sambrook for their masterly advice on social history; Henrietta Bredin, Ann Cleverly, Julia Crittall, Anne French, James Le Fanu, Jane Mee, Jane Ramsden, Christopher Ridgway, Karen Snowden, Mark Studer, Martin Watts and Alicia Weisberg-Roberts for much information and help; my inestimable agent Felicity Rubinstein and her colleague Sarah Lutyens; and at Headline, Hazel Orme, Leah Woodburn, Richard Green and above all my perceptive and inspiring editor Charlotte Mendelson.

Part One

'That is the gate,' he said. 'Beyond that gate is your new home, my dear.'

Ellen refused to be afraid. This was the back drive, she could tell. There was no lodge here, just a gate propped open and not quite straight, leading to what was little better than a track. She wondered if the gate was closed at night. After all, there was a long brick wall stretching round the park, they had been following it for at least a mile – it was surely meant to keep people out. Perhaps it kept people inside, too. What if she wanted to leave, once she was part of this place? Would she be locked inside and forced to stay?

'Inside'. It sounded like a workhouse. Or a prison. Not that this place looked like a prison, with the oaks standing proudly on either side of the drive and the cow parsley in full flower and the cows munching in the fields. Still, would she be able to escape? She'd been told there would hardly ever be a chance to leave the place, once she was in service.

She must have trembled. Her father, who was driving the cart, turned to her and said, 'Nearly there now.' He went on: 'There's nothing to be afraid of, my girl, your sister is here, and our cousin Mrs Rundell will take care of you. And it's a great house, this is, one of the best in Yorkshire, not so much large as ancient. The Markhams have been here since 1538 when they were given the land by the King, old Henry VIII that was. It belonged to an abbey, you know.' Her father was extremely interested in history and was a leading figure in the Literary and Philosophical Society in Malton. Though he made his living, more or less, as an apothecary, what he liked to do was to read, and read he would, night and day. Her mother would look at him and shake her head, knowing how much work he had to finish, and how badly the business was doing, but she knew she could not stop him reading.

No use thinking about home in Malton, forty miles and a day's drive away. Ellen swallowed hard. She would not be seeing her family for a while, and even then, not very often. She would be allowed home only once a year, she believed. She could hardly go there and back all in one day, what with Father having to collect her. She would not see her mother and her father and her little brothers and sisters for a long time, much longer than she cared to think. Probably they would forget her. She would write to them, of course, she had the paper all ready in her trunk.

A tear trickled down her cheek. And then another. She knew she must not cry, her father would hate it so, and she did not want the servants at the big house to think she was a little girl who burst into tears when she left home. After all, she was an adult now. The horse stopped, and she felt her father's hand on her shoulder. 'Now then, lass,' he said. 'You give your father a proper kiss, since in a minute we shall not be on our own.' He took her in his arms, held her closely and kissed her, almost solemnly. He touched her cheek with the back of his hand, gentle, loving man that he was, and said, 'Always my favourite child, and I hate to lose you, Ellen, but it's not really loss, we'll be seeing each other soon enough.' As though talking to himself, he went on, 'We'd not choose to send our children into service, but things being as they are and with five daughters, what are we to do? And, Ellen, we're not far away and if you feel lonely you just think of your mother and me and remember that we'll be thinking of you just as fondly as you do of us. And you have your sister here to keep you company.'

They turned a corner in the drive and there was the house. Ellen was disappointed. She'd thought the house would be like Castle Howard, but it was not. This house was not at all impressive, at least not the back of the building, which was what they must be looking at, so grey and rough-looking and irregular. As they came closer she could see that the windows were all different, large and small, some sashed but mostly with black diamond patterns in them. It was a very tall house, four floors at least, and there were attic windows as well – she supposed her room would be up there. Great black drainpipes ran up the height of the building, making it even uglier. Would she like living here? No, she thought she could never be happy here. She could feel the tears rising again.

Her father noticed – he never missed such things. 'None of that,' he said. 'No more puling, my girl, you're a grown-up person now. Sit up straight and let them see you're as good as your sister Agnes. She never cried when I brought her here. She was as calm as Queen Elizabeth herself on one of her progresses.'

Ellen sat up straight at once. In any case, as the cart rolled nearer to her new life, she felt both nervousness and anticipation. She certainly did not want to seem less grown-up than her sister. Agnes was the eldest girl and three years older than she was, and had already been in service for three years at Markham Thorpe. She would come home from time to time. During her visits she made it clear that she found her parents' house excessively small, and the way they lived excessively plain. She had started as a junior housemaid, but now she was a very important person (or so she said), and was lady's maid to Miss Emily Markham. Miss Emily gave her a great many clothes, which she liked to sport when she returned to Malton. Very pretty they were, and gave her quite an air of fashion. Their mother had never seen such clothes on anyone she knew, and loved to examine and caress them, glancing at Agnes now and again as though awed but still not quite sure that her daughter should be dressed so richly. When Agnes walked through the market-place at Malton, as she chose to do several times each day, a great many heads were turned. Not least her own, her mother would say. Agnes treated Ellen with kindly condescension, and told her a good deal about life at the big house and how last year the family went to London for the Season. Next year, Agnes would be going too. 'And I dare say you will accompany the family as well, one of these days,' she had remarked, on her last visit home, 'that is, if a suitable position can be found for you.'

Ellen was not altogether pleased at the thought of seeing her sister Agnes again. They might have to share a room, and then she'd have to listen to Agnes prattling away, largely about herself. Agnes had always regarded herself as the best, and now that she could dress herself like a dressmaker's dummy she evidently considered herself a most remarkable person. Soon she would forget her father was an apothecary, and possibly the least successful of the four in Malton — and that her mother had been in service herself as a young girl. At the thought of how hoity-toity Agnes could be, Ellen straightened her straw bonnet and pulled crossly at the ribbon under her chin, as a warrior might tighten his stirrups before battle.

'It will be good to see Agnes,' said her father. 'And I hope we shall be given some tea before I set off home. It's a warm day, it certainly is, and after sitting in the sun all these hours . . .'

As the cart approached the house, the door opened. Out came Agnes, smoothing her dress. She looked more ladylike than ever, Ellen thought, and had done something complicated to her hair. Evidently at work she wore a plain black dress, but even workaday clothes had an elegant air on her, with their close fit and the tiny white apron. She was smiling genteelly. Well, at least it was a smile: Agnes could be very unfriendly when she was in the temper for it. When she saw them she exerted herself so far as to wave, raising her right arm in the air and twiddling her fingers in a refined manner.

'Well, here you are at last,' she said, as they approached, and then immediately, 'what a comic old cart that is, Papa.' This was most annoying, Ellen thought, and typical of her sister to be so patronising and to say 'Papa', which they never did in the family.

'It's very good to see you, Aggie,' said her father, 'looking so well and prosperous. And it is good of you to greet us the moment we arrive.' He had a way of imputing kind motives to people, which made them appear better than they really were. 'I have a precious cargo today.'

'Precious enough, I suppose. Welcome, my dear,' said Agnes, to her sister. She said this rather as a duchess might greet her younger sister, or so Ellen imagined from the novels about high society she read with such enthusiasm. They gave each other a tentative handshake, and then Agnes said, 'Ah, we can do better than that,' and kissed her quite warmly. Ellen felt that perhaps her sister was not so disagreeable after all, particularly when Agnes went on, 'You will be tired after your journey and we have some tea for you in Mrs Rundell's room, and if you would like to stay the night, Papa, Mrs Rundell has a bed for you.'

'I should be going home,' he said. 'I'm expected home, your mother would be alarmed if I did not return . . .'

'Well, just as you please, if you want to be driving the cart through the night,' Agnes interrupted briskly. 'The room is there if you want it. It's the steward's room, we have no steward just at present — Mrs Rundell deals with most of that work.' And to her sister, 'Don't you be troubling yourself with your trunk, Ellen. Jem will bring it in for you, Jem is always ready to be helpful. At least, when I ask him, he is.' Simpering a little, she raised her voice as they walked towards the house, and cried his name, as though he were bound to be in earshot. 'The family are all away at the moment,' she went on. 'Sir Richard is in London dealing with business affairs and enjoying the Season, and Mr James is in London too, and Miss Emily is also visiting her friends down south.' She looked at her father archly as she said this — clearly the remark meant more than appeared. 'Normally I would be with Miss Emily, but in view of your arrival, she said she didn't need me for a few days. Very thoughtful she is.' Ellen wanted to ask how old Miss Emily was but was too nervous to open her mouth. Agnes led them through the open door into a hall which was so dark that, coming from the bright day, Ellen could hardly see. This hall smelt of polish and leather and vegetables. Agnes turned towards them with another of her elegant gestures and said, 'Welcome to Markham Thorpe. Don't suppose, Ellen, it's always as quiet as it is today. This is the back hall and it's the way we always come into the house, we never ever use the front door, it's always this way for the servants. Will you come upstairs, then, to see Mrs Rundell? She doesn't like to be kept waiting.' The back hall had a flagged stone floor and pale earth-coloured walls, which had not been painted for many years, with odd little windows high up. There was a row of pegs covered with coats and shawls, and four or five dark brown doors, all closed.

'And my trunk, will it be all right?' asked Ellen, nervously.

'Yes, yes, Jem will deal with that. You have a room to yourself. It used to be mine, a nice room it is too. The household is less big than it used to be, so there's space enough. If you are ever frightened on a winter's night – and, my goodness, the wind does whistle round the house – you can move in with me. Will you leave your coat, Papa?' she said. 'And take off that shawl of yours, Ellen. Wherever did you get it? How very quaint it is. Put them on that table, why don't you? You can consider yourselves quite at home.'

And she led them with firm step to the room of Mrs Rundell.

The way to Mrs Rundell was complicated. Mr Braithwaite and Ellen, deferential and silent (though Ellen was smarting over the remark about the shawl, a very nice one in her view until that moment, though now she found herself despising it), followed Agnes. 'The kitchen's that way,' she said, 'and the servants' hall there. You'll soon come to know it all. Mrs Rundell has a room quite a way away, up with the family really,' and as she said this she seemed to smile. 'The old housekeeper's room was down that passage but as Mrs R pointed out to Sir Richard it looked on to the back court and was dark and she didn't see why she had to spend her time in the twilight staring at drainpipes when there are so many fine rooms empty. So Sir Richard gave her a much more pleasant room. It looks out on the garden it does . . .' They had gone up some stairs and down another passage, also painted brown with stains here and there, and rush matting on the wooden floor.

When Agnes pushed open a swinging door, they seemed to be in a different house. Not that the passage was expensively furnished, but it was lit by a window at the end with a view over fields, and the walls were a beautiful pale colour. Ellen could not find a name for it: she had never seen such a colour. The prints hanging on the walls showed hunting scenes, and a strip of red carpet stretched beneath their feet. 'This is the still room, on the right,' said Agnes, and Ellen had a glimpse of a light, pretty room lined with shelves full of jars and bottles and cups and saucers. 'That's Lucy's department, we don't go in there very much at all. Mrs R's bedroom is over there, and here we are and expected.' As she paused at the door and raised her hand to knock, she gave them a quick glance, as though to check that they were looking presentable. 'You're both a little travel stained,' she said, as though to herself. 'Still, that's to be expected and will be excused.' And she knocked.

The housekeeper's room was a large one, and struck you as light and well furnished, but when you went in, it was not the room you were aware of. It was the occupant. Mrs Rundell sat at a round table in the middle of the room, and seemed to fill the space. Her eyes were bright and sparkling, and bulged a little, her face was as pale as the finest lady's, and her strong black eyebrows under her handsome forehead were surmounted by a white cap. Her black hair, gleaming so that it almost reflected the light, was plaited on each side of her head, thick curling plaits, so you wondered how she would look if her hair were released and tumbled round her shoulders. She had a commanding air; only her mouth, small and pretty and surprisingly red, seemed feminine. She must be quite old, Ellen thought, at least forty, but she did not seem old, she was so full of energy. She wore a full-cut shiny black dress with a white collar, but it looked to be made of expensive material, rich and glossy. From her waist hung a metal chain with a bunch of keys at the end, which she was playing with as they came in. Every so often her hand returned to these keys. Mrs Rundell was the pink of prosperity.

As her guests (Is that we what are? Am I a guest, coming into service as I am? Ellen wondered) came into the room, Mrs Rundell remained seated. She surveyed them all, just long enough to make it clear what she was doing.

'Cousin Braithwaite,' she said, in a deep rich voice, but very ladylike, Ellen thought, 'I am glad to see you. We are so pleased with your Agnes, she looks after her duties in a most satisfactory manner. And now you are bringing us another girl. I hope she will be as sensible as her sister. Did you have a pleasant journey?' she enquired graciously, as though the Braithwaites were calling on her in their carriage. 'And so this is Ellen?' Ellen wondered whether she should curtsy or nod, and did both in an embarrassed way. 'Do sit down, Cousin, and let me give you some tea. Lucy.' For the first time Ellen noticed a person standing in the background, a woman rather older than herself, dressed in dark green with a white apron. 'Lucy, see to the kettle, and here is the key for the tea caddies.' She looked Ellen up and down once again, and smiled, but somehow not as though she were including Ellen in the smile. 'Good. You have a sweet daughter, Cousin Braithwaite, though of course that will not be any advantage to her here, not at all. Smaller than Agnes, I see. Even allowing for the difference in age, she's a small child. Strong, I hope, we can only have strong girls here. No vapours, no fainting fits?'

As she spoke she took the tea caddies from Lucy. One was a plain black one but the other was very handsome, Ellen noticed, while trying not to feel hurt: it was decorated with black and gold panels, with a little figure of a Chinaman on the top. Mrs Rundell spooned a generous amount of tea into a large pot from one of the caddies and an almost equally large amount into another pot from the other.

'Oh, yes,' said her father. 'She's a grand girl, she can do anything. Of course, she's young but growing all the time.' And he shot a look at his daughter to apologise for speaking about her like this.

'Good,' said Mrs Rundell. 'Her hands will be needed. Everything she learns here will be useful to her in later life, to whatever station she may be called. You may sit down, dear,' she said to Ellen, 'and you too, of course,' with a glance at Agnes. 'But this is the last time you will be seated in my room, young Ellen, cousins though we are.'

'I have something for you,' said Mr Braithwaite, 'very modest but we hope you will like it. We remembered that you are very partial to tea,' and he presented her with the package that he had been discussing anxiously with his wife for several weeks. It was a pound of the finest China tea from China, from the best tea merchant in Hull, and considerably more expensive than any tea they bought for themselves.

'Thank you,' said Mrs Rundell, as though paid her proper dues. 'May I unwrap it?'

'Oh, yes, I hope you will, so that I can tell Mrs Braithwaite whether you are pleased,' he answered nervously.

Mrs Rundell settled herself yet more firmly at the table and unwrapped the parcel. She paused to inspect the shop label, and nodded. The paper was unfolded scrupulously, and placed on one side as though for future use. When she came to the tea itself she looked at the packet label, and said, 'Ah, my favourite, how did you know? Nobody else likes it. It is one of my exotic tastes so I am afraid I drink it on my own. Hence the two pots.' She lifted the packet as though to weigh it, and smiled graciously at her cousin.

Ellen found her father's behaviour surprising. It was as though he were fascinated by Mrs Rundell, somehow in her debt and afraid of not pleasing her. She had observed this once before when Mrs Rundell had visited them in Malton and had spent an hour closeted with her parents, just before it had been decided that Ellen would go into service at Markham Thorpe, but then she had only seen the lady for a few moments.

'We are very pleased to have Ellen with us,' remarked Mrs Rundell. 'I have no doubt that, being your daughter, she reads and writes very well. She will be quite unusual in this household, where we have some ignorant people who can hardly read a word.'

She nodded at Lucy with 'Fetch the tea-things, would you? Cousin Braithwaite, how is your dear wife, and the dear children? I remember them fondly. I hope to be able to assist them all one of these days. I suppose you had dinner on the way, but I thought some of our modest Markham Thorpe victuals would not go amiss.' Ellen, who had not eaten all day, having been too nervous to have any breakfast or eat anything from the little parcel her mother had made, felt hunger returning. The maid laid on the table a china dish piled high with scones and another with very thin white bread and butter, a glass pot filled with fruit preserve, a fruit cake, and another big white cake decorated with pink icing and candied fruit.

'Yes,' her father was saying, 'a very good pupil she's always been. I've taught her myself, and now she is the best scholar in the family . . . She's almost fit to go out as a governess.'

'Lord, you are ambitious, Cousin Braithwaite,' said Mrs Rundell, handing out plates. Such plates they were, with gold edges and dark blue borders decorated with golden garlands and the purest white in the middle. She gave one to everybody except Lucy. 'Governess, indeed! Well, she will have to rise a long way to achieve that. We have a sort of a governess here, by the name of Fisher, left over from when the children were young, more a stranded fish than a fisher. Sir Richard was too kind to tell her to leave, she's lived here for so long. Poor creature, nobody would employ her now. But she likes to let us know she is a lady. Very proper spoken she is, Miss Fisher. We are always made aware of how learned she is.' She rolled her eyes and rubbed her breast with her large white ringed hand. 'So you're well educated, are you, dear? However educated you are, you'll be paid the same as any maid starting here: seven pounds a year, with a pound a year tea-money.' She inserted a piece of scone piled with cream and jam into her mouth, and chewed pleasurably. 'Though, of course, you may be promoted, one way or another. Why, even Agnes started at the bottom.'

'Yes,' said Agnes demurely, 'but not for long.'

'No, Miss Emily took a fancy to her and when she needed her own maid there was no question who it should be. Nearly the same age, they are. Miss Em is only one year older than Agnes, and now, of course, we've just heard she's going to be married . . .'

'And to whom is she to be married?' Mr Braithwaite asked, swallowing a large piece of scone.

'Mr William Dykes, the heir to Sir Francis Dykes, you know, a very good Yorkshire family. They have an estate near Bridlington, but also they have other properties in the south and they are in London for the Season, naturally. That is where Miss Emily met Mr Dykes last year, when she was coming out.' Her voice assumed a reverential quality. 'They met at a great ball in Piccadilly, you know. Love at first sight, they say . . . And it is such a good thing he comes from a good Yorkshire family.' She favoured them all with a benevolent smile, as though generally pleased with life and its effect on the Markham family and herself.

'Of course,' Mrs Rundell went on, 'things will change, I suppose, now that we have the main-line railway from London to York. Why, people are able to reach York from the capital in only five hours. Just imagine how many strangers we shall have in this country, when people become used to travelling on the railway. It is quite an alarming conception, is it not? Why, Miss Emily thinks nothing of going to London for a week or so.'

Mr Braithwaite was not interested in the railways. 'Will our Agnes be travelling with her mistress? That is, will she go away with Miss Emily when she marries?'

'That is to be seen. It depends, of course, on Miss Emily's wishes. She may seek a trained lady's maid, possibly from France. French maids are very much in favour with the fashionable.'

Ellen stole a glance at her sister. Agnes was sitting upright, flushed, her lips pursed.

Mr Braithwaite tried to enquire about the history of the house but Mrs Rundell always turned the talk back to the family. The household was considerably smaller, she said, than when she had come to Markham Thorpe nine years before, after Lady Markham's death. There was Mr Fellows, the old butler, who valeted for Sir Richard, and Jem the footman, who answered the doorbell and helped Mr James with his clothes and served at table and polished the furniture, and Billy, a young boy who dealt with the lamps and did the odd jobs. Below Mrs Rundell the most important woman servant was Mrs Saunders, the cook. She had been with the family for ten years, 'a good plain cook, you understand, her Yorkshire puddings are crediting, and she can do a roast quite nicely, but French cuisine is not something she holds with. Miss Emily is always eager to try new dishes she has tasted in big houses but Mrs Saunders will have none of it . . .' Then there was Lucy, and the housemaids, and two laundry-maids from the village who came in by the day.

Mrs Rundell brushed a few crumbs from her third piece of cake off her skirt on to the carpet. It was not she who would be sweeping the carpet, clearly. 'The first housemaid, Katherine, does very well considering her physical weaknesses, and then there is

Beth, and then young Ellen here. Low in the pecking order, I'm afraid, Ellen, but we must all start at the bottom, must we not? Even the Quality have their own pecking order in the county.'

'And where do the Markhams come in the county pecking order?' asked Mr Braithwaite, curiously.

Mrs Rundell looked reflective, and coughed. Then she spoke ponderously, as though conducting a party of visitors round the house. 'The Markhams of Markham Thorpe have enjoyed the baronetcy since 1621 and have been seated here since that date. Lord and Lady Carlisle may possess more acres, but nobody in the three kingdoms is prouder or more respected than a Yorkshire baronet.' She rolled her eyes and raised her nose, like a hunting dog sniffing the morning air. 'More tea, Cousin Braithwaite? I think I will have a drop myself. Can I offer you a little comfort in your tea?' she asked, lifting a glass flask from the table. 'I am sure it will do you good.' She poured a little something into his cup and rather more into her own. 'As for the outside establishment,' she went on, 'there we are well provided for. Six gardeners under Mr Hurst, four men in the stables, and the gamekeepers under Mr Andrews. They live out, of course.'

Mr Braithwaite looked impressed. 'Why are there so few men working in the house?' he wanted to know.

'Sir Richard does not like them. He thinks butlers steal the wine. And he considers footmen a nuisance, always making a noise and . . .' Here she whispered into Mr Braithwaite's ear, glancing at Ellen. 'I make sure Jem is busy. Sir Richard has permitted Mr Fellows to stay, even though he is well past seventy. He's very attached to Mr Fellows, is Sir Richard. They've known each other ever since Mr Fellows came here as a young man and worked for

Sir Richard's father. He helped to bring Sir Richard up, I have heard. Very loyal Mr Fellows is, you know.' And she chuckled. 'Mr Fellows can still manage occasions, as long as I'm there to keep him steady, though I have presumed most of his duties.' She stroked her black silk front. 'I help him with the wines, I have a key to the silver safe, and Mr Fellows is grateful. He spends most of his time in his cottage.' She looked out of the window for a moment, proprietorially. 'A woman can supervise a household as well as a man, Cousin.'

She was becoming more confiding as each minute passed, until Agnes sneezed. This seemed to change Mrs Rundell's mood. She moved imposingly in her chair, the light playing patterns over the silk of her dress. 'A little more cake?' she asked her cousin. 'No?' More cake was not offered to the girls. 'Then may I invite you on a tour of the house?'

'I should be delighted,' he said.

Mrs Rundell rang a silver bell. Lucy reappeared. 'Clear the table, Lucy,' said the housekeeper. 'The fruit cake was good, the sponge a little dry.'

'Thank you,' said Lucy, casting down her eyes. The woman seemed to have no character, and waited on Mrs Rundell like a devoted personal servant.

'The tea caddies,' said Mrs Rundell, locking up the little boxes. Lucy locked them in a cupboard, returning the key to Mrs Rundell.

'Will you take my arm, Cousin Braithwaite, down the great stairs?' Turning to the sisters, she went on, 'Agnes, show Ellen everything, will you?' When Mr Braithwaite looked dismayed and asked if he would not be able to say goodbye to his daughters, she said, 'Of course you may. We will ring for the girls when we are ready.' And down the corridor she sailed, her head high, her cap straightened with a few deft gestures, her skirts following her obediently.

The three women were left in the housekeeper's room. 'You've not met Lucy,' said Agnes, as though it were a matter of indifference.

'I'm very glad to meet you,' said Ellen, putting out her hand.

Lucy looked at the hand doubtfully, as one might inspect the last piece of meat on a market stall, and took it briefly and feebly. Then she raised her eyes to the new maid and lifted the corners of her mouth. 'Welcome to Markham Thorpe,' she said. 'Some folks like it, and some don't. Well, I must get on. There's no time here for chattering, not if you work for Mrs Rundell. She likes things done properly, and quite right too.'

'You must tell me more about the family, and her ladyship,' said Ellen.

'You'll soon learn what there is to be learnt, if you are attentive. We're very quiet here,' and Lucy shot a glance at Agnes, who raised her eyebrows. 'And we shall be even more so, with Miss Emily leaving us. What life will be like with just the two gentlemen in the house, I don't know. I'm sorry if the sponge was a trifle dry, but at least you managed to eat a good deal of it.'

'It wasn't dry at all,' said Ellen, trying to be pleasant.

Lucy smiled coolly. 'Well, that's all right, then. Don't imagine that I will be serving you again, young Ellen.' She looked at the girl with an unfriendly air, as though suspicious of her. Ellen could not imagine why.

'No,' replied Ellen, 'I'm sure you won't.'

'In fact,' Lucy went on, 'one of your duties is to wait on the upper servants.'

'I'm afraid, my dear,' said her sister, 'you will have to get used to me being an upper servant while you are not. That means I take dessert here with Mrs Rundell, while you stay in the servants' hall. You'll grow accustomed to it. And perhaps you'll be promoted too.'

'No doubt you will,' said Lucy, 'you being one of Mrs Rundell's family,' and she leant over the ravaged table. She cut a slice of cake and ate it thoughtfully.

'In some families, you know,' said Agnes, 'a lower housemaid never speaks to a lady's maid, even if they are related – it is not thought proper. But the Markhams are more easy-going and I can talk to you as much as I wish, though in public we need to be correct, you understand?' Ellen nodded dumbly. 'When you speak to me with anybody else present, you call me Miss Braithwaite. Do you understand?'

'Yes, Agnes.'

'No, not "Yes, Agnes" but "Yes, Miss Braithwaite". Don't forget. I'll take you to your room.'

As they walked down the passage with the prints towards the swinging door, Ellen was remarking, 'Now, tell me, Agnes, do, who is that Lucy . . .' when her sister put her finger to her lips.

Only when they had passed through the door did Agnes say, 'No chattering in the passage, Ellen. It's not permitted, and what is more, it's not wise. Walls have ears, and in this house especially.'

Once in the back hall, Agnes whispered in Ellen's ear, 'Keep on the right side of our cousin, whatever you do, but never mention your cousinhood. If she chooses to remember you're her family she will.' She looked at Ellen appraisingly. 'You did well just now. Remember, it is Mrs Rundell carries the keys of the house. Do you follow me?'

'I suppose so,' said Ellen, but she was remembering that she still had to say goodbye to her father.

Agnes tapped her sharply on the elbow. 'There's no time for crying,' she said. 'I'll show you your room. Bring your little bag there. Jem will have taken your trunk upstairs. Usually Jem and the other men never go up the maids' stairs, and the outdoor men even less.' They set off up a small staircase. Long ago this staircase must have been painted light brown; now it was a dark sludge colour. 'These are the stairs to the women's bedrooms. The men's bedrooms are a long way off. There's no reason for you to know where.'

'Really not?' asked Ellen, who was so used to her little brothers and sisters tumbling all over each other that she could not see the need for such secrecy.

'You'll know where they are, soon enough, but there's no call for you to go up to them. If you ever do, it's trouble. The men and the maids meet downstairs and that's it.'

They reached the top of the second flight of stairs and turned into a long, carpetless passage. It was lit by not very clean windows looking out on to a roof with a glimpse of trees beyond. The walls were painted dark brown with a border of dark green below. Facing the windows was a row of closed doors.

The fourth door was Ellen's. 'Here is your room,' said Agnes, throwing open the door. Ellen's spirits rose. It was quite a large room, with a paper of little pink roses on what had once been a white background. She liked her new abode at once. It was a nice room and the first of her own she'd ever had. The bed was covered with a coloured counterpane and on the other side of the room stood a large chest of drawers. There were three chairs, and a washstand with a jug and basin decorated with flowers, and a round table with carved legs, old like all the other things but well made. On the table was a little vase of roses. Her trunk was waiting for her beside the door.

'I hope you like it,' said Agnes. 'It is one of the best maids' rooms, I made sure you had it. There are so many empty rooms at the moment that we can choose, and we don't have to share, as the maids do in many houses. Mrs Rundell is very kind. It's too good a room for the third housemaid, really.'

'Roses!' said Ellen. 'Roses in my room, how did that come to be? I never expected roses.'

'I remembered you liked them,' said Agnes. 'The gardeners will give you flowers if you want them, as long as it's nothing too special. You just have to make yourself pleasant to them, but not too pleasant, mind.'

'You're very good to me, Agnes,' said Ellen.

'I know you will be feeling strange,' replied her sister, 'but you have no reason to be lonely. You'll soon feel quite at home.'

Ellen was hardly listening. 'It is such a pretty room,' she said. 'And such fine furniture too.'

'Most of this furniture was in Miss Emily's room till lately,' said Agnes. 'But when Miss Emily left the schoolroom, she asked her papa if she could have some smart new furniture and he said yes, as he always does to her, so the old stuff came upstairs. Do you like it? I would rather have something light and pretty, myself, like Miss Emily.' She looked thoughtful. 'Well, one day I may. Or, rather, one day I firmly intend to.'

'What do you mean, Agnes?' asked Ellen, startled by Agnes's confidence. 'How will you get light and pretty furniture like Miss Emily's?'

'I may be a servant now,' said her sister, 'but I don't mean to be one for long. There's no need to stay a servant if you don't choose to. And I don't. Lady's maid is the first step up the ladder, and not the ladder to housekeeper.' And she tossed her head unsmilingly. 'I hope you've brought all the clothes we said you'd need? By the by, hanging in the closet are two work dresses of mine you'll find useful. I no longer require such things. Unpack your bags, and I'll take you downstairs.'

Downstairs in a little while they went. Ellen had not unpacked, merely stared out of the window and looked into the drawers of the chest. She wondered who had slept in the room before and whether they'd been happy. She liked the view on to the flat lead roof and the chimney stacks with a glimpse of the lawn beyond. She could climb out easily, though no doubt that was forbidden.

At the bottom of the stairs her father was waiting for her, with Mrs Rundell beside him. 'Ah, there they are,' she said. 'So, I bid you farewell, Cousin Braithwaite. Give my best wishes to Mrs Braithwaite, and here is something you may enjoy on winter evenings,' and she handed him a parcel. She gathered up her skirts and disappeared.

'Goodbye, Papa,' said Agnes, briskly. 'I will write and give you the news. I'll be over to visit soon. Give my love to Mamma and the children.'

23

Ellen had no words. All she felt able to do was cry. She tried not to, and made a choking noise.

'Why don't you go outside to say goodbye?' suggested her sister. 'Be quick, it's less painful that way,' and she pushed them out of the door.

Once outside neither could say anything. They kissed hurriedly. Mr Braithwaite climbed into his cart and set off down the drive. Ellen worried he would not be home until it was completely dark. She waved after him until the cart turned the bend. She felt quite alone in this place she did not understand, which seemed to be full of difficulties and even dangers that she did not understand, either.

When, reluctantly, she went inside, her sister was waiting. 'There,' said Agnes, 'not so bad, was it? Next time it will be much easier. Now, come into the kitchen and meet everybody.'

Hours and hours later, as it seemed to her, Ellen lay on her new bed and thought about the day. Was she going to be happy here? Should she even expect to be happy? Was this a happy house? She had no answers. What she did know was that she liked her attic. She'd opened her window, and although at first the heat from the leads seemed to have invaded the room, as the night became cooler and a breeze arose a smell of flowers and freshly cut grass stole into the heavy atmosphere. For a moment, tired but unwilling to go to bed, she lay naked on her bed. This would never do at home, in the room she shared with her little sister. But at Markham Thorpe she felt a free person, an adult, who would not be told what to do, at least by her mother. In the last glimmer of twilight she looked down at her body and ran her hands over her bosom and on to her hips, something she had never done before. She was ready to frown as usual at her tiny breasts and meagre form, but in the pale light she thought that she was filling out.

I'm becoming a woman, she thought, and laughed.

During the evening she had met crowds of people. The first person she was presented to was the cook. Mrs Saunders came from Whitby, quite some way away. She was old, too, about thirty-five, and quite stout, and fair, with pink cheeks that glowed in the heat of the kitchen, and dressed all in white. She had blue eyes, which pierced you, and a giggle, which burst forth more often than you might expect, and when she was not busy she would be looking about the kitchen table and at the shelves of the dresser, and now and then would seize a bit of food and push it into her mouth, then chat away again. Mrs Saunders who was talking when Agnes led Ellen into the kitchen stopped as soon as she saw the sisters. She glanced at them with her head on one side, and said, 'Oh, Miss Agnes, and how are we today? And is this your sister? And what are we to call her?'

'My name is Ellen, please, madam,' said Ellen, at which Mrs Saunders and the other people in the kitchen burst into laughter, Ellen had no idea why. She was not sure about Mrs Saunders, who seemed ready not to like her. Cheerful but spiteful, Mrs Saunders appeared to be. Indeed, the house seemed to be full of people who were suspicious of her, she could not understand why.

After a moment Mrs Saunders nodded, to say it was time they left the kitchen. There was a little girl running around, but Mrs Saunders did not introduce her.

The servants' hall was a long, tall room with windows so high you could hardly see out of them and on the wall a painted sign saying, 'Waste Not, Want Not'. Two maids were sitting there, and a young boy. Katherine, the head housemaid, hardly looked at Ellen but told her to be in the back hall at six the next morning. She seemed tired and serious and wore her hair scraped back from her forehead in a bun. She walked with a limp. The second housemaid, Beth, was not much more than her own age and, for a change, looked quite pleased to meet Ellen. The boy, Billy, simply gaped at her – he was so small she wanted to give him a hug as though he were one of her little brothers. After a while there was a bustle outside and the door was pushed open and in came a large young man in outdoor clothes. 'Good evening, girls,' he said, in a jolly manner. 'Last day of the holidays so let's enjoy it, sing a serenade to Mrs Rundell, shall we?' And seeing Ellen, he went on, 'And who would this bonny person be?'

'None of that,' said Agnes. 'This is my sister Ellen, and mind you be respectful to her. Ellen, this is Jem.'

'Delighted, I'm sure,' said the young man, 'and mind you be respectful to me too, Ellen, since I'm a very important person, am I not, Miss Agnes? And how do you like Markham Thorpe, Ellen?' He smiled at her cheerfully.

Ellen felt rather better. 'I like it very well, thank you, sir,' she said.

'Jem, not "sir",' he answered. 'And what's a girl like you doing in a servants' hall in Yorkshire, when you could have the whole world at your feet?'

'Ellen is learning to be a housemaid, starting at six tomorrow morning, that's what's she's doing,' said Agnes, severely. And then more people came into the servants' hall, and introduced themselves to Ellen, and on the table appeared plates of cold meat and cheese and bread and pickles, and Ellen sat in a blur while they talked over and above her, and wished she was at home.

'Will you come and see the garden?' Beth said to Ellen later, when they had been dismissed from the kitchen. 'When the family's not here we can walk wherever we like. It's ever so beautiful. You haven't seen it, have you?'

Out of the back door they went, into the courtyard. Beth pointed out the offices: brewery, laundry, game larder, coal house. At the end stood a shrubbery, high and thick – 'so that the family can't see the back court,' she explained, 'but actually they're in and out of here all the time, on their way to the stables.' Round the shrubbery they walked, on to a narrow gravel path with a high wall on the other side. 'You'd like to see the walled garden, wouldn't you? It's locked evenings but I know where the key is and no one will mind if we walk there. Come with me,' and she led Ellen to an iron gate in the wall, decorated with scrolls and a coat of arms. Under a pot was the key, which opened the door to Paradise. In front of them and to either side stretched paths of hard black tiles with trellises above and roses growing over them, and flower borders on either side. 'This is the cutting garden,' explained Beth, 'for flowers for the house, though they don't have flowers indoors much when the young ladies are not here. Sir Richard and Mr James don't trouble themselves with flowers. Mrs Rundell likes them, though, she has flowers every day now. Her ladyship used to come here almost every morning in summer and she'd decide what the head gardener should send up. Some head gardeners make difficulties, you know, but ours loved to gratify her ladyship. They would talk together about the garden, for hours on end.' She paused, gazing at the flowerbed, looking for a moment like somebody much older than herself. 'Over there's the vegetable garden. They grow all the vegetables for the house and the estate here, we never buy anything in. There are peaches and apricots – you can see the netting to keep the birds away.'

'How do you know the garden so well?' asked Ellen. 'You can't have been here long.'

'Oh, yes, I have,' said Beth, 'I've always lived here. It's my home. My dad is the head gardener, Mr Hurst. He lives in that brick house.'

'Is he indeed?' asked Ellen. 'That must be so nice, living next to your family. Don't you want to go and see them now?'

Beth hesitated. 'No, not just now. They'll be so busy, with Sir Richard coming home so soon.'

'And if they live so close, why don't you stay at home?'

'Oh, the house is awfully small,' said Beth. 'Why would I want to be sharing a room with two of my sisters, and helping my mother with the housework, when I could be living in my own room in the big house? Come, I'll show you the pond. My father is a champion gardener, you know, his flowers are the best in the West Riding, and when he exhibits at the Great Northern Show it's a very bad year if he doesn't win at least six Gold Medals. Come!' and she pulled Ellen by the hand.

'Will I meet your father?' asked Ellen, charmed by the gardener's house, with its brightly shining panes and window-boxes, and the low box hedge in front.

'Yes, you will. It must be like coming home for you, coming

to this house where you have your sister and your aunt.' She spoke carefully. Ellen felt that she was being tested, even though she did not know what the test was.

'My aunt? Oh, Mrs Rundell is not my aunt. She's my father's first cousin. I don't think that makes her an aunt.'

'We thought she was your aunt. But you must be very fond of her. I expect you've known her all your life.'

'No,' said Ellen, 'I hardly know her. She's been to visit us in Malton two or three times, but not lately. I was just a child when she last came. I've hardly spoken to her before today. She used to say she didn't like children overmuch, so we kept out of her way.'

'Was there ever a Mr Rundell?' Beth wanted to know. 'We've never liked to ask Agnes. She doesn't care to talk about Mrs Rundell, I don't know why.'

'Oh, I don't think so, she's just called Mrs because she's so important, isn't she?'

Beth smiled. 'That's what I thought. But you must be so pleased to see her now,' she said. Her questions were oddly persistent, it seemed to Ellen, as though she felt suspicious.

'No, not so very much, I've only met her once or twice before. She is so very imposing and grand, like a queen almost.'

'Oh,' said Beth, as though satisfied, 'I see.' They arrived at a round pond at one end of the garden. Two curved benches faced one another across the water, and the flowerbeds were filled with stocks and wallflowers, snapdragons and sweet peas. 'We call this Lady Markham's Pond,' said Beth. 'Her ladyship used to love sitting here. She taught me to read here, when I was a little girl, along with Miss Emily. She was a lovely lady, she was indeed, so kind.

29

In the morning you would hear her singing as she walked. If she saw me playing she'd open her arms and I would run right into them. It was as though I was her own child. Shall we sit down?' They sat on the low parapet beside the pond, and trailed their hands in the water. Beth was silent, and Ellen saw there were tears in her eyes. 'Since she died Sir Richard never comes here, he can't bear it. But I come as often as I can, and my father looks after the flowers for her memory's sake. They're all flowers she chose, you know.' There was hardly a sound in the garden, only the wood-pigeons from the great trees outside the wall. 'It's a lovely smell, isn't it? That's the tobacco plants. Her ladyship used to plant them – she loved their scent in the evening.'

'And do you all miss her?' asked Ellen.

'Oh, yes, we do. Terrible it was when she died. Sir Richard hardly spoke for a year or two.'

'Did he never want to marry again, Sir Richard, when his lady died?'

'Well,' said Beth, and laughed, 'to be sure he could have married as easy as anything – the widow ladies of Yorkshire were all over the place, trying to cheer him up. And not just widow ladies either, young ones too, with their mothers making sure the girls made themselves as pleasant as could be. But, no, he was never interested in any of them, not one bit, or so I've been told.'

'I suppose he'll never remarry now.'

Beth shot a glance at Ellen. 'No, I suppose not. Anyway, why should you be asking that? You won't be having dreams, will you? Many a girl thinks she might marry into the Quality, but it never happens. The Markhams are proud of their ancestry, and they're hard headed too, good Yorkshire folk. They'd never lower their standards. At least, I don't think so . . .' She looked thoughtfully at the ground.

'I suppose,' said Ellen. 'I've read so many stories about the gentry that I see their lives like a beautiful romance.'

'It's no fairy story when you're sweeping out the fireplaces at dawn, I can tell you.' She looked sharply at Ellen. 'If anyone ought to be getting themselves married, it's Mr James. Though I'm not sure quite who he'd choose to marry, or who'd choose to marry him, either.'

'Is he not a good man, Mr James, then?'

'A good man, Mr James?' Beth turned down the corners of her mouth. 'He changed, Mr James, when his mother died. There was trouble then, soon after she died, but there's no reason to tell you that story. You'll see him, in a while, and you can judge for yourself.' She looked at Ellen severely for a moment. 'Just mind you keep an eye on him. I won't say more than that.'

Ellen considered all this, with surprise. Markham Thorpe seemed to her a perfect place, at least the part where the family lived; she could not imagine its inhabitants not being perfect too. 'Isn't this a happy house?' she asked.

'You mean for the family? Well, I don't know that I'd say that. It used to be, but . . . I suppose Sir Richard is cheerful enough nowadays. As for Mr James, there's no saying what goes on in his mind. Miss Emily finds life here very slow since she did the London Season last summer. She hardly comes here any more.' She stirred the water of the pond. 'We used to be such friends, Miss Emily and I, when we were little girls. We played together all day – not in the house, of course, I didn't have the clothes, but in the garden. But when she became older, you know, she could only play with other young ladies. I was only the gardener's daughter, though we're still friends, I like to think. We each have our own level, that's what we're born to, and if you try to change your level it can be dangerous . . .'

It was warm and sheltering in the walled garden, as though the day's sun were trapped in the brick walls.

'I thought perhaps I would be her maid, you know, when she came out, but no, they chose – well, they chose your sister. Mrs Rundell said Agnes knew more about clothes than I did, she would be better suited to the position.' She looked sad for a moment. 'Well, you're more ladylike than I am, you and your sister. I'm just a country girl, I can't expect too much.'

Ellen was very embarrassed. 'I'm sorry,' she said. 'Would you have liked that position?'

'I would have liked to work for Miss Emily but I don't think I would have liked travelling around all the time. Now it's all changed and there are things to keep me here, one way or another. I'll tell you one of these days,' and she smiled. 'The birds will be going to bed. And we shall have to be going to bed soon ourselves. The back door is locked at ten and after that you have to ring the bell, and Mrs Rundell knows. Or you get Jem to let you in, if you can find him, that's not usually too difficult.'

'He seems such a nice man.'

Beth laughed. 'Oh, yes, indeed he is a nice man, but don't you go being too charmed by his smiles. He smiles at all the girls, and who knows? He may have a sweetheart of his own. Yes, he'd let us in, but Mrs Rundell keeps a good look-out. Now and again she inspects our rooms to make sure we're all where we ought

to be of an evening. Very strict, is Mrs Rundell. Usually, that is.'
She giggled. 'We'll go indoors, shall we?'

Ellen found it hard to go to bed. She wandered round her
room, unpacked her trunk, and stood at the window gazing out
at the leads. And when she did go to bed, she could not sleep,
so crowded was her mind. In the silence that settled upon the
house, she heard the stable clock chime midnight and the half-
hour and one o'clock, and still she could not sleep. Agnes had
knocked on her door and sat on her bed and talked about the
Markhams (everyone here seemed to talk about them constantly)
and how it was forbidden for the maids to carry on with the
menservants. 'Anyway,' she said, 'don't you be tempted. You can
do a great deal better for yourself than one of the stable lads
here, if you'll only be a bit patient.'

In the morning Ellen was woken by a tap on her door. It was still
very early – half past five, she saw from her clock – but at least
it was light outside. Waking up at half past five was earlier than
she was used to, or liked. She had to be in the back hall at six,
ready (she'd been told) to work and work and work. She forced
herself out of bed, found the new print dress and the apron she
had never worn before, washed her face (it looked pale and wan)
in last night's water, tied her shoes, reluctantly put on her white
cap, and hurried down the stairs as the stable clock chimed. At
the bottom of the stairs stood Katherine and Beth.

'Good morning,' said Katherine, not unkindly.

'Good morning,' mumbled Ellen.

'I'll take you round the family side,' said Katherine. 'This is a
good moment, there's no one here. If you meet a member of the

family in the passage, stand close to the wall and keep your eyes on the ground as you curtsy. In some houses you have to face the wall, and in a few houses I've heard of, you are dismissed if the family sees you at all, but not here.'

The house was quiet, and chilly, and shadowy. The early-morning sun could hardly penetrate the thick velvet curtains and muslin hangings, and the walls were mostly covered with dark panelling and wallpaper with large floral patterns. They went round rapidly. 'This is the Great Hall,' said Katherine. 'You can come in by that door or by the little door over there. As you see, there's a huge grate – it's such a difficulty to clean it, the outside men clear it out after a big party. We don't have a fire here often. It's very cold in the winter: you have to travel across the room as fast as you can. We clean the Great Hall once a week or so, no more, nobody stays here very much except in summer.' They entered a large light room in the corner of the house, the walls covered with lilac silk. 'This is the drawing room, where the family receive. It was all redone by her ladyship, as a young bride, it's never been changed. Nor will it ever be changed, not by Sir Richard.' It's a beautiful room, Ellen thought, clasping her hands in excitement. Katherine was pragmatic. 'It has to be kept swept and polished, though you will not be polishing, it's Jem and Billy who do that work downstairs. The same applies to the picture frames. Don't ever touch them, you need training for that. This room is tidied and dusted every morning when the family are here, or after a visitor has been, and then we tidy it again when the family go in to dinner. Sir Richard doesn't use the room if he's here on his own, that is to say only with his son, not since her ladyship died. She would keep the peace between them. The two gentlemen do not care to be in the same room, you know. They never have been friends, not since Mr James was a little boy, his father never could abide him.' She looked around at the flat surfaces as she spoke, as though in pursuit of a rogue fluff of dust. 'Make sure, if you move anything, you put it back exactly where it was. Everything must be kept in its exact place, as though we'd never come in. Put a hand behind a piece of furniture when you move it back against the wall. You never touch the writing table, that is looked after by Mr Fellows, the butler. There's a housemaid's closet here, in the passage.' On down the passage they went, and into another room with bookcases on each wall, filled with books, mostly in brown leather bindings, that looked as though they were never read. 'This is the library, it's not used much by the family. The governess comes here sometimes, I believe. More books than you could possibly want. I don't see the use of them at all.'

Back across the Great Hall, into another very large room. She could not understand why her father had described the house as not very large. 'Here is the dining room. This is used for all the meals except tea.' She sighed. 'The dining room has to be done every day. It means a deal of cleaning.' Out into the passage, with swords and animals' heads hanging on the walls, and along, and then down to another door. Ellen did not care for the next room, which was gloomy with only one window, and the walls painted dark red and paintings of horses and dogs and an old Turkey carpet. There was a huge table in the middle covered with a mass of papers all higgledy-piggledy, and a general air of disorder, and a smell of tobacco and alcohol and leather. 'This is the smoking room, and Mr James is often here, alone or sometimes with his friends. It's a room for the men. Don't look at the books or the pictures or anything you might find lying about – there's stuff here not suitable for a young girl's eyes. And if you are ever working in here and Mr James comes in, then you curtsy and leave the room. You should not be alone in a room with a young gentleman. It is permissible for me, but not for a young girl like yourself, and particularly such a pretty and innocent young girl.' She avoided looking at Ellen as she said this. 'That's all there is on the ground floor. Do you follow me?'

'Yes,' said Ellen. She was consumed with curiosity about not being in the same room as Mr James – on the whole she rather liked the idea – and about the books and the pictures she was not supposed to look at and she wondered whether she would be able to restrain her curiosity when she was working alone in the room. On the whole she thought she would not succeed.

'Upstairs now,' said Katherine, and then to Beth, who had been following them about, 'there's no need for you to stay. See the library and the drawing room are in order. And the dining room, of course.'

'Yes, Katherine,' said Beth, and disappeared.

The other two set off up the massive black staircase, with its carved beast holding a shield on the lowest post, and rows of dark family portraits in shabby frames that must once have been gold. Katherine continued her commentary: 'The stairs have to be dusted every day, and polished once a week. That's the only time you ever go up or down them, do you understand? Though Mrs Rundell uses them all the time, and the other upper servants, sometimes.'

'Aren't you an upper servant, Katherine?' asked Ellen.

Katherine raised her eyebrows. 'Yes,' she said, 'yes, I am now that I am head housemaid. I take my pudding with Mrs Rundell and Mr Fellows, and Agnes, of course, for what that's worth.' They were standing in a broad passage, hung with portraits and pictures of landscapes, with settees and chairs lining the walls, that stretched along the middle of the first floor. It was shabby but comfortable, Ellen thought. 'Now, you must see the bedrooms. This door leads to the master bedroom, the Blue Bedroom. When her ladyship was taken Sir Richard moved into the dressing room next door. The Blue Bedroom is locked, we never go in there. Next to it is the boudoir. That was her ladyship's sitting room, that's never used either.' She opened a door on the other side of the passage. 'This is the Pink Bedroom, Miss Lavinia's, she sleeps here when she visits. The family don't like change.' They walked along the passage, Katherine opening doors from time to time, into shadowy bedrooms with the blinds drawn and dustsheets over the furniture. 'The Chinese Room. King Charles the First's room – King Charles stayed here during those wars he had to fight. That's Miss Emily's bedroom, and her sitting room next to it. Mr James's bedroom is down the passage and through that door at the end, away from the rest of the house.' She sniffed. 'In that direction, through the blue door, are the apartments of Mrs Rundell, her sitting room, which you've already had the privilege of seeing, as I understand it, and her bedroom. The still room is off to the left, where Lucy is to be found. The main back stairs come up into the passage down here, so Mrs Rundell can see what is going on in the house. Do you understand?'

'Yes,' said Ellen. What was there to understand, except that there were a great many bedrooms?

'Up the back stairs you'll find another floor. That's where the nurseries are, and Miss Fisher's rooms, and a few more bedrooms.' She looked at Ellen sceptically. 'I suppose you know how to clean a room properly? Your sister certainly did, though she never stopped complaining, but fortunately for her she was not a housemaid for long. You come from a good house, I would say. Follow me,' and they went into Sir Richard's room. 'This room is ready, the bed was aired yesterday. I want you to sweep the carpet and dust the surfaces, that's all. Do you know how to sweep a carpet?' Ellen nodded, as though surprised. 'There's little to do since they've been away. I'll be back in a while to see how you're getting on. Then there will be breakfast. No noise on the family's side, mind, no singing or talking, even when they are away, and no clattering of brooms and pans. You're not here to be heard or seen, you are here to work.'

Alone in Sir Richard's room, she felt strange. It seemed odd to be admitted to the bedroom of such an important man, free to study him and his possessions and habits, even though she'd probably scarcely ever speak to him. It was quite a small room, with a single bed and a rug on the floor. You could see that it had once been very comfortable and even handsome, but it had a worn look now. The armchairs were tattered, and the carpet was rubbed where Sir Richard moved from his bed to the washstand and the wardrobe. Desk, two upright chairs, a trouser press, a few books. The wallpaper, which was decorated with oak leaves, was hung with some prints of people hunting.

Ellen could not resist a little inspection. How much the room could tell her! She picked out a row of little paintings above the mantelpiece. The central one, in a gold frame carved with roses, showed a beautiful young woman in a white dress, with brown ringlets, gazing at the viewer, her lips slightly parted. This must be Sir Richard's wife. Right and left hung miniature paintings of two little girls, pretty they were, elegant, in their white frocks. Then there was a portrait of a young man, and of Sir Richard and his wife together. She stared at them all, trying to make out their characters, till she recalled that soon Katherine would be back. She bustled round the room, dusting, tidying, plumping cushions. On future mornings, she knew, she would be carrying trays of tea upstairs, and lifting heavy coal scuttles (that was the worst job, her mother had told her, and the menservants almost never helped because it was not their job to carry coals, and if they did offer, you should be wary, never trust a friendly manservant), lighting fires, taking hot water to the rooms, removing chamber-pots, all the while pretending she did not exist. As her mother had told her, nobody was interested in a housemaid: she was a machine. Her mother had hated being in service, and hated sending her daughter into servitude, as she put it.

Once again Ellen felt a tremor. Was this work, this drudgery – that seemed the right word – all she was good for? What sort of a life would it be? How many years must she spend cleaning and polishing someone else's house? If her father's business were not almost failing, might she not now be learning how to teach in a school? Or working in a shop, at least?

Miss Emily's room looked south, on to the lawn, and even with the blinds down was full of light, and so fresh and new. The walls were adorned with a paper of pink roses on a trellis. The light wooden furniture was upholstered in pale pink satin, and the bed too was covered with pink satin, and a huge gilt mirror hung over the fireplace and the carpet, too, was decorated with roses. Ellen had never seen anything so charming in all her life. It was like a box filled with flowers. On the walls were paintings, done in watercolour, she supposed. Perhaps Miss Emily had done them herself, they were signed 'E. M.'. Ellen was so enchanted, she could hardly bring herself to work. She let herself imagine that one day she, too, might live in such a room. For a moment she stroked the soft pink silk that covered the little armchairs on either side of the fireplace, and dreamt that one day she would sit on such chairs in a room of her own, which would be quite as pretty as this one – though she did not dare to sit down in one of the chairs now.

She was bending over to fetch out an awkward bit of fluff and humming quietly, when she heard a voice. It was Katherine.

'Are you done?' she asked.

'I've tried my best,' said Ellen.

'Yes,' said Katherine, looking about her with a professional eye, 'I can see you've tried. You have much to learn, but I can see you've tried. It's time for breakfast.'

At breakfast the main subject of talk was Sir Richard's return. That, and the visit of Mr Dykes a few days later. Apart from Agnes (who nodded distantly at Ellen, as though she hardly knew her), none of them had even seen him. With Mrs Rundell absent, the atmosphere was easy. The men came and went, the maids chatted. Though Sir Richard had been away only a month they seemed pleased he was coming back. Having the family at home seemed to give the servants a proper reason for being there themselves. 'It's nice when the family are away, it's quiet, you can take your time a little,' Beth had said to Ellen, 'but it can be dull.' All morning, as Ellen swept the stairs and polished the brass knocker on the front door and brushed the rug in the Great Hall, she was aware of urgent activity all around her. Mrs Rundell appeared at ten o'clock, laced up and severe. She greeted Katherine with 'Is everything in order, Katherine?' to which Katherine replied, 'As you see, Mrs Rundell.' Mrs Rundell subjected Ellen to a brief unsmiling inspection before saying to Katherine, 'Has the new girl been instructed how to conduct herself in the presence of the family?'

'Yes, Mrs Rundell. I am sure she will know how to behave,' Katherine answered. She emphasised the word 'she' in a curious way.

The Great Hall and the drawing room, the dining room and Sir Richard's bedroom gleamed with cleanliness. The head gardener had arranged flowers in all the rooms, and the newspapers were laid out in the library. Upstairs, Sir Richard's laundry had been put away in his chest of drawers and his boots polished. A sense of welcome reigned throughout the house. Mrs Rundell passed from room to room, examining each surface, each corner, not sparing a speck of dust or shadow of cobweb. At the sight of anything wrong, she would flick her fingers at Katherine and point to the annoyance. While the fault was being righted Mrs Rundell, confident her orders would be carried out impeccably, would turn away and look out for further omissions. At the end of her tour of the ground floor she nodded at Katherine, remarked, 'I hope there is nothing to be done in the bedrooms,' and advanced upstairs. Katherine followed, with Beth behind her.

During the morning Ellen encountered two further members

of the household. As she was dusting the Great Hall, in hurried a small elderly man in a black jacket with striped trousers, peering around him busily. She looked up timidly, not sure whether to stand. He greeted her. 'Ah, Ellen, is it? The new girl, Mrs Rundell's niece? Yes, good, I hope you'll be happy here, yes, no, don't get up, no need at all, glad to see you are so much at home already, oh, I'm Mr Fellows by the way, won't be in your way too much, ha ha ha, Mrs Rundell is the one who will tell you what to do, by the way have you seen her? Oh, upstairs is she? Good good good,' and with a little pecking smile in her direction off he went up the main stairs.

The next meeting was less amiable. Ellen was crossing the Great Hall when she saw a lady advancing slowly down the stairs, holding a little dog. The lady wore a pale grey dress and her abundant black hair was pinned into place with long metal pins under a very small black cap, and her face was white with a protuberant nose, which was slightly pink at the tip. A white rose was pinned to her bosom. She looked at Ellen and yet did not look at Ellen and patted her dog, and when she reached the bottom of the stairs she put it on to the ground and said, 'Go, Diogenes, go, walkies,' and again looked through Ellen, who was still attempting a curtsy to this mysterious person, and walked across the Great Hall and out of the front door, with her dog, which, like her, was black and white and twitchy, in front of her.

At twelve the servants assembled in the servants' hall. They had been told to change into their best clothes and brush their hair, ready to salute Sir Richard. Ellen, sent upstairs to wash her face and change into a clean dress, was so tired she could hardly reach the top floor, but when she saw the others she noticed that her sister was attired in an elegant pale grey dress. After a rapid inspection by the housekeeper and butler they walked in two orderly lines, with Mrs Rundell and Mr Fellows at the head, through the house and out of the front door ('You can go out of this door on special occasions like this,' whispered Beth to Ellen, 'but you can't come in this way, not ever.'). Once on the gravel in front of the house, they formed into a line.

Punctually, a carriage trotted up the drive, wheeled smartly round the circular lawn, where the fountain was now playing, and stopped with the front wheels precisely on a line with the front door. The footman jumped off the box and opened the carriage door, and out stepped Sir Richard.

The master of the household was very old, about sixty. He had a solid red face – that was the first thing Ellen noticed – and a thick neck and broad shoulders. Though not tall he was big and strong-looking. He wore a dark grey coat, like the solicitor in Malton, but more expensive. She could not make out his face very well against the sun, but she saw dark heavy eyebrows and a large nose. All the servants bowed or curtsied.

Sir Richard smiled and gripped the butler warmly by the hand. 'Afternoon, very good to see you again,' he said. Mr Fellows beamed. The baronet moved easily on down the line and paused again. 'Afternoon, Mrs Rundell. It's nice to be home. All well? Any new faces, Mrs R?'

'Ellen Braithwaite, Sir Richard,' said Mrs Rundell.

'Ah, yes,' he said, 'Agnes's little sister, is that right?' And he looked at Ellen. She was confused, and not being sure what to do, she curtsied again. 'Hmm, very good, very good,' he said. 'Charming niece you have, Mrs R.' And to Ellen, 'Well, I hope you will be happy. You're very welcome here.' He laughed. 'We shall soon have the house entirely filled with your family, Mrs Rundell.'

Being too eminent to notice the collective behaviour of his household, Sir Richard was unaware that this remark occasioned a rustling, coughing and stiffening of shoulders among the servants. He was advancing towards the front door, where the lady Ellen had seen that morning was waiting to greet him. She did not curtsy, but held out her hand, while her little dog yapped at his ankles.

'Miss Fisher,' he said genially, 'and how are we? Keeping the schoolroom in order, I hope?' Into the house he went, followed at two or three paces by the grey lady, and then by Mr Fellows and Mrs Rundell. The others proceeded round the side of the building to the servants' hall.

'Who was that lady?' Ellen asked Beth. 'I saw her in the hall this morning, but she wouldn't speak to me.'

'Oh, that's Miss Fisher, the governess,' answered Beth. 'She's been here for years and years, taught all the children, you know. Taught me to read, too – it was her ladyship's idea. Don't you mind if she doesn't say anything to you at first, she's quite harmless. She just has her ways.'

Walking in two straight lines at first, once out of view the servants straggled into little groups, chattering in the bright sunshine. Ellen, silent and feeling as if she was gasping for air, sat down in the servants' hall and waited for the next instructions. They were still only half-way through the day, and she was so tired, yet this was supposed to be an easy day. What a hard one might be like she couldn't imagine. She wished she was at home, something she had not felt for at least five hours.

What was next, was dinner. After a moment there was a good deal of noise outside and in came five or six men, mostly young. 'They're the gardeners, the ones who aren't married. They're taking their meals here just for the time being because Mrs Hurst who usually looks after them is expecting,' whispered Agnes in Ellen's ear. They all came up to Ellen and shook her hand and said their names. She had never seen so many young men altogether in one room — outside church, at least. She found it rather pleasant.

The clock struck six. At this signal everybody in the room divided. The men went to one side of the long table, which stretched the length of the hall, the women to the other. Each clearly had an appointed place. Agnes sat close to the top end of the women's side near the window, but Ellen was told to sit at the lower end of the table. Beth was on one side of her, an empty place on the other. Jem established himself at one end of the table, Ellen's end, with a serious air. The other end of the table was empty. Conversation flickered out. They waited. After a moment, the door opened. Mrs Rundell came into the room, looked around at everyone with a slow, comprehensive stare, and advanced majestically into the silence. She took up her position at the far end of the table from Jem. Then she raised her head and looked in his direction, though not exactly at Jem himself. He cleared his throat, and said loudly, in a rather fine voice, 'For what we are about to receive may the Lord make us truly thankful.' Upon which they sat down. Then the door opened again for Mrs Saunders, bearing a large tureen and followed by the little kitchenmaid.

Ellen was used to dull meals at home. Food was not a thing

for enjoyment in her family, it was a necessary routine, and her mother just managed on the modest weekly allowance from her husband, sometimes hardly enough for her to feed the family. At Markham Thorpe, judging by the rich, exotic smell from the tureen and the general look of anticipation, food appeared to be a pleasure. As Mrs Rundell ladled out the soup, everyone stared.

'What have we here, Mrs Saunders?' asked Jem. 'One of your experiments?'

'Mulligatawny soup, Jem,' replied Mrs Saunders. 'Curry soup, from India.'

'I've never heard of it,' said Jem.

'Miss Emily asked for it in particular, and so she is getting it. I found the curry in Ripon, where we have some very good shops.'

There was some mirth over this on the other side of the table among the gardeners.

'Is this a very expensive soup, Mrs Saunders?' asked Mrs Rundell, as she ladled.

'No, Mrs Rundell, it is not,' replied Mrs Saunders. 'It is relatively economical. I am trying it out today, to see if it would be enjoyed in the dining room and to be sure I have it right.'

'What makes you suppose, Mrs Saunders, that what we like in the hall will be enjoyed in the dining room?' asked Jem. The others sat and listened, or peered into their soup inquisitively. As far as Ellen could make out, it was only those at each end of the table, Mrs Rundell and Jem and Mrs Saunders, who were allowed to start a conversation. 'After all,' Jem went on, 'as common people, we cannot appreciate the refined tastes of upstairs.'

Mrs Saunders seemed unflurried. 'I have always found that what is enjoyed here is enjoyed there. Even though the Quality may have some unusual ideas about what is good to eat, we all have the same stomachs in the end.'

Jem was not deterred. 'Would you not agree, Mrs Rundell, you who know the family so well, that their tastes are more polite than ours are? It is hard for us to judge what might please them. Though you are probably able to do so, being so close to them.' Seated at the head of the table Jem was transformed into someone strong and bull-like, superior in status to the man who carried bags to people's rooms. His nostrils flared. He was, Ellen thought, very handsome. Indeed, so many of the men were handsome, she was rather confused by it all.

By this time all the plates had been filled. Mrs Rundell lifted up her spoon and immediately so did everybody else. They attacked their soup with curiosity, except for Jem. He still seemed dissatisfied. 'You've not answered my question, Mrs Rundell,' he said. 'Do the Quality like a different sort of food from us on the other side of the baize door?'

Mrs Rundell looked coldly down the table at him. 'The food at Markham Thorpe is always good, Mr Thwaites. Everybody, I hope, enjoys what they are called upon to eat – after all, it is our duty to thank the Lord for all that he graciously bestows upon us.'

Mrs Saunders nodded at this tribute, as though it had been made to her. Jem stopped looking angry, and smirked. 'Thank you for these pious thoughts, Mrs Rundell, they are most edifying,' he said.

'Mrs Rundell, do you approve of the experiment?' asked the cook.

'Of course I have eaten such soup before, in London,' she replied, 'and I would say it was an excellent mulligatawny.'

'Very good soup,' said Jem, 'though a little too spicy for my taste. But, then, I'm not a gentleman.'

Mrs Rundell interrupted the noisy silence. 'At least, Mr Thwaites, you know all about the Quality even if you cannot claim to be one of them. Having served in the Army with Mr James, I forget in what capacity, you will have observed officers closely. I believe during your military days you served at table rather than in the field.'

'Both, Mrs Rundell, both,' he answered. 'There would have been little call for firing guns in the officers' mess, it would not have been appreciated. In any case, I hope you are not sneering at personal service, you who have spent so very many years engaged in it.'

There was a mild stir at this. The table was on Jem's side rather than Mrs Rundell's, Ellen felt.

The tureen and the plates were removed. Mrs Saunders and the kitchenmaid appeared a few moments later, the cook bearing a huge platter with a metal cover, the girl struggling with a tray piled with dishes.

'Mutton stew,' announced Mrs Saunders, placing the platter in front of Jem.

Ellen found this dinner so full of ceremony and so different from what she was used to that she gaped about her, until she saw one of the young men opposite wink. She blushed violently. Beth gently touched her side.

'Mrs R,' she whispered. Ellen stole a glance up the table and saw this lady looking towards her. She blushed again, particularly when she realised that the young man across the table was grinning at her, and not just him, but the next one too, and raising their horn cups, filled with beer from the jug that had been pushed down the table on a little wagon, in her direction. She stared downwards at her place, mechanically passing on the plates that arrived in front of her up the table, until one stopped at her place. She did not know what to do. After a while, Beth put a large Yorkshire pudding on her plate, followed by potatoes, and the girl on the other side gave her a pile of cabbage. Ellen had never liked it, but this was rich green cabbage, not like the limp vegetable at home. For a moment she wanted to be at home where she knew how to behave and there was no housekeeper to frown her down or young lads to wink at her or rules about who spoke and who kept quiet. But there were compensations. The mutton stew was more delicious than any stew she'd ever eaten, the pieces of meat lying in a rich brown juice full of soft carrots and onions. It revived her, and she forgot her embarrassment over the young man opposite. She would certainly not be looking at him again.

Talk turned to the family.

'And do you have any information from Sir Richard, Mrs Rundell?' asked Jem. 'Has he enjoyed his visit to London?'

Mrs Rundell assumed an important air, as though making an official announcement. 'It has been a most satisfactory visit. Sir Richard has concluded all his business, and met the family of Miss Emily's intended. And he has attended a number of society parties. Mr James has accompanied him on a number of these occasions.'

This information was received in silence, like an official bulletin. Then Jem spoke. 'Some of us may wonder,' he said, 'if Mr James is attending the Season for particular reasons. Is it possible that he is seeking a bride of his own, now the family's become so matrimonial?' Nobody commented on this. 'The same might apply to Sir Richard, for that matter. After all, it's almost ten years since her ladyship passed away. He might well be seeking consolation.'

'I don't think,' said Mrs Rundell, 'that speculations of that sort are considerable, Mr Thwaites.' There was a ripple of amusement down the table, quenched by another of Mrs Rundell's looks, clearly an important feature of life at Markham Thorpe.

Under cover of this conversation, Ellen caught the eye of the young man opposite, who nudged his neighbour. Would he never be turning his eyes away?

Mrs Rundell was continuing: 'Miss Emily will be returning to Markham Thorpe on Friday, together with Mr James and Mr William Dykes and one or two of their friends. Sir William and Lady Dykes will be arriving on Sunday. We shall be very busy.'

'I hope they are all content with good Yorkshire food,' said Mrs Saunders, 'and won't be asking me for fricassées and souf-flés.'

'Indeed, the Dykeses do live in the most fashionable circles,' Mrs Rundell announced, 'and are used to the best cuisine. That is certainly most veracious.' She pronounced this word with relish and a quick downward look at the remains of her stew. 'There was talk on the family's part of employing a caterer.' As she spoke Mrs Saunders opened her mouth and eyes wide. 'But I told Sir Richard that if that happened we should be having to find a new cook, and the idea was abrogated.' Ellen wondered what this word might mean, but Mrs Saunders seemed satisfied. Subsiding, she left the room, kitchenmaid behind her, returning with an enormous platter, which filled the hall with the smell of sugar and sponge.

Was there no limit to this lovely food, Ellen wondered. As she watched the pudding being ladled out, Mrs Rundell said, 'Mr Thwaites?' Upon which Jem stood up, and so did Mrs Rundell, and Agnes, and everybody else. Holding their laden plates in front of them, the upper servants walked in a line out of the room.

'They're off to the housekeeper's room,' said Beth to her, as the remaining servants began to talk freely. 'They always go there at the end of dinner. Lucy will go and pour their tea in a minute. Very stiff the company is, she says, especially since Mr Fellows hardly ever comes in to dinner, these days. Jem can't abide Mrs Rundell, though she quite likes him – she likes a well-made man, does Mrs Rundell.'

The pudding was treacle sponge, so soft and smooth that it made you feel there was nothing better in the world. There was a good deal of chat, but Ellen did not listen to it, so exhausted was she by all this new experience. She just ate, with keen enjoyment. When she raised her eyes again she realised with horror that all the men at her end of the table were watching her.

'I see young Ellen likes treacle sponge,' said the young man opposite, who had been grinning, and they all laughed. She blushed violently. She had never realised before how easily she blushed, and they laughed further. But it was not scornful laughter. She raised her eyes and smiled, just a little, to show she was not frightened. She firmly did not look, let alone smile, at the boy opposite, who had winked at her in the first place, only noticed out of the corner of her eye that he had flaxen hair and a fresh, ruddy face, and that he had a nice voice, as though he were well educated.

Part Two

Two days later, Ellen was even more exhausted. There had been so much dusting of rooms and scrubbing of floors and making of beds and cleaning of brass and carrying upstairs of hot water and mending of linen, so many comments from Katherine and lofty suggestions from Agnes, so many orders (delivered through the head housemaid) from Mrs Rundell, so many rules and customs to be learnt, so much curtsying and sliding out of the way when Sir Richard was sighted (he bobbed up all over the house, accompanied by Mrs Rundell, worrying about arrangements for the house party), so much changing from morning work dress to afternoon black frock. It was torture to wake up in the morning and she was always tired, because late at night when she was on her own she could not resist slipping on to the leads to sit in the dark and think about her new life.

When she woke on the third morning she knew she was late. She crawled out of bed, hardly opening her eyes, and pulled on her clothes. She hated her working dress, such a drab thing, nasty striped cotton with ugly buttons, and deliberately too big so she could grow into it. With her hair scraped into a bun with a cap on top, and a huge white apron, she looked and felt anything but herself, not Ellen at all. She could see herself in the glass, a servant, frowsty and tired. She ran down the stairs to the sound of furious activity in the kitchen, and into the Great Hall. There Katherine was walking up and down.

'You're late,' said Katherine. 'It's ten past six, you're ten minutes late. On your third day. It's only your third day.'

Ellen felt miserable and ashamed. Would she be sent away? Not that she wanted to stay here, but if she were dismissed it would disappoint her parents, and she would not get a character, and then how could she help support the family? 'I'm so sorry,' she said, 'really I am, Katherine. I overslept. I'm so sorry . . .' and she felt tears pushing into her eyes.

'That's all right,' said Katherine, 'you've worked hard these past days and I see you have the makings of a good girl. Only don't be late again.' Later, Ellen wondered why she'd felt so proud at these words. 'The makings of a good girl' – what was that to be proud of? A good cleaner – was that all she wanted to be?

She was told that her duties would include taking tea to Mrs Rundell at seven o'clock every morning. 'The lower servants wait on the upper servants in any good house,' said Katherine to her. 'After a while you will find it quite easy.'

At noon they were again on parade. This time it was the whole family arriving, and their guests. 'We wouldn't normally be greeting the family,' said Beth, 'but since all the children are coming and they're not often here together, Mrs Rundell thought it would be suitable. All the family here and eight guests, it makes a large company. It'll be just like the old times. They always used to have a big party for Ebor Day at York Races.' She sounded pleased. 'And then there are the visiting servants, six of them, I believe – you can never know what they will be like. The Dykeses have come to talk about plans for Miss Emily's wedding, you know.' Beth enjoyed a gossip, and most of what Ellen learnt came from her. 'Miss Emily's been wanting to have more people to stay for a while, but Sir Richard's always asked her to wait, said he wasn't ready, it was too soon after her mother's death . . . But he's so pleased they're coming now, wants the old house to look its best.'

As they waited in the sunshine, with the fountain playing once again, Ellen thought how alike the women servants looked in their best black dresses. She could already recognise almost all of them, although this time – was it to make the household appear larger? – the grooms were lined up as well, along with the gardeners and two women Ellen had not seen before. Mrs Saunders had refused to attend, telling the housekeeper she was too busy with luncheon. 'It's not my face the family are interested in,' she had said, 'it's my food. You can have Joan instead of me,' and she pushed forward the kitchenmaid, who always looked as though she were about to cry and now more than ever. Ellen studied Mrs Rundell, who dominated the proceedings. The housekeeper was especially imposing today. Her large bosom was rising and falling majestically, her eyes were bulging, and a smile was firmly attached to her face. She stood close to Sir Richard, murmuring into his ear. Sir Richard looked pleased to have her there, and would pluck at her arm if she made to leave him. Only as hoofs were heard beyond the trees did she take her place at the head of the line of servants.

Meanwhile Ellen shot a glance in the direction of the gardener who stared at her so much. She liked to think of him as her gardener though of course there was no sense in that. She knew his name was Harry but had never ventured to use it. She had not thought about him very much these past few days, she told herself, and she certainly did not want to be exchanging smiles with him here and now, with the entire household (who were highly observant) as audience. So she had ignored him in the servants' hall, and she was determined to ignore him now. A little glance, on the other hand, would not do any harm. He was wearing his Sunday best, like all the men, and she had to admit to herself that when he was well dressed, with his hair brushed and everything in place, he was a fine-looking fellow. What she had noticed about him was that he had very good manners, and spoke properly; he was not just a simple country lad. Beth had told her that he came from Ripon, where his father owned the most successful provisions business. Harry had insisted that he wanted to be a gardener, and Sir Richard had found him a place.

He was chatting to one of the other gardeners, not looking in her direction. Very fortunate. From what Agnes said, there was little to be gained from taking an interest in gardeners, though he was certainly a cut above all the other gardeners and indeed above most of the other servants. In any case, it was difficult to get to know him better, since when he was working in the garden in the morning she was in the house, and in the afternoon she had to do sewing under Katherine's eye, and when everyone met in the servants' hall there were so many people around. On Sundays, Beth had told her, he went to see his family in Ripon. Altogether there was no point in taking an interest in him at all.

The visiting party arrived in three carriages. The first two stopped in front of the house while the third, which was piled with luggage and people, disappeared towards the yard. Never had Ellen seen such an event as the arrival of the Markhams and their guests; it was so impressive and yet apparently so easy for everyone. The first person to be assisted by the coachman out of the front carriage was a young lady whom she recognised from the portraits as Lavinia, Sir Richard's elder daughter. She seemed to Ellen as fine as a lady could be, tall and handsome, her fair hair piled on her head in a much more elegant version of the style favoured by Mrs Rundell, wearing a dress of lilac silk, her travelling cloak a slightly darker shade. If only I could look like that, Ellen thought, but she knew she never would, not unless she ceased to be respectable, like Lydia in *A Kiss Too Far*, and she had no plans of that sort. Miss Lavinia (as they still seemed to call her, though she was really Mrs Wentworth) walked down the line of servants with a polite smile, nodding as they curtsied and bowed but not greeting them individually. When she reached Mr Fellows she took his hands in hers and smiled warmly, for the first time. To Mrs Rundell she extended her hand and gave a frigid nod. Miss Fisher she kissed before moving on to her father.

Even more interesting was Miss Emily. Miss Emily, it was clear, was perfect. You couldn't feel anything but admiration for such a person. She was quite small but not too small, with soft white skin and gold ringlets, and a laughing face under a huge straw hat. Her white dress was so delicate and ribboned and lacy that Ellen could have admired it all afternoon. She seemed the prettiest person in the world. There were no stiff bows from her: this was her home, obviously. Though she had been away for only a month she moved slowly down the line, greeting all the servants by name, asking laughingly, 'Where is Mrs Saunders? I suppose she refused to come?' She took Agnes by the arm with 'I'm back to trouble you, Agnes, no peace for you now. I have so many new dresses to show you, you will be quite amazed.' When she saw Ellen, who was hiding behind Beth, she said, 'And this must be Agnes's little sister. I could tell you were sisters at once. I hope you will be happy here.'

So fascinated was Ellen by this person that she did not at first notice that the rest of the guests had emerged from the carriages and were advancing towards the house. The group consisted of a young lady and four gentlemen, all young, tall, confident. They seemed wholly uninterested in the servants, all except for one gentleman who smiled in their direction. This must be Mr James, though this dark-faced, tall and heavy-set man, not so young when you looked at him, did not much resemble the handsome youth in the portrait. As her friends advanced towards Miss Emily and called her name, she turned away from Katherine in mid-sentence to seize the arm of one of the young men. He was not the tallest or handsomest but, as Ellen could tell instantly, he was as kind and good a man as you could find. This must be Miss Emily's future husband, then, Mr Dykes. The curiosity he aroused in the servants was evident from their stares, but he showed no sign of noticing them. Miss Emily was now surrounded by these young gentlemen. To Ellen they appeared united in an elegant band of graceful nobility, just as the admirers of the Honourable Adeline de Mowbray were described at the great ball at Northam Towers, in *Sir Evelyn de Mowbray*. The group moved slowly across the gravel towards the front door to meet Sir Richard. They seemed to Ellen to belong to a sphere of existence entirely different from her own, a world of assured and beautiful and indeed truly blessed ladies and gentlemen. This, indeed, was the Quality. Whereas Sir Richard struck her as an older gruffer version of her own father, these beautiful young people were unlike anyone she had ever seen.

The sun, which had been hidden behind clouds, burst out as the arriving guests greeted their host. It flooded with light the burnished heads of the gentlemen and the rich hats of the ladies, caressing their shining clothes, their smiling faces. Their voices rose into a chorus of greetings and laughter as hands were shaken, shoulders slapped and cheeks kissed. The party moved into the house, the girls on each side of their father. The governess, Mrs Rundell and Mr Fellows followed them through the front door.

As the servants walked round the side of the house, they discussed everything, but in particular Miss Emily's young man. He had made a favourable impression, as though he were almost good enough for their dear Miss Emily who, to the older servants, seemed more and more like her mother every time they saw her.

'How are you getting along, then?' said Jem to Ellen, as they hurried across the lawn.

'Oh, very well,' she said, 'I think so anyway, though I was ten minutes late this morning. That was very bad, wasn't it?'

He laughed. 'Yes, I heard you were late.'

Beyond him she could see Harry. He was gazing at her now, but not smiling. She did not mind his looking at her, if he was going to do it in a respectful sort of way, as he was doing now. She returned his look, not smiling, but not frowning, either. It would be hard to frown at him.

*   *   *

There was no time for thinking in the next few days. Hardly any time for sleeping, or eating, and certainly none for sitting on the leads or wandering in the garden. 'We're not prepared for this sort of entertaining,' said Agnes to her sister, on the third night of the house party, when they were sitting in her room and brushing their hair. 'We've never had anything like this while I've been here. There's Miss Emily wanting everything to be as fine as can be and needing her clothes to be just so, and the master wanting to show he can keep up standards, and Miss Lavinia expecting the house to be as comfortable as the grand houses she stays in. The fact is,' and in her fatigue she spoke more freely than she usually would to the third housemaid, 'they've reduced the household so much we can't really do a big affair like this one. We can just manage in the kitchen but where's the butlers and the footmen? And, anyway, this is an old sort of a house, and even when her ladyship was alive they never thought much about comfort.' She yawned and looked at herself in the mirror and frowned, rubbing her cheeks. 'Poor old Mr Fellows can't last a full day, what with being called here and there and everywhere. In the evening he's so tired he can't serve the dinner. Our Jem's very good but he can't do everything and the boy's very little. There should be two or three footmen in the house for an event like this, and you can't rely on the visiting servants. They're running about after their own masters and mistresses and they don't know how anything works. And there's the big dinner party tomorrow night, and I only hope you can do what you need to, my girl.' Ellen had been told she would be helping at the side-board for the dinner the next night. She was as nervous as anyone could be. Agnes went on, 'And when you have to stay up, like me, till your mistress chooses to go to bed, which was one o'clock last night, and up at six to have all the clothes ready, well, you do get tired.' She looked at her sister who was almost asleep, though trying to pay attention. 'Poor lamb, you must be exhausted too. I'll tell you one thing, though, if you wake up, that is.'

'Yes?' said Ellen, blinking and smiling as her head drooped like a peony soaked in rain.

'You've been noticed by the family, and they're very pleased with you, that they are. Miss Emily spoke to me this evening, she said, "What a sweet sister you have, Agnes, what a good girl. I'm sure she'll fit in here as well as can be."'

Ellen smiled. 'That's very kind of Miss Emily. I didn't know she'd noticed me.'

'Oh, yes, she notices everything, just like her mother, they say. Everything – and if anything is not quite right she says so, too. You don't think the Quality are aware of you sometimes, except as machines to do the work, but they see you without looking at you, as though they had a third eye. The only thing they don't notice is if you're tired. None of the gentry notices that, however kind they are. They couldn't, it might spoil their fun. The men might look at the girls, of course, but we don't need to pay attention to that.' She nudged her sister, whose eyes were closing again. 'Don't worry too much about the dinner tomorrow. I'm sure you'll manage. Just do what Mr Fellows and Jem tell you. Oh, Lord, Mr Fellows was very shaky at dinner, he spilt sauce down Sir Richard's sleeve, but Sir Richard never said anything.'

'Why doesn't Mr Fellows retire, then?' Ellen asked sleepily.

'Sir Richard asked him if he'd retire and he said no and Sir

Richard is too kind to send him away, so he stays. He's been here more than fifty years, you know, ever since he was a boy.' She looked at her sister consideringly. 'By the way, Ellen, I have to tell you something else. Miss Emily is not the only one who has noticed you.'

'No?' said Ellen. What did this mean?

'Yes,' Agnes went on, 'it's Mr James. Mr James has noticed you. You need to be careful. Mr James, you see, is not married.'

'No,' said Ellen, 'I know that. That doesn't make him a bad man, does it?'

'I suppose I should tell you the story about Mr James, it was a while ago, of course, but then . . . You just need to be careful of him.'

'Oh,' said Ellen, not sure whether to be alarmed or to laugh. 'That's very bad. I will be careful if you say so.' But even the fascination of hearing about Mr James could not keep her awake, and she fell fast asleep. Agnes laid a blanket over her, and tenderly pushed her hair back from her forehead.

The dinner party took place in the Great Hall, eighteen people sitting at the long table in the middle of the room. The table had always been there, they told Ellen, the house had been built around it; it had been carved by an estate carpenter long ago from the trunk of a single oak tree. The house was full of stories like that, all of them showing how old and fine the family and their house were. People were working in the Hall all day. From time to time the head gardener brought in flowers to be arranged by Miss Emily and Mr Dykes. They took a great deal of time over their flowers. This was a pleasure for Ellen, who, during the afternoon, had to carry tray after tray of knives and forks and plates and glasses into the Great Hall. She did it as slowly and in as many separate journeys as she could, to allow her to spend as much time as possible looking at Miss Emily. She knew she was not allowed to stare at Miss Emily, so she just peered at her out of the corner of her eye. It was difficult to know how hard she and her young gentleman were really working – so much of their time was spent staring into each other's eyes or by Mr Dykes twining flowers in her hair. They seemed unaware of Ellen, so she peeped at them a good deal. At one moment she was bold enough to approach and say, 'Is there anything I can do for you, Miss Emily?'

To which Miss Emily smiled and said, 'No, we have everything we need.' Then she thought for a moment, as though needing to remember who Ellen was, and said, 'I hope you are happy, here at Markham Thorpe.'

Ellen answered, 'Yes, thank you, miss.' It was true, she supposed, in a way. She hesitated for a moment but Miss Emily had ceased to notice her and was back staring at Mr Dykes.

When Mr Fellows and Jem and Billy set about laying the table, Ellen was told to watch them. They laid out four knives and two spoons and four forks for each person, the butler measuring the distance between each place with a rule. 'Yes, yes,' Mr Fellows would say, 'just a little to the left, just a little to the left, just a little to – oh, no, just a little to the right. Come now, Billy, don't you see that's wrong?' and he laughed and darted out of the room. A moment or two later, puffing rather, he emerged from the back of the house with tall silver candelabra and curved silver dishes and placed them on the damask tablecloth. Now and again Mrs Rundell would come in, keys clinking, hands resting on capacious skirts, and confer with the butler while surveying the details of the room. Whenever she passed Miss Emily and Mr Dykes she would look in their direction, though not quite at them, bowing her head slightly, as though she wished to be noticed by them and even included in their conversation. But once Miss Emily had remarked, in a neutral voice, 'Good afternoon, Mrs Rundell, isn't it a beautiful day?' they paid no attention to her. It was curious how they could go on playing with their flowers, oblivious of all the people observing them.

Outside, the rest of the house party played croquet. They did not play very seriously, but larked around and laughed, and now and again they would all cry aloud. Ellen watched them from a window. The day was hot, and the ladies wore white or lavender dresses, the gentlemen striped jackets, though one or two had taken off their jackets and rolled up their sleeves. Ellen looked curiously at Mr James, wondering whether a girl could ever find him handsome. He was like Sir Roderick, the bad baronet in *The Curse of the Despards*, she thought, but Sir Roderick had turned out good in the end and married the clergyman's daughter, who had always loved him but whom he had despised because she was less high-born than he was, even though she had the fairest white skin of anyone in the county and soft trusting eyes, with a voice like a bell. (How long would her own hands stay white, Ellen wondered, with all the cleaning and scrubbing she had to do? Not long at all, probably: they were already redder and rougher than they used to be.) She did not think Mr James resembled Sir Roderick, who was tall with glowing eyes and long dark locks that he tossed sideways when he was angry (which was quite often): Mr James did have dark hair, but it was matted in a not very romantic way and cut rather short, and he had a reddish face like his father and was not at all like Childe Harold. He had a confident air at times, though: this morning when he had passed her in the corridor he had not looked shy at all but had smiled at her, with a rather impudent air. She was not sure she liked this.

Altogether, it was not easy to understand what sort of a man he was. Among all this gaiety, he was so stiff and ill at ease. Though he spoke sometimes to the men, he hardly addressed the ladies.

'Are you cleaning the window with your eyes?' said a voice behind her.

Ellen shuddered, and turned to face Mrs Rundell, motionless at the far end of the passage. 'I saw something on the floor,' she said, 'and I wanted to pick it up, it was in the way . . .'

'Yes,' said Mrs Rundell, thankfully not asking what it was Ellen had wanted to pick up, 'no doubt you did. Now go about your duties, my girl, there's no time to be wasted. There is never time to be wasted, and particularly not now.'

She turned and moved majestically away, while Ellen sidled back to the kitchen.

What a dinner it was, such a dinner as Ellen had never seen. Nine ladies and nine gentlemen, the ladies in low-cut dresses and sparkling earrings and necklaces, the gentlemen in black tail coats and stiff white collars. The silver candelabra that Mr Fellows had produced that afternoon were lined along the table, and there were candles on the side tables, even though it was still quite light outside. And the flowers . . . She had never seen anything so beautiful. And the food . . .

There had been much discussion in the servants' hall about the way the dinner would be served. Up to now they had always put the first course, a dozen or so dishes, on the table for people to serve themselves, followed after a while by a second course. But Miss Emily wanted it done the new way, Russian, it was said to be, one course after another with each offered individually to every guest. This seemed to require a good deal more work, though fortunately they had two visiting menservants to help. The company had rich, succulent soup (Ellen tasted it when no one was looking), then a huge salmon, and after that a princely piece of roast beef carved by Sir Richard and accompanied by Yorkshire puddings, and an enormous trifle and tarts, then a savoury, and wine and more wine and yet more wine. Ellen had eaten her own supper at six o'clock but she felt hungrier and hungrier as the dishes followed one another into the Great Hall. As they came out she took just a little of the leftovers from each tray she had to carry to its right destination: the silver and glass to the butler's pantry, the plates upstairs to the still room, and the serving dishes to the scullery. She was wearing her best black dress and a white apron, better than her horrid everyday dress but still remarkably unbecoming.

In the kitchen Mrs Saunders was growing hotter and crosser and crosser and hotter. Ellen stayed by the sideboard, helping as directed by Mr Fellows and Jem and the two visiting menservants. From where she was she could hear the conversation going on. The talk was loud and cheerful but disappointing, she thought. It was not at all like the smart banter in the novels she read, no more interesting and a good deal less learned than her father's conversations with his friends from the Literary and Philosophical Society. They talked about the new railway station at York and Mr

Hudson the railway king and whether it was safe to invest in the railways (some thought it was very rash) and racing and what was going on at Castle Howard. A few of the ladies and gentlemen held low, whispered exchanges with each other, which involved much smiling and blushing. Miss Emily, who sat next to Mr Dykes, talked to him almost all evening in a soft voice accompanied by many sidelong glances.

Ellen felt horribly self-conscious at first, standing there by the sideboard, then clearing the plates and bringing new ones in. She told herself that the Quality would not even see a maidservant like herself, they only noticed each other, but still it seemed to her as she stood there, unobtrusively as she hoped, that though they pretended only to be interested in each other they were quite aware of her, the gentlemen in particular. Then she heard Mrs Wentworth, who was sitting at one end of the table facing her father, say, 'Yes, she's a nice little girl, one of the housekeeper's family. Pretty? Well, I suppose she is, in a servantish sort of way. Funny how you can always tell, can't you? They always look like servants, don't they?' Who did she mean? Herself, Ellen? But she was too busy concentrating on what had to be done to brood over these cruel remarks. The brooding would have to be saved up for later.

Later in the evening, as Ellen rested for a moment and allowed herself a little yawn, she saw one of the gentlemen staring at her intently. She could not think what he was doing, he was so old, and why should he be interested in her when he was so old? Really, there was no reason at all.

Sir Richard drank a great deal of wine and as the evening drew on became vague and silent until prodded into conversation. Once he fell asleep, his head drooping on to his chest. Mr James grew redder and redder and several times leant closely towards the lady on his right, so that she drew back and put her hands over her breast. The ladies of the family were more correct, Mrs Wentworth the perfect lady, grand and stiff-backed, aware of everything going on at the table, occasionally beckoning to Mr Fellows or leaning over to speak to someone who had no one to talk to. At one point she caught Miss Emily's eye and nodded sharply, at which Miss Emily coloured and turned to her other neighbour.

It was interesting to watch all these people, as though you were not in the room. That is, you were in the room but not in their company.

After a while Mr Fellows tapped her shoulder and motioned to her to leave. As soon as she was outside the door, there was a sound of scraping chairs and rustling skirts and footsteps in the Great Hall. Jem came out of the room and said to her, 'You've done very well.'

'What's happening in there?' she wanted to know.

'It's the ladies leaving to go to the drawing room, the gentlemen stay in the Hall. You're not needed, off to the kitchen with you.'

Back to the kitchen she went, past the servants' hall, from which came a great deal of noise made no doubt by the visitors' coachmen, who were being handsomely entertained according to the traditions of the house. In the kitchen she found Mrs Saunders, still rosy but calmer, sitting in her own chair in the window, and popping little pieces of the savoury into her mouth. 'They liked their dinner, did they, they liked it?' she was saying. 'What was it Sir Richard said? Tell me again what he said.' The women from the village were eating leftovers and Mrs Rundell was standing in a corner, looking more amiable than usual. There was a general atmosphere of celebration. The kitchen was still extremely hot but the windows high in the wall were open, letting in the cool evening air. Late as it was, outside there was still a little light. You could smell the tobacco plants outside.

'And here's Ellen,' said Mrs Saunders, 'and a good girl you've been. You have a good niece, Mrs Rundell,' and to the surprise of all she turned to this lady and offered something resembling a smile, to which Mrs Rundell responded with a twitching of the lips.

'There's plenty more work to do,' said Mrs Saunders. 'Ellen, you take that silver to the pantry for Jem to wash, and then the glasses, all the glasses on those trays. Joan is in the scullery along with a few dozen dishes, and that's where you belong too, Ellen and Beth. There's a golden rule in this kitchen – no one goes to bed while there's one dirty dish in the sink. And there's a second – I don't wash a single one.' As the evening advanced, the girls in their drowsy state almost fell into the suds. There seemed no end to the serving dishes and the kitchen equipment that had to be washed.

On the family side the party was continuing. Mr Fellows, staggering rather, and Jem, seeking a moment of relief from his washing of the silver and glass, came into the kitchen from time to time and reported on progress on the other side. The gentlemen stayed a long time at their port, and very uproarious they were when they left to join the ladies.

Around midnight Jem told Mr Fellows to go home. A while later the carriages were ordered, and the coachmen lurched out to bring them round. 'Full moon,' the coachmen said, as they went into the yard, where the cobblestones glistened in the moonlight. 'Should have no trouble getting home.'

In a little while and after many cries of gratitude and hearty kisses the guests had all gone and it was one o'clock. Sir Richard, the older Dykeses and the Wentworths retired and their maids and valets, some a little flushed after their convivial evening in the housekeeper's room, disappeared to attend to their needs. Miss Lavinia's maid, a pale young woman from France who had hardly spoken since she arrived, looked rather odd as she went upstairs. The young members of the house party, however, were not tired at all. In the Great Hall they romped and broke a glass and played Ring a Ring o' Roses and Grandmother's Footsteps and all sorts of other children's games, including Tag, which involved (as Ellen discovered, peering through the door when Mrs Rundell was busy elsewhere) running up and down after each other, with the young gentlemen in pursuit and the young ladies submitting to forfeits (invariably kisses) when caught. After a while Mr James went to bed and still the work in the scullery and the games in the Great Hall continued. Only as two o'clock struck from the stable clock could Beth and Ellen and Joan look at each other and say, 'It's done.'

'Time for bed, girls,' said Mrs Saunders, preparing to retire to her bedroom beside the kitchen, 'no dawdling, but Mrs Rundell says you can start your duties at half past six tomorrow. The family will not be up early. Thank you for your hard work.'

On her way upstairs Ellen wondered where her sister was. She knocked on her door. No answer. She must be waiting for Miss Emily in her bedroom. Did Ellen dare to find her, to say good night? As soon as the other maids were in their rooms, she crept down the back stairs and pushed open the green door to the family side. The gas lamps were burning softly along the Red Corridor but there was no one around, only a faint rustling from one or two rooms. Some of the doors were open, and in one bedroom she could see one of the visiting lady's maids yawning by the fire. She pushed open the door of the Pink Room, and there was Agnes. She was asleep, quite asleep, in an armchair, a book on the floor beside her, the candles burning low and the fire almost out. 'Agnes,' she whispered.

Agnes shot to her feet. When she saw her sister she looked startled and then angry. 'What are you doing here?' she said. 'It's forbidden to you, at this time of night. What time is it?'

'I only came to bid you good night,' said Ellen, and then tried saying, 'Sister', by means of propitiation.

'It's forbidden to you, this part of the house, at this time of the day,' said Agnes. 'And it's Miss Braithwaite to you now. We are colleagues, not sisters, during work hours.'

'It's past two, Agnes. Anyway, it's quite reasonable for me to come and see how you are.'

Agnes stopped being severe, she scarcely had the energy for it. 'I'm so tired,' she said. 'Will Miss Emily never come? That evening dress of hers, it takes quite twenty minutes to remove, and as long to put away, and there's her hair to unpin – ah, well, at least she won't be rising early.'

They heard distant voices. Agnes, who had been yawning again, patted her hair into shape, poked the fire, and pulled at her dress. 'Go to bed, Ellen, and if they see you pretend you are on an errand.' Ellen negotiated the Red Corridor carefully as the merry voices became louder, and slipped upstairs.

* * *

The house party stayed seven more days after the dinner party. Very pleasant days they were for the guests, filled with picnics and excursions to ruined abbeys and famous beauty spots, and visits from the neighbours and games of croquet and a cricket match in the next village and best of all – for those who went – Ebor Day, the great racing day of the year for Yorkshire society, an event that needed hours and hours of preparation and dressing up, and from which the party returned happy and crumpled. And meals and more meals. How could anyone eat so much, Ellen wondered, these enormous breakfasts and the cold meat and hot dishes at lunchtime, and afternoon tea (not something she'd known at home, where they had proper tea at six), and long dinners, and all that drinking, at least by the men? They ate a great deal in the servants' hall, too. Often Mrs Saunders would prepare much more of a dish than could possibly be eaten in the dining room and it would be finished in the servants' hall, with much discussion of its fine points. They talked about the family and the guests in detail (though they had to be careful with the visiting servants who might be expected to gossip to their masters and mistresses and would not welcome criticism), the beautiful manners of Lady Dykes and how pleasant Mr William was and how happy Miss Emily would be and how Miss Lavinia had changed.

They also talked endlessly about Mrs Rundell. 'It's her first really big occasion,' Katherine had remarked, 'and she's putting everything she has into it.'

'And that's a great deal,' Jem had replied – since by and large the servants considered Mrs Rundell's two cousins were on their side, not hers. Mr Fellows was discreet about what he heard at table, but Jem would offer minute descriptions of the conversation and how much had been eaten and drunk – three helpings of the meat, Mr Wentworth had had, and all the while looking so pompous and cold as though he were reading a brief, not gobbling down large lumps of meat smothered in sauce. Jem was a fine mimic and could easily be persuaded to do an imitation of two of the visitors who were courting. They used their own baby language, unaware that Jem was listening closely in order to convulse the servants' hall with his rendering of 'Who's a naughty little loveykins, then?' and 'Who's a great big slyboots Jack?' If the Quality knew how they were observed, Ellen reflected, they might be more careful . . .

Three days before the house party was due to end, there was a crisis: Miss Lavinia's maid fell ill and could hardly leave her bed. Miss Lavinia was helpless without a maid and told Agnes she would have to act as her lady's maid as well as her sister's. Agnes, who was not afraid of Miss Lavinia (or of anyone, apparently), suggested that Ellen might help her: though untrained she was intelligent and nicely brought-up. Ellen was delighted to oblige. After a day or two watching her sister, Ellen found she could help Miss Lavinia fairly well, preparing her clothes, helping her dress, brushing her hair. When they were on their own, Miss Lavinia was pleasanter than she was when surrounded by guests. She asked Ellen about herself, seemed interested to find how well she expressed herself, asked what she wanted to do, said thank you in a way she never did downstairs. They had a nice way with them, this family, Ellen thought. Even Mr James (whom at first she had thought so rude and hasty) always said thank you when you brought him something.

When the family doctor was called to see the French lady's maid he asked to speak to Miss Lavinia. It was almost immediately known in the servants' hall – how was it known, how did such things get around? – that the unfortunate maid was very ill indeed, and would be unable to work for a long time.

Soon after, Agnes found Ellen, seized her by the hand and drew her into an empty room. There she told her, in an urgent whisper, that Miss Lavinia was going to invite Ellen to become her lady's maid for a trial period. Agnes said this was a wonderful opportunity, and that she must accept.

Ellen was summoned to speak to Miss Lavinia in the library. Miss Lavinia was with her husband. She seemed nervous. His face was hidden behind the newspaper. Miss Lavinia cleared her throat. She smiled charmingly. She made her offer. Ellen demurred for a moment, as seemed suitable, and then accepted. Miss Lavinia looked pleased. Ellen asked whether she should give notice to Mrs Rundell.

'No,' said Miss Lavinia, 'it's all in the family. There's no need.'

As it turned out, Miss Lavinia was wrong. That evening the family were alone for dinner when the butler entered the dining-room and asked his master whether Mrs Rundell might speak to him urgently. The alarming interview that followed was revealed to the servants' hall by remarks Miss Emily made to Agnes and by the butler who remained close by the corridor, in case he was needed. Mrs Rundell had flown into such a rage that the family had been quite alarmed. She had said that if Ellen was to leave the house in the next few days with Miss Lavinia, there would be so few servants left under her charge that the place would become unmanageable, and there was no chance of recruiting anyone at short notice. She could not maintain any standards if the family was going to steal servants from their own father – or put up with London people's belief that country servants were there for the taking. Ellen was her cousin and she, Mrs Rundell, who acted *in loco parentis*, had not been consulted, not one single word had been said. She was training the girl up, and hard work it was, and what sort of rules allowed the family to snatch a young servant from her care? She forbade Ellen to go, and Ellen's parents would say the same. If Miss Lavinia carried out her plan, she, Mrs Rundell, would give notice immediately. Then she stalked out.

Agnes told Ellen this story in an awed voice. What had struck her most was that Miss Emily had spoken of Mrs Rundell almost with fear. Apparently, when Mrs Rundell had left the dining room, Sir Richard had lost his temper, shouting at Miss Lavinia and her husband, calling them names never heard in that house, and concluding that if Mrs Rundell went he might as well close Markham Thorpe since life there would be insupportable.

The next morning Ellen took tea to the housekeeper as usual. It was quite a business, this early-morning tea, since Mrs Rundell's tea was different from everyone else's, and a small supply for this purpose was kept in the still room in the caddy with the Chinaman on top and Ellen had to make her a special pot. She had wondered about tasting it but had never quite dared to, Mrs R being so particular about it. This morning Mrs Rundell, in the silk gown that she liked to wear in the morning, was seated in her armchair by the fireplace. This was most unusual – usually she was lying in bed, and scarcely spoke. Mrs Rundell stood up when Ellen came in, also a most unusual act. She was holding her bunch of keys, something she usually did only when her feelings were particularly strong. Though Ellen kept her eyes on the ground, she was very aware of this formidable physical presence in front of her. As for Mrs Rundell, she shifted the keys from one hand to the other and stared hard at her little cousin.

'Sit down, Ellen,' said Mrs Rundell. Ellen sat down and burst into tears.

But Mrs Rundell did not appear to be angry with her. She gave Ellen a large white handkerchief trimmed with lace. When Ellen dared look up, she saw that Mrs Rundell was looking at her intently. What a lot of Mrs Rundell there was, how very many acres of black silk.

'You've no need to be afraid,' said Mrs Rundell. 'I don't blame you at all. Indeed, I am gratified you have made such a good impression on the family. I am not pleased with that silly sister of yours, persuading you to accept this offer. A little success – not her own doing – has gone to Agnes's head.' She paused, her eyes still fixed on Ellen. 'As for you, I have some advice, child. You need to stay here at Markham Thorpe. This is a much better place for you than London. And you're too young to be a lady's maid, it's only a month you've been in service. Believe me, I have your interests at heart. You may think I've not observed you, but if so you're deceived. You are a good girl. The only danger is that you are very pretty.'

'No, Mrs Rundell,' said Ellen. 'I mean, yes, Mrs Rundell.' Why was being pretty such a danger?

'Rather too pretty for a maid, but then you may not remain a maid,' she went on. Mrs Rundell was calming down. 'Have faith in me, my dear. If you receive other such offers, always consult me, not that sister of yours. Let me be your guide – I know what is best for you. Is that understood?'

'Yes, Mrs Rundell,' said Ellen. She was grateful to her cousin for looking after her, she thought, but she found herself wondering why Mrs Rundell took such an interest in her, whether she had some plan for Ellen that Ellen did not know about.

Mrs Rundell won her battle without difficulty. The Wentworths left the next day, much earlier than expected, and they did not take Ellen with them.

The weather continued hot, and life at Markham Thorpe became steadily slower. The blackboard in the passage outside the servants' hall, which recorded which guest had which room, emptied. The family and their future in-laws spent most of their time discussing the forthcoming wedding. It was to take place in Yorkshire next April. The service would be in Ripon Cathedral, which could hold great numbers. Not all the guests for the wedding could be asked to the wedding breakfast, since there would be a garden party at the house the day before. Places to stay had to be found for dozens of guests, and neighbours the Markhams had not entertained for years would be asked to hold house parties, since hospitality of this sort was part of their duty to the county. A firm of caterers from York had been engaged for the wedding breakfast.

Everyone agreed that nowadays, with the railways, such a wedding would be quite different from what it had been in the past. Now that people could come up to Yorkshire in only a few hours, hundreds might be expected whereas in the past it would have been dozens. It might be pleasant for a wedding, but generally it was very confusing, very unsettling, all this movement. There was little to be said for having the county filled with strangers – having Leeds so close was quite bad enough.

The number of guests was discussed at length. The Markhams and the Dykeses decided they would be asking only two hundred people. Then they counted the numbers on their various lists. These would come to five hundred. When they cut down the numbers, they found that, what with godparents and aunts and cousins and ancient friends who might leave bequests and the Lord Lieutenant and the Master of Fox Hounds and two retired nannies and important neighbours, the only people who could safely be eliminated were the ones they really wanted. A table in the drawing room was covered with sheets of paper bearing lists of names, crossed out and reinstated and crossed out again. When Ellen was cleaning the room she would look at these lists to see how they had changed, and think how lucky all these people were to be invited to such a magnificent event.

Sir Richard disliked these discussions. He would puff heavily and become even ruddier than usual if they went on too long. Mr James avoided them if he could, shaking his shoulders and retiring to the smoking room. When Ellen cleaned the smoking room she would find it full of cigar butts and smelling of whisky. It was sad to think of Mr James sitting there on his own, drinking away and staring at the ceiling, she supposed, since there was nothing else to do but read his sporting papers. But at every meal-time the discussions continued. Sir Richard would sit at his end of the table, looking bored, while Miss Emily talked at length, deferring to her father but definite in her views. Dear Mr Dykes always sat close to Miss Emily and said not very much although when he did speak his gentle voice was delightful to the ears ('There's no point in me being sweet on him,' Ellen told herself, 'though it's hard not to like him.'). His parents, sitting good and upright, made helpful suggestions, while Miss Fisher, who appeared at meals when the family had no guests in particular, occasionally pointed out important facts that the others had forgotten. It seemed to Ellen from the odd overheard remark (why did they think she would not listen?) that the Dykeses were offering to contribute financially, and that Sir Richard was too proud to accept.

Then the Dykeses left. Miss Emily stayed on, but only for a week. Her heart was not there, they could tell: it was straying after her young man. She was listless and fretful. From time to time she quarrelled with her brother, and Ellen overheard her telling him he was horribly lazy and must spend his time more profitably. 'Why don't you marry?' she said to him. 'It would make you much happier. But when we introduce a nice young woman to you, you just turn your back on her and pretend to be a clown.' To which he only growled. What did this mean? Ellen used to wonder. Did he not like women? Was he afraid of them?

As the house became quieter, Ellen occasionally had a moment to herself. In the early mornings she would linger in the library, looking at the shelves. Many of the books, in their brown calf bindings, were legal volumes and county histories and Latin texts, but one corner contained more interesting material. She found a set of recent books, all of them with a bookplate showing the family coat of arms with the name Sophia Markham. This must be Lady Markham, Ellen supposed, since some of the books were only ten years or so old, and on the bottom shelf was an unopened brown-paper parcel labelled 'Lady Markham, Markham Thorpe, Ripon, Yorkshire'. Lady Markham had bought novels and history books and books about natural history and many other things besides. When Ellen put her face into a book, she was transported back to a pleasure she had almost forgotten, before remembering that her duty was not to read but to clean.

One morning she slipped into the library with, she thought, ten minutes to spare. She had worked on the drawing room with great speed and it looked all right. Nobody had used the library for a few days and there was nothing very much for her to do but she had to make sure everything was in order. She had found an old novel, a book called *Pamela*, about a maidservant, which she had already started. Would anyone notice, she wondered, if she smuggled it to her room? Sitting herself down on the library steps, she reopened *Pamela*. The book was quite as interesting as she'd hoped — she felt so strongly for the poor girl, trapped in a country house with a wicked housekeeper and persecuted by a master who wanted things of her she could not possibly give. As she read, an internal voice kept telling her she must stop reading, that Katherine might find her or, still worse, Mrs Rundell, but she could not stop. She was just turning the page (the last page that morning, definitely) when she heard a cough. She looked up. It was Miss Fisher, in her grey dress, regarding her with surprise.

'Oh!' said Ellen, and put the book back on the shelf while standing up and brushing down her dress. 'I'm so sorry. It was just for a moment . . .'

Miss Fisher did not seem annoyed, however. She merely said, 'You can read, can you, or are you just looking at the pictures?'

'Yes, indeed I can read,' said Ellen. 'At home I used to read all the time. I hardly have time here . . .'

'It is not very usual for a housemaid to read proper books,' observed Miss Fisher. 'We used to have a library for the servants but it was thrown away. It was a silly collection of little tales and tracts. What do you read, then?'

'I read novels mostly. But my father is very fond of history and I have read a number of historical works . . . I hope you won't tell anyone, Miss Fisher, I hardly ever do this, but then there are so many interesting things here . . .'

'Poor Lady Markham was a great reader. So was Emily when she was young and I had great hopes of her, but her head has been turned lately towards other things. James never touched a book, only the sporting prints. He was an intelligent little boy, in a way, but he found reading so difficult. He could not, he simply could not, sort out the words or write straightforwardly. I used to think he was being contrary. He changed so when his mother died, she was the only one who could handle him. He would be so angry, throw his toys around the nursery when he was a little boy, and he was no better when he came into the schoolroom. But she could always soothe him . . .' She seemed to recollect herself. 'Why am I telling you all this?' She peered at Ellen as though unsure to whom she was talking. 'I instructed all the children, you know, but of course James went to his private school when he was eleven. But the girls I taught all the way through, even though they are not at all studious now. They write a pretty letter, at least.'

Ellen gazed at Miss Fisher, as she thought, rather stupidly, and wondered whether she should be going back to her cleaning, though it was most interesting to hear about the young ladies as pupils. She dusted a shelf tentatively to indicate that she was working, but Miss Fisher did not seem to care whether or not she was doing housework.

'When Emily left the schoolroom a year ago,' she went on, as though half to herself, 'I thought I would have to leave, find another situation, which would not be easy at my time of life. But no, Sir Richard said I was not to go on any account, I was part of the family, he said, and James said so too. I was surprised, but he always had a good heart, that boy, always affectionate if you knew how to handle him. So here I am. They tell me my job is to catalogue the library, so that is what I do. There are some interesting books here, you know, some going back to the early days of printing – but I don't suppose that means much to you.'

Stung, Ellen replied, 'Indeed it does. My father told me all about Caxton, and how he introduced printing.'

'Did he indeed? Well! So that's good. Your father must be a man of education. What is his occupation?'

'He is an apothecary,' said Ellen, 'but what he likes to do is to study, and particularly to read history. But I must . . .' and Ellen waved her duster and her brush in the air.

'I will ask Sir Richard if you may borrow some books for your own reading, if you would like that? I'm sure he will say yes.'

'I suppose Mrs Rundell will not mind?' said Ellen, innocently.

The name was not well received. 'The opinions of Mrs Rundell on books are not worth listening to,' replied Miss Fisher. 'Or on any matter beyond housekeeping, one might say. Of course, she is your aunt, is she not? Ha!' She looked Ellen over once more. 'Well, I will speak to Sir Richard.' And with a curious flutter of her skirts, which Ellen realised was caused by the little dog that had been sitting at her feet, Miss Fisher turned and went out.

* * *

One evening, quite late, Agnes came into her sister's room and told her that Miss Emily would be leaving in two days' time and that Agnes would be going with her. 'Will you miss me, my dear?' she asked.

'Yes, I shall miss you very much,' said Ellen.

Then Agnes prattled on about how Miss Emily was going to London to choose her trousseau and staying at various great houses and that there would be an enormous number of new clothes to look after. All of this, in Ellen's view, was not very interesting if one's own fate was to stay in Yorkshire and dust the drawing room. Still, she did not like the idea of Agnes leaving her to be on her own with all these people who still almost seemed strangers, in this house, which was full of mysteries she did not understand.

So Miss Emily left for Lincolnshire with Agnes dressed up as elegantly as could be, the two sitting in the carriage like two young girls going to a party – you could hardly tell which was mistress and which was maid. Though Emily would be back soon, Sir Richard seemed dejected. 'Close the drawing room, would you, Mrs Rundell?' he said, the day after Miss Emily had gone, but this was unnecessary: Mrs Rundell did not need to be told what to do – she was quite capable of making decisions herself. She had already given instructions for the blinds to be drawn down and the covers put over the chairs and the pictures, and the door locked. The blinds came down in almost all of the bedrooms and the guests' corridor fell into darkness, and the house, with none of the family there but father and son, quietened almost into silence.

The two Markhams resumed their old unsociable habit of taking their meals at different times and in different places, Mr James in the smoking room and Sir Richard sometimes in a little upstairs room, close to Mrs Rundell's apartments, and sometimes in the dining room. Miss Fisher usually dined with Sir Richard in the dining room, as she had for many years. For dinner she would change her grey day dress for a grey or even lavender evening dress, with a pale shawl in summer and a dark one in winter. She took a good deal of trouble over her clothes for dinner, though she did not possess an extensive wardrobe. Evidently she wished to look her best.

All summer the weather was fine. There was so little rain that the lawns began to lose their greenness, and the water in the lake sank and sank. In the herbaceous borders the dahlias and the delphiniums glowed against the old brick walls and the dark shrubs. Mr Hurst, the head gardener, could be seen on his morning rounds, shaking his head and looking up at the sky, as though asking whether its pitiless azure would ever be broken. It never was, all the way through July and August and into September.

Hard and dull as Ellen's work generally was, she found she was becoming attached to the place. This was partly, perhaps, because she and Beth spent so much time together, and Beth adored the estate where she had spent all her life – she had been twice to York, but no further. In the evenings the two girls would slip into the garden. They would walk hand in hand along the path that took you all the way round the lake to the furthest point where you reached the darkness of the West Woods, and could see the hall across the water, distant and small. If you timed it right, the windows would be aflame in the sunset. The two girls became the closest friends, telling each other every secret. Ellen learnt that Beth was engaged to Jem, that nobody knew except her parents, and she was planning to marry him as soon as possible, when they had made enough money in service to set up house together. 'Does that mean you will be leaving us?' cried Ellen. Beth said she might be able to stay for a while, given that her father worked there, even though maids usually left service when they married, but she wanted to have a family and Jem might not care to stay in service for long. They would laugh over Billy, who was captivated by Ellen and would gaze at her adoringly. They would wander into the walled garden and call on Beth's parents, who had been rather reserved in their manner towards Ellen at first but were friendlier now, and gave them lemonade and little cakes.

Ellen began to take pride in the way her rooms (as she thought of them) looked, even though so few were now being used. She made the smoking room, still an alarmingly masculine apartment to her, as clean and comfortable and well polished as she could. In spite of what Katherine had said, she never found anything in the least shocking. She liked to think that this might cheer Mr James during his long evenings there. What she did enjoy was the library, where she spent as many hours as she could. She tried to do this secretly, though it was extraordinary how everybody (except Mrs Rundell, she hoped, since Mrs R was known to despise book learning) seemed to know exactly what she was doing, even though it was hardly very interesting.

In the library she had another encounter with Miss Fisher. On her regular exploration of the shelves, she found herself drawn towards those that contained what she knew to be French books, published in the seventeenth and eighteenth centuries and many of them filled with engravings. One day Miss Fisher, armed with a large black book and several pencils, found her there, kneeling in front of the shelves, staring at a book.

'I didn't know you read French. What is your name, girl? Ah, don't tell me – Ellen.'

'No, Miss Fisher, I don't read French. But I wish I did. I would love to read another language, but I suppose I never shall. There is no call for that in a housemaid, no call to read at all, except the laundry lists.'

Miss Fisher looked at her consideringly. 'Well, I suppose I could teach you,' she said. 'Emily was not a very taxing pupil and we rather abandoned French, but I dare say I could try again. It was quite good, my French, once. It would amuse me, that is at least if you prove to be intelligent.' And teach her she did, for fifteen minutes or so most afternoons, in the schoolroom at the top of the house. It was a room Ellen came to know well. Though the furniture was plain and battered, Miss Fisher had covered every flat surface with cloths and rugs and crammed the room with books and pictures and drawings the children had done and shells and assorted souvenirs the children had given her. One thing that struck Ellen was how many portraits of the family there were, in particular pictures of Sir Richard, sketches and a miniature and a little oil painting and a daguerreotype, a great novelty. And piles and piles of books: on her table Ellen found a volume of German philosophy, and a play about Dr Faustus, and two huge dusty volumes about natural history, and the fables of La Fontaine. She wished she could spend all day reading, instead of cleaning and sewing.

The other servants found Ellen's French lessons eccentric but harmless, especially since Ellen worked so hard the rest of the day. She worried that Mrs Rundell (who did not conceal her contempt for the governess) might forbid them. But no – she remarked to Lucy, who told Ellen, that if the girl wanted to improve herself it could do no harm at all, as long as she did the work expected of her.

One Sunday evening in mid-September the weather broke. For a few days it had been so hot and sultry that nobody in the house had had the energy to do more than walk through their daily routines. The attic bedrooms were stifling, one could hardly sleep, even with the door open (which was normally forbidden). Only at one or two o'clock did the housemaids fall into an uneasy slumber. In the mornings of these hot days they left their beds later than usual and might not be at their duties until as late as seven. Nobody, they discovered to their amazement, seemed to mind. Even Katherine, usually so punctilious, was not to be seen till then, so that Beth and Ellen saw no reason to come downstairs at six. Mrs Rundell, in this hot weather, retained the full-bodied dignity of her black dress but seemed to melt into a less energetic being than the one they were used to. Often she was not seen downstairs until noon and no one knew what she was doing. Even Lucy was not allowed into her rooms but was sent away to work elsewhere. Nor was Sir Richard seen: he had his breakfast taken to his room and then he stayed upstairs, resting, perhaps.

If anything Mrs Rundell seemed more amiable than otherwise at this period, or at least abstracted. Something was preoccupying her. She smiled to herself (though not much to others), and when she passed the other servants in the corridor she even sometimes noticed them.

The Sunday that followed this heat was so stifling that the sun was hardly visible for the thick, yellowish light. Mr James was out for the day, the cook was away visiting her family, there was hardly any work to be done, and Sunday afternoon was free for most of the household. In the afternoon Ellen sat in a corner of the walled garden with her book. No one else was there, other than Beth's younger brothers and sisters playing in the distance. Dozing, dreaming of this and that, she woke suddenly with a feeling that something important was happening. She was right. Something was happening, on the main path leading to the pool where she was sitting, Lady Markham's Way, as it was known. As she took in this spectacle, she heard a distant growl in the sky, and then another. These forewarnings were followed by a whistling, rustling sound in the trees, and then a few distinct and very large raindrops, which sizzled as they hit the stone around the fountain where Ellen was sitting. The opaque sky was beginning to change colour, no longer hot and yellowish but grey, changing rapidly to black. Here at last was the thunderstorm they had been waiting for.

Ellen was about to run out of the walled garden towards the house, but as she began to move she saw two people walking towards the place where she was standing, unaware of her presence. She did not want to meet them, not at all: even though they might be annoyed at being observed, their annoyance would be nothing to her embarrassment. After a moment she peered again round the hollyhocks, which she had been hiding behind, and saw the path was now empty. Just as well, because as she did so the rain exploded, violent and intensive, battering the fragile flowers. Protecting her precious book in her shawl, she ran for the shelter of the gardener's house.

She was warmly received by the Hursts. From their talk about the thunder, it was clear they had not seen what she had. She decided to say nothing, even though this spectacle, conducted in the open, invited observation. Her mother had always told her that a chattering tongue was the scourge of womankind – and as the board of 'Rules for Conduct in this Family', displayed in the servants' hall at Markham, explained, a servant should engage in 'No tale-bearing. No tattling'. She held her tongue, though with some difficulty, and did not (at least for the moment) tell even Beth that she had seen Sir Richard walking slowly through the walled garden with, on his arm, dressed not in her usual black but in a floral print dress that fully revealed her form in a way her housekeeper's dress did not, Mrs Rundell. They clearly thought, from the way in which they walked, that nobody would see them.

It rained hard for an hour. When the rain stopped and only heavy drops falling from the trees on to the ground recalled the storm, Ellen walked back to the hall. The garden smelt over-poweringly sweet, the scents of the summer stirred by the down-pour, as though one were walking through a perfumed landscape. Everything at Markham Thorpe seemed so beautiful after the storm. But she did not like what she had seen: Sir Richard with his arm tightly clasped around Mrs Rundell's waist, and his face so close to hers, nuzzling up against her, with his tongue popping out of his mouth. It was unpleasant to see such old people doing such a thing. Even more upsetting was the fact that it was the master of the house and his servant – surely this could not be right? The more she thought about this little scene, the more it seemed to explain certain actions and words of Mrs Rundell. Ellen did not at all care to imagine what Mrs Rundell's intentions for the future might be.

Part Three

In October Ellen fell in love. With Harry, the gardener's boy. She'd often wondered about him. After seeming so interested in her when she arrived at Markham Thorpe, he then avoided even looking at her. They met now and again, even though the gardeners were no longer taking their meals in the servants' hall. Not that she was in the least interested in him, but she did find herself wondering about him a great deal of the time. He had a kind face, she thought. Eventually Beth explained. Harry's father provided the more high-class groceries to the house. Very soon after Ellen's arrival he had had an argument with Mr James – or was it Mrs Rundell? – over their account, claiming the Hall was more than a year in arrears. Harry was almost dismissed, not for any fault of his own but because of his father. The matter was resolved when the head gardener told Mr James what a good boy Harry was, but he had thought it best to be seen as little as possible in the house.

Courting the housekeeper's cousin was unwise. But one October morning when Ellen was walking across the yard to empty a bucket she met Harry. It was a bright morning. There was nobody else around. The sun shone full on his face, which glowed as though a candle were burning inside it. He looked at her, she looked at him, in the way anyone might when they met in the morning, but not quite in the same way. He opened his mouth to say, 'Good morning,' but then did not speak. He simply stared at her. She blushed. He blushed too. Then he gave a laugh, but it was not a laugh of amusement, more as though he recognised that something important had happened.

'Well,' he said, 'Ellen. So there you are.' There was a pause, and he smiled more cheerfully. 'I must be getting my breakfast.'

'Yes,' she said.

'Will you be having your breakfast?'

'Yes,' she said, 'when I've emptied my bucket.'

Harry took the bucket from her. She followed him across the yard. 'There,' she said. 'You empty it there.' Actually she was not thinking about what to do with the bucket at all, but how extraordinary life could be. He turned round and gazed at her, tilting his head, looking at her ears and her nose and her hair tied up at the back, and her white neck emerging from her print work dress.

She did not want him to see her rough red hands, and hid them behind her back. 'You'd better be going to your breakfast,' she said.

'Yes,' he said. 'I had. So had you.' And he looked at her in a way no one had ever looked at her before, somehow as though she was his. She liked this feeling, she thought she liked it very much. It made her feel safe.

After that, life was transformed. They knew they were meant for each other, they said so to one another often, so it must be

96

true. If Ellen felt low or tired, she would think about Harry and cheer up. But it was not easy to meet privately. 'Nobody must know,' he said to her. 'We would both be in trouble – we could be dismissed. Don't say a word to anyone, certainly not that sister of yours.'

'Not even Beth? She'd never tell anyone and, besides, it would make things much easier if Beth knew we were friends.' So Beth was told, and did not express much surprise, only cautioned Ellen not to be carried away – though what this meant, Ellen was unsure.

Harry was very insistent that they should meet as often as possible, even when it was difficult for her. She appreciated his insistence, even though she was occasionally frightened of being found with him. He and Ellen met whenever they could, usually in a corner of the garden, in the afternoon when she was supposed to be sewing with the other maids. It was quite easy to escape, since they hardly saw Mrs Rundell, and Katherine was not very interested in enforcing rules. Indeed, she did not seem very interested in anything some days, and looked pale and weak. Ellen became known in the servants' hall for her fondness for taking walks, however wet or windy the weather might be. They would talk about what they had been doing and thinking, and then they would break off and simply look at each other. After the first time or two he kissed her. They kissed each other a good deal. She realised what Beth had meant by not being carried away. Though Harry did not suggest anything more than kissing, she sometimes wished he would, and thought being carried away sounded a good idea. He would bring her little posies. Though she liked these very much they were a difficulty: she had to smuggle them into the house and hide them in her room, away from the questing eye of Mrs Rundell.

'Are you happy?' Beth said to her one day, watching her come humming down the stairs.

Yes, she supposed she was. Harry made living in someone else's house and doing the same tedious work day after day more or less tolerable. She realised that she was beginning to find life at Markham Thorpe comfortable, like being part of a big family.

The other person who made life interesting was Miss Fisher. Miss Fisher knew so much. She could read not only French but German and a little Italian; she could recite long passages of poetry; she had travelled in her youth and could speak about Rome and Dresden; she knew about paintings and history. She was not exactly friendly to Ellen, treated her as a schoolmistress treats her pupils, but when she was in a good humour she talked in the most interesting way. One of the most memorable events of her life, it seemed, had been a journey that she had taken, many years before, with the Markhams to Italy – a journey she loved to refer to. She seldom talked about herself – 'I don't have a past,' she said once. 'Governesses don't have pasts, only duties.' She preferred to talk about the Markhams, the centre of her world for thirty years, describing the children as they grew up, and how Lady Markham used to visit the schoolroom and listen to the lessons, saying from time to time, 'I am your pupil too, Miss Fisher.' She was an angel, Lady Markham, according to Miss Fisher. When she was alive the house was an almost heavenly place. She would often mention Sir Richard, too. 'Such a fine-looking man,' she would say, 'especially when he was young, before he met the sorrows of this world. You should see Sir Richard on a horse –

nobody manages a horse like Sir Richard. Indeed, he taught me to ride, such a kind instructor he was.' And then they would return to their French lesson.

Now and again Miss Fisher asked Ellen about her aunt Mrs Rundell, slyly as it were, slipping the questions into her conversation. She wanted to know what Mrs Rundell ('Rundell', she always called her) talked about, and how long Ellen had known her, and whether she had been married before, and whether Sir Richard took tea with her very often. Some of these questions Ellen could answer, but not many, and after a while she realised that it might be wiser to say as little as possible. Why did Miss Fisher need all this information?

During the autumn Mrs Rundell was not much seen below stairs. She kept to her own rooms. An announcement was made one day that she would no longer be regularly attending meals in the servants' hall, and after a while she never appeared there, except when she entered unexpectedly, to check that everything was in order. Lucy would carry large trays from the kitchen to the housekeeper's sitting room. This room Mrs Rundell was making extremely comfortable, as Ellen found on her visits there from time to time. One day a gentleman from the upholsterer's in Ripon arrived and was taken up to the housekeeper's rooms, emerging some time later with a slightly flushed air. Two weeks later a carriage arrived from the same establishment, containing two fitters and several rolls of carpet. None of the servants except Lucy went into the housekeeper's room regularly, and Lucy told the others nothing, so it was some time before any of them – it was Ellen, who was invited in – had the chance to note the new carpet. It was Wilton, she was sure, with red, green and gold swirls and a wide border filled with flowers, a fitted carpet what was more, reaching to the walls and so thick your feet sank into it. 'Odd, isn't it, that our Mrs Rundell should be enjoying a splendid carpet when poor Mr James's rooms have not had a lick of paint for ten years, not to mention such a thing as a new carpet?' Katherine remarked. She often spoke in his support. 'He never has any money given to him by his father. It's a wonder he can manage at all.'

Whether Sir Richard and Mrs Rundell still went walking arm in arm in the walled garden, Ellen did not know. She never saw them there again. But they were often observed walking, though not arm in arm, across the lawns or down the drive, Mrs Rundell assisting Sir Richard when they reached the steps. His health was evidently declining, and the doctor called now and again. He must enjoy the comfort of her guiding hand.

In November another change occurred. Sir Richard announced, through Mrs Rundell, that he would no longer be taking his meals in the dining room. The dining room would only be used if there were guests, and there seldom were. In future all Mr James's meals would be served in the smoking room, even if he had guests. Mr James protested, but was told that keeping a fire in the dining room was an unnecessary expense, especially since he had one in the smoking room. Miss Fisher was also affected. For years she and Sir Richard had chatted over their meals and she had kept him amused, but now she was banished to her upstairs sitting room, once the schoolroom, where she sat alone. She hardly saw Sir Richard, unless she made an appointment through Mrs Rundell. Having to ask a favour of the housekeeper made Miss Fisher screw up her little face, as though in pain. As the weeks passed she became pale and sad, though Ellen tried to cheer her.

Ellen was summoned to Mrs Rundell's presence from time to time. Her cousin would look at her closely and comment on her appearance and her hair. Ellen was given a new work dress, made of better material than her old one, and in blue and white stripes rather than plain grey. As she realised when she tried it on, it even had some shape to it. Mrs Rundell did not explain this gift, merely remarking that it was a pity that a pretty girl from a respectable family should have to wear such plain clothing. Ellen would be asked about her progress at housework, and her work for Mr James, and whether Mr James was kind to her. She hardly saw him, Ellen would say, but he was very considerate in the way he left his rooms, as tidy as could be. To which Mrs Rundell hummed, presumably in approval.

At the end of the first of these conversations, Mrs Rundell offered Ellen some refreshment. At first she said no, out of shyness, but her cousin's frown told her this was a mistake. She changed her mind apologetically, and was given marsala in a dainty glass with the Markham coat of arms on it, and a most delicious soft biscuit shaped like a shell. While she consumed these delicacies, still standing, the housekeeper would watch her as though pleased with what she saw. She would leave these meetings, which took place every three weeks or so, confused and yet flattered.

What she did not like was the way the other servants would look at her after these visits, inquisitive but not willing to ask about them, their eyes narrowed and unfriendly.

The event that increasingly preoccupied the household was Christmas. Christmas had always been a great event at Markham Thorpe. 'They may not be as rich as they were,' Beth would say, 'but they do know how to celebrate Christmas.' The daughters would be coming home, the whole house would be opened up, there would be a tenants' party on Boxing Day and a servants' ball at New Year. Even Mrs Rundell, fond as she was of economies, could not stop this happening.

As Christmas neared, the house began to change. The sleeping rooms reawoke. In the drawing room, the dust sheets were removed amid vigorous dusting and polishing. The cook was to be seen poring over long lists in the kitchen, and the tradesmen from Ripon delivered not just everyday items but large packages that clinked excitingly and were hastily removed to the house-keeper's storeroom. On one or two occasions Mrs Saunders was heard to complain that she was not being allowed to spend as much as she usually did, that 'that woman' was cutting down on the Christmas fare, that there would hardly be any celebration worth mentioning this year – but still the packages arrived, not only from Ripon but from York and even London. 'That'll be from Miss Lavinia,' Beth would remark. 'Mrs R would never order anything from London.'

Ellen's duties changed. For many years Mr Fellows had acted as valet for Sir Richard. Mrs Rundell was prone to remark that 'poor Mr Fellows' was finding the business of putting out and tidying his clothes and shoes, and keeping his linen in order, more than he could deal with. He must do less. She was right, as all could see, though the old butler was determined to work as long as he could, and would look away as though he had not heard whenever Mrs Rundell asked him (as she did often, with a note of strong concern) whether he was tired. Sometimes Mr Fellows appeared not quite to know where he was or what he was doing, especially when Mrs Rundell delivered a flurry of questions at him, at great speed. He would say, 'Oh, yes, yes, Mrs Rundell, of course you must, of course we must do that, of course we must, yes, yes, indeed,' and she would smile, shaking her head and saying, 'Oh dear, oh dear, poor old Mr Fellows,' in a way that suggested pitying contempt.

In due course Mrs Rundell announced, on one of her periodic visits to the servants' hall, that in future Jem would be looking after Sir Richard while Ellen would be responsible for Mr James. They would each be paid an additional pound a year for these duties.

There was some commotion in the servants' hall when these changes were announced. No one was surprised that Jem was to look after Sir Richard: that was only proper. But people did find it strange that Ellen was to valet Mr James, as she heard partly from them directly and partly from overheard conversations and looks that came her way. She had no experience, and one of the other housemaids could surely do it, and was it right that such a young girl should be in and out of Mr James's rooms? What was Mrs Rundell thinking of, since the plan was hers? What might she have in mind for Ellen? they even asked.

As it turned out, these duties were not too onerous. Indeed, she even quite enjoyed them. She already knew Mr James from cleaning the smoking room, where the prints showed hunting scenes and the books were all about sport and agriculture. She was intrigued to know more about him – she felt she knew him very little, and she was curious about this man of whom the older servants, at least, tended to speak fondly, though sometimes perhaps with a note of pity.

She did learn more about him, though not all at once. Mr James tended to wear the same clothes every day, though he liked his linen as clean as could be. Since he had been a young boy he had occupied the same rooms – his bedroom, his dressing room and a little room he used as a study – at the back of the house, looking over the stables. They were dark, and rather shabby, but spare and masculine, as a sailor's might be. They contained little that was not useful, other than a print labelled 'Eton College' and two or three pictures of ships at sea. Being the reflective girl she was, she tried to work out from their contents the character of the person who inhabited these undemonstrative rooms. They were so different from the smoking room, the other part of his territory, quieter and more personal, like the rooms of a man who does not have many friends.

Only twice did Mr James appear while she was cleaning his rooms. Each time he apologised, muttered into his moustache, and moved silently round the room as though in search of something. When she suggested she should leave, he said, 'Oh, no, oh, no, don't let me disturb you,' and slid out.

Ellen found herself, for some reason she could not quite understand, taking pride in the appearance of his rooms. When she started they had an uncared-for look, even though Katherine had done her best to keep them in order. She hesitated to move objects around – perhaps he liked the untidiness – but after a while she ventured to tidy some of the papers and arrange his shoes and boots more neatly in the cupboards. She was relieved that he did not move anything back. On the contrary, he became tidier, putting away books on the shelves (he read a good deal, though mostly books about racing and shooting, which were of no interest to her) and picking up his clothes instead of leaving them on the floor, though he did not go so far as to hang them up. His mantelpiece, in particular, she worried about – it was so piled with odds and ends, pieces of paper and invitations (almost all of them old ones), a heap of corks from wine bottles, a wooden carving of a fox, a little box of butterflies, things he must have been given as a child. In the middle was a little portrait of a young lady – his mother, she was sure. Ellen wanted, if possible, to make this mantelpiece look less desolate – as she saw it, here was his childhood and his young manhood, all higgledy-piggledy and covered with confusion and dust. These looked, she thought, like the possessions of someone who had never truly grown up, who in his heart was still a boy.

One day she tried some very mild rearranging. No reaction. She tried a little more. Still no comment. After a week or so of this, the mantelpiece looked, if not tidy, at least better. Then, to her amazement, when she went in one morning, a small vase of flowers, something she had never seen in those rooms, was standing on the chimneypiece. She was pleased to see it, but where had it come from? Had he arranged the flowers? Had somebody else, and if so who could this have been?

She found making his bed difficult. It felt so much like him. In the morning the bedclothes might be curved neatly in the shape of his body, or sometimes twisted into strange shapes as though he had been agitated in his sleep. There was a particular smell to him, not at all unpleasant, of tobacco and eau-de-Cologne and the open air, and when she drew back the bedclothes she would sense this smell, very faintly, in the sheets. Ellen felt the bed was a part of him, as though in touching it she were not exactly touching him but coming very close. So she would make the bed as quickly as she could, hiding the sheets under the huge red counterpane.

The flowers in his vase died and she took them away as the petals began to fall on to the table. That, she thought, must be the right thing for her to do. No other flowers appeared, and though she thought now and again of picking him some more from the garden – where the chrysanthemums were richly profuse – she knew she could not do that. Arranging flowers, after all, was something ladies did, and it hardly seemed right to ask Harry to give her flowers for Mr James. Though she came to know his habits, and could tell his mood when she went into his rooms in the morning, even when he was not there, after two months she had hardly said more to him than 'Good morning, sir', or he more than 'Good morning, Ellen' or 'Thank you, Ellen' to her. She knew so much about him, or so at least she thought. He knew nothing about her.

The housekeeper regularly asked Ellen about her duties. She would mention Mr James's rooms and enquire whether Ellen found it difficult to look after a man's clothing. 'You may think gentlemen don't notice their clothes, Ellen,' she said, 'but even the most careless will be aware at once if everything is not done as they like it. Of course, Mr James is not careless, but equally he is not fussy, shall we say? They live by rules, gentlemen, and ladies too, and if we do not make it easy for them to obey their rules, they will make their feelings known. That is the job of us servants, to make it possible for our masters and mistresses to be ladies and gentlemen without the discomfort of doing any work.' She smiled and her hand tightened its grip over the keys on her table.

'I never see Mr James,' said Ellen, 'and so I don't know if he is satisfied or not. He has not complained, has he? I do my best.'

'I'm sure you do, my dear,' said Mrs Rundell. 'Indeed, when I made an inspection last week, I found the rooms very neat and tidy. I perceived, in fact, that you had tidied the chimneypiece, something nobody has done for many a month, certainly not that silly Katherine,' and she chuckled.

'Has Mr James said anything to you about me?' She was not sure why she wanted to know this.

'Well,' and Mrs Rundell rolled her eyes ruminatively about the room, 'well . . . it's curious that you should ask that. No, he has said nothing.' She stirred her tea. It was remarkable how much tea she drank, pints of it every day, fortified by milk and sugar. On the whole she did not offer this to her guests. 'Well, that is to say,' and she laughed, deep down in her throat, with a sort of gurgle, 'that is to say, he has remarked that you are a good girl – which we know – and look after him very well. So, you see, you give satisfaction. And that is very satisfactory to me, as your cousin and almost your aunt.' And she laughed once more. 'He comes to see me sometimes, you know, and we have a good talk. I do my best to make him comfortable and to be a bridge between him and his papa.' She stroked herself in a satisfied way.

'There's things I know. Sit down, girl, sit down, and don't stare at me with those big eyes of yours.' She contemplated Ellen once again. 'Now, there's something else I want to talk to you about, the servants' ball at New Year.' Again Ellen felt a curious satisfaction that Mrs Rundell would want to talk to her in private about anything. 'The servants look forward to it so much,' she remarked, in a patronising manner, as though she were not a servant herself. 'They have few enough amusements, poor things, that one can't begrudge this modest pleasure. They like to dress up, you know, and the ladies' maids can look very fine in their ladies' cast-off dresses. Your sister looked most refined last Christmas, very ladylike, almost too elegant, you might say. Sometimes – not in this house, but in some of the houses I have known – the maids cut more of a dash than the young ladies, when they have the occasion to dress themselves. And, of course, the young ladies can't laugh at their maids for making mistakes with their hair or their rouge since the girls know all the secrets – and, of course, they know that rouge is very little worn now-adays by respectable women.' Her eyes narrowed. She was not laughing now. 'The young gentlemen always enjoy these events, of course, since they have the chance to dance with the maids. Sometimes they've been itching to get their hands on them, and the chance of a dance is very tempting . . .' She looked at Ellen thoughtfully. 'Of course it's easier for the ladies' maids to make themselves gaudy, and I've no doubt your sister Agnes will be even more fancy this year than last, especially now she's learning the London fashions. It's not so easy for a housemaid, especially one who's never even been to York.'

'I have been to York,' said Ellen, 'twice.'

'Ah, you've been to York twice, that makes you quite a cosmo-pole. So what will you wear, my girl?'

Ellen was quite cast down. She had no idea what she would wear. She only had her work dresses, and the simple clothes she had brought from home, and they would not do at all for a ball. A ball! Imagine trying to dress up, and having to dance in front of all those people, and then – could she dance with the person she wanted to dance with, and could she dance with him all evening, and what would the others say, and would she be forced to dance with Sir Richard or whoever it might be?

'I suppose Agnes might lend me something,' she said finally.

'Agnes might indeed lend you something, but whether she would want to be outshone by her little sister I don't know. Besides, Agnes is four inches taller than you, and quite different in form, quite a different shape, Juno-like, as they say, not a slender little thing like you, with hardly a curve to be seen. And I don't know that the young ladies will give you anything. Miss Lavinia is considerately taller than you, and Miss Emily by a little way, but they would not think of it, even at Christmas the season of goodwill. You would be the last person on their minds. In any case, I don't think we want to be beholding to them, do we? I'll have to see if I can assist you myself.' She smiled. This was a relief. There was, Ellen felt, a compelling force about Mrs Rundell. In her presence, you did not feel completely in command of yourself. She seemed to know what you were thinking.

Mrs Rundell was scrutinising Ellen and nodding. 'Turn to the side, Ellen,' she commanded. Then she stood up and advanced upon the girl, who stepped back. Her cousin laughed. 'You have no need to be afraid of me, my dear. I am your kin, after all. Other people may need to look out for themselves, but not you. Just stand there.' She held a tape measure, which she laid down Ellen's leg, across her shoulders, the length of her arms. Then she stretched her hands round Ellen's waist. She stood very close as she did this so that the girl could feel the stiff black dress with pieces of black jet interwoven in the material, smell her perfumed hair, the rich soap she used and something else, perhaps the comforting liquid she put in her tea. Mrs Rundell stood for several moments gripping Ellen. The girl was uncertain whether to pull in her waist. She did not quite like this powerful body, breathing deeply and rapidly, so close to her own. Then Mrs Rundell remarked, 'A very pretty waist, and as small as any lady's, though perhaps not quite as small as it used to be – we feed you well here, don't we?' Released, Ellen stepped back, perplexed. 'I think we can find you something for the ball,' said Mrs Rundell. 'In a few weeks I should be able to contrive something. You don't have any jewels, I suppose?'

'No, none, I never did. I've never worn a jewel.'

'Well, you shall, just for the evening. We want our child to be as pretty as a picture, don't we? As pretty as a girl can be.' She nodded at Ellen, to dismiss her. 'You must go back to your duties, Ellen, you can't be spending the day here seeking admiration.' This was hardly fair. As Ellen said to herself, she had not gone to Mrs Rundell's room seeking admiration.

Ellen told Harry about this occasion as soon as she saw him. He had no reason to like Mrs Rundell and he was not pleased. 'What's she buying you clothes for, then?' he asked crossly. 'I know she's your relation but what's she buying you clothes for?' And when she said there was no reason to think Mrs Rundell was buying her anything, he looked even more angry and stubborn, and said, 'Well, maybe she's borrowing something from the pawnbroker, even worse. At least if she's going to help you she could do her best for you.' Ellen said Mrs Rundell had seemed proud of her, making Harry even angrier. 'Well,' he said, 'maybe you prefer whatever Mrs R can find for you. Maybe you should go to her to settle your future. Maybe she can offer you something I can't.' He scowled and drew away from her. They were standing in the shadow of the kitchen-garden wall, where they usually met when it was not raining. The huge elms and the shrubs clustering against the walls made a little grove where they could not be seen, and Harry could pretend to be working if anyone disturbed them. It was very quiet there, and they felt more inclined than ever to speak in low tones, but as he became angry his voice rose.

'Hush, Harry,' she said, 'hush, my dear. Somebody will hear us.'

'What does that matter?' he said. 'Most of them know we are walking out, though perhaps you don't want to be doing that any more. Perhaps Mrs R has other plans for you.' He looked handsomer than ever, standing proudly upright, his eyes boring into her. She had never seen him angry before.

'No,' she said. 'Mrs R may have other plans for me but that's of no interest to me, not at all. It's you I love, Harry my dear, not old Mrs R.'

He still looked furious, then suddenly laughed. 'Well, that's all right, then,' he said. 'But you be careful of Mrs R. There's no knowing what that old woman may be up to. You just be wary of her.'

After a while she said to him, 'Do you really think most of the people here know we're courting?'

'Some of them do,' he said. 'Beth knows, of course, and I think her dad may have guessed. If they think we . . .' He blushed deeply and looked at the ground.

'If they think we what, Harry?' But he would say no more, and only that evening did Ellen realise what he had meant.

*　　*　　*

Since Mrs Rundell and Mr Fellows had ceased to take part in meals in the servants' hall, life there had become much easier. With Jem presiding in his easy-going way, they talked freely, even though not all of them were friends. When Lucy appeared she would stay silent and leave as soon as she had finished. Her only contact with the others was the occasional hostile glance. Ellen thought these glances were directed particularly at her, though why, she had no idea. Katherine, on the other hand, would become quite animated, particularly after her pint of beer. She was fond of telling stories about her early life at Markham Thorpe and how things had been twenty-five years before, and how her ladyship had found the house so sad and old fashioned, and had set about making it prettier. Now and again she would remark on Mrs Rundell, as they all liked to do, but Katherine knew more about her than the rest. She would tell them how previously Mrs R had worked in a small house in Lincolnshire, with hardly any servants at all, looking after an old lady for a long time until the old lady did as she was bade and not the other way round. 'I understand the lady was generous to her in her will, and our Mrs Rundell has quite a little fortune stacked away in the bank.' She would shoot glances now and again towards Ellen, as she talked in this way. Though Ellen tried to look unconcerned she felt uncomfortable. She knew everyone in the servants' hall was aware that Mrs R had offered favours to her little cousin, favours she had not refused . . .

One evening they were sitting rather late in the hall, which, along with the kitchen next door, was much the warmest room in the house and a pleasant place to sit about in as the evenings grew chillier. Several flagons of beer, over and above the daily allowance, had appeared on the table, and Jem was smoking, and the dishes from supper were still on the table so that they could nibble at cheese and the apple pie Mrs Saunders had produced because it was a Saturday night, and they all felt most comfortable. As they chatted, complaining in a mild way about everything and wondering whether it would be a cold winter and when the family would be arriving and whether Mr Dykes would be spending Christmas at Markham, Jem stood up and coughed commandingly. 'I have an announcement to make,' he said. They gaped at him. 'A very important announcement. I have asked Beth to be my wife, and she has accepted my hand, and her father has given us his blessing.' There was a silence, and then they all clapped and cheered, and shook his hand, and kissed her cheek. And when were they to be married – next year, he said – and would they be staying at Markham Thorpe? Yes, for the moment at least, but Beth would not be working as housemaid after they were married, only coming in now and again to help, that was what Mrs Rundell had suggested, but Jem would be continuing, and they would be moving into a cottage just near the house.

'So I suppose we shall be seeing some new faces,' someone remarked. 'There are few enough of us here now.'

'Maybe Mrs Rundell has some more nieces,' remarked Mrs Saunders. They all giggled, all except Ellen who was not listening. She was thinking about Beth and the life she was going to lead with Jem, a pleasant way of life, Ellen thought, perhaps the sort of life she might lead herself, one day, with Harry.

A few weeks before Christmas, Ellen was summoned to Mrs Rundell's room. The housekeeper was seated by the fire, toasting her feet on the fender. Beside her on her sewing table was a long brown card box, which revealed nothing about the contents. She smiled in that way she had, mouth curving, eyes cold. 'I have something for you.'

'Yes, Mrs Rundell?'

'I hope you will like it. First we must see how it fits. Stand over there, in front of the glass.'

Ellen obeyed.

'Take off that dress.'

Ellen was reluctant to obey. She did not like the idea of standing in her petticoat and her little white undershirt in front of Mrs Rundell. She hesitated.

'Do as I say. You can't try on a dress if you have one on already. Take it off.'

Ellen removed her black maid's dress. Looking in the long cheval glass, she was reminded of how hideous her underclothes were, though her face looked all right. She saw a black figure moving behind her, holding something white and floating with pink silk ribbons entwined in it. The figure moved towards her.

'Turn round and face me,' said Mrs Rundell. 'Hold up your arms. Stand still. Put on this petticoat. Put on this other petticoat. Now the dress.' Ellen found herself encased in a dress such as she had never worn, made of soft, caressing material. Mrs Rundell tutted and told her to stand straight, fastened the ribbons at the back, tied her sash, smoothed her sleeves, put a shawl round her shoulders. She stood back and looked at her handiwork, up and down, and gestured to the girl to turn sideways. Pursing her lips, she took Ellen's head between her hands, twisting it round sharply so that the girl cried out. Mrs Rundell pulled the hairpins out of Ellen's hair, tied in a neat bun. Her soft fair hair sprang into life. The older woman gestured at the girl, telling her to shake her head. The hair fell round her shoulders.

'Well,' said the housekeeper, her voice expressing satisfaction and more. 'You don't look like a housemaid at all, Ellen, you look like a lady, a real proper lady. That dress is much too good for a housemaid, even at a servants' ball.' She sat down heavily in her chair and poured herself a little more tea. 'But youth's blossom soon fades. We must enjoy it while it lasts. Look at yourself in the glass, my dear.'

Ellen did not recognise herself or anyone she had ever been, not the drab housemaid or the plain schoolgirl, in the person she saw in the mirror. 'Is that me?' she said, knowing at once that the question must sound absurd. 'Is that me?'

'It's you, all right, Ellen, it's you, even though you don't look like a housemaid but a lady. For the ball you will need no cosmetics, just a little powder since you have a tendency to flush, but no rouge. We will have to see about putting up your hair becomingly, but otherwise, my dear, you are all ready.'

Mrs Rundell turned away towards the window, her fists clenched. 'This will teach them,' she whispered, as though speaking only to herself. 'This'll teach those young ladies.' She turned back to Ellen, who was still standing, entranced, in front of the mirror. 'Now, take that dress off,' she went on. 'The fit is perfect, your figure is ideal. Oh, before you do, there's a scarf,' and out of another parcel she took a green silk scarf. 'Try this on, Ellen,' she said, in a way that was both imperious and affectionate. 'I'll arrange it for you.' She stood in front of her young cousin, assessing her, looking at the scarf, then at Ellen's face and gently heaving breast. She raised the shawl over Ellen's head, let it fall on to her shoulders, pulled it this way and that, patted it into the position she wanted, all the time her narrowed eyes assessing the effect. 'Yes,' said Mrs Rundell, 'that will certainly do. I think the gentlemen will like that – one gentleman in particular.'

'Why are you doing this for me, Mrs Rundell?' asked Ellen.

'You are my very own girl,' said Mrs Rundell, 'a pretty girl, and a sweet one, and I want to do my best for you. And who knows? We may even find you a husband.' But as Ellen continued to stare at herself in the mirror, Mrs Rundell's mood changed abruptly. 'Now, take it all off, Ellen.' And as the girl was slow to respond, 'Do as I say at once. We've spent enough time on this business.'

Mrs Rundell became peculiarly brisk and decisive. Fortifying herself now and again with sips of tea, she rapidly, almost roughly, removed the shawl and laid it on the table, unfastened the dress, told Ellen to step out of the petticoats, and left her almost naked in the middle of the floor. 'Enough of this, for the moment at least. Back into your own clothes,' she said. 'You won't be seeing this costume again until the servants' ball. That's all, you can go.'

Ellen was used to being hastily dismissed and was no longer offended. She left feeling excited about her new clothes but at the same time puzzled. The dress had, she thought, been made for her specially – who had paid for it, then? Would the money be taken out of her wages? Would her parents have to pay for it? Or was Mrs Rundell doing this out of kindness or, indeed, for some other reason that Ellen did not understand?

*   *   *

When Miss Emily came home in December, the atmosphere in the household changed at once. The dining room and drawing room came back into use, and Sir Richard returned to meals with the family and Miss Fisher. The housekeeper, no longer almost invisible, supervised the house with alarming energy. In place of the slow routine that had developed, the maids again found themselves working fifteen or so hours a day. Mrs Saunders, reanimated, cooked as she had not for months, doing all she could to please Miss Emily and prepare for the festivities. Mr Fellows put on his best coat again (he had been wearing his second-best coat that from black had turned to green with age, since his master hardly saw him and Mr James did not notice) and tried to appear brisk, more successfully in the morning than the evening, when he would sometimes slow to an almost complete halt. From time to time he would give pieces of advice to Ellen on etiquette and correct behaviour, such as the occasions when a servant should show he was aware of the Quality's conversation and when not. Even Mr James seemed more cheerful. He brushed his hair regularly again, emerging frequently from the back of the house to help his sister make ivy wreaths, or climbing on a ladder to push holly behind the pictures while Billy nervously held down the ladder with his foot. Ellen hardly had time to talk to her sister, only to note the elegant clothes and fashionable airs Agnes had acquired. Her voice had become more ladylike than ever and she would smile patronisingly – it was hard to bear. Nor did she have time to see her young man privately, and had to wave at him occasionally from an upstairs window.

When the Wentworths arrived, the bustle increased. Meals were served ceremoniously and punctually in the dining room with all of the family present. At dinner in the servants' hall Mrs Rundell and Mr Fellows presided as before. The Great Hall, decorated with a huge bunch of mistletoe hanging from the chandelier, looked grand, especially when the candles were lit in the sconces and a fire was burning. It was finer than anything Ellen had ever seen, even the subscription rooms in Malton when she went there once as a child for a Christmas entertainment.

You especially felt the family's kindness at Christmas time. They gave a party for the tenants and their children in the Great Hall, ninety or a hundred people. The village choir played their instruments, there was dancing and games for the children, a bran tub, presents for everyone, a speech of welcome from Sir Richard. On Christmas Day the family and servants walked to church across the park to hear the Christmas sermon Mr Walters the rector had delivered every year as long as anyone could remember. After church all the servants were invited to the Great Hall to open their presents. This was a moment of high excitement, since unlike many families the Markhams did not give each maid a length of cloth, but found everyone something individual: a brooch for one, a necklace for another, riding boots for Jem, and for Ellen a small mirror framed in what she thought must be ebony and mother-of-pearl. She had other presents, too: a book sent her by her father, a pair of mittens from her mother, a velvet purse from her sister. She was very happy to have these things, but it made her sad to think of her family miles away, celebrating their Christmas without her. She knew from earlier Christmases, after Agnes had left home, how much her parents missed her. And then there was a silver chain, the prettiest chain, which she put on at once. It came from someone who did not reveal their name, but she had no doubt who this was.

For Christmas dinner in the Great Hall, for the Markhams and the rector's family and an old aunt or two, the table was covered with silver and bowls of grapes and crystallised fruit and marzipan. Quantities of wine were drunk, notably by the rector and Mrs Walters, who gave the impression of competing in a wassailing competition. Dinner afterwards in the servants' hall was almost equally fine, dampened for Ellen only by the fact that Harry was away with his family. Such goose there was, and chestnut stuffing, and roast potatoes, and sausages, and plum pudding, and red wine, something she'd never tasted. Ellen laughed a great deal during dinner, feeling ever more cheerful and boisterous until her sister removed her glass.

The highlight of the festivities was the servants' ball, which was to happen on the Saturday evening three days after Christmas. As she worked her way through the day, observing the preparations for the evening, the arrival of three women from the village to help (she hardly knew them, the village was a foreign country to her) and of trays of food brought in by caterers from Ripon, the tuning up of the band, she grew increasingly excited, yet nervous. Would she have a chance to dance with Harry? That was the great question. Would the dress Mrs Rundell had promised really be available? How would she manage if Mrs R had changed her mind?

'What are you wearing this evening, child?' Agnes asked her, that morning. 'You have nothing to wear at all, do you? I suppose I'll have to lend you something.'

'I think I do have something,' said Ellen.

'And what does that mean?' her sister wanted to know. 'What can you possibly have, a little thing like you?'

'I have something to wear,' said Ellen, stubbornly, unwilling to let her sister know where her dress was coming from. Mrs Rundell had never provided a dress for Agnes, as far as Ellen knew.

'Don't be so contrary, child,' cried Agnes, turning to her sister with an impatient stare. 'Tell me what you have to wear. That gardener's boy can't have found you a dress, surely. You can't have bought anything – they've hardly paid you yet. Has Miss Emily given you something of hers? Tell me. As your sister I need to know. It's not something from Mr James, is it?'

Agnes had never been more annoying and Ellen had never felt so provoked. 'No,' said Ellen. 'I won't tell you.'

The ball was to start at six. At half past four, Ellen was summoned to Mrs Rundell's room. The housekeeper was already attired in a rich purple silk dress, which showed her shoulders and upper arms, which were handsome and white, as Ellen noticed with some surprise, never having thought what might lie beneath the black silk. 'I have your clothes ready,' Mrs Rundell announced, 'and I will help you into them. At the end of these proceedings you will help me out of my clothes. Lucy is so ill tempered today I can't ask her to do it. Come . . .'

An hour or so later, her face very lightly powdered, her hair skilfully arranged by Mrs Rundell, her petticoats smoothed down, her legs encased in white stockings, her feet in little dancing shoes with white ribbons, and her whole self embraced by the white dress she had been dreaming about for several nights – Ellen looked at herself in the mirror, and drew in her breath sharply.

She realised, for the first time, that when people said she was very pretty (as they quite often did) they meant it. She seemed to glow in these clothes.

'Very pretty,' said Mrs Rundell, 'very nice indeed.' And as Ellen started to wriggle and shift in the sheer pleasure of being so beautifully dressed, her cousin clasped her by the waist to stop her moving and said, 'Stand still, there's something else. You can't go to a ball without a necklace, can you, my dear? Your fairy godmother has no glass slippers for you, my little Cinderella, but she has something just as nice – your jewellery or, rather, my jewellery. An innocent young girl does not wear very much jewellery, but since this is a Christmas party, I have something for you.' And she unlocked her bureau and took out a small blue leather case with gold writing on the front, which she handed to Ellen. In her exaltation, Ellen hardly knew what to do with it.

'Open it,' she said, looking expectantly at Ellen.

The case contained a necklace of blue stones intertwined with flowers in gold, and quite beautiful. 'Do you like it?'

She could scarcely speak. Mrs Rundell put the necklace round Ellen's neck tenderly but firmly, letting her hands slide from her neck on to Ellen's shoulders. Then she stood back to judge the effect. 'Yes,' she said, 'a turquoise necklace, it is perfect for you. Really, I have chosen the wrong profession.'

'Oh, thank you,' Ellen breathed, 'thank you, Cousin Rundell. You are so kind to me . . .'

'Well, you have no reason to be so grateful. This pretty necklace doesn't belong to you, child, it's mine. I am only lending it to you. But then, you never know, one of these days it might be yours, I suppose. Though, of course, one day you may have so many jewels of your own you won't need anything of your Cousin Rundell's.' She sat down for a moment, while Ellen, unable to resist, gravitated again to the mirror. From some old lesson of her mother's she knew that vanity was wrong and led to all sorts of dreadful things, but it was so very pleasant to see herself looking – she had to admit – so fine.

But Mrs Rundell had not finished with her advice. 'Now, Ellen, mind how you behave yourself this evening. Not very much to drink, not too much to eat. You're very fair, your face will go red if you partake too much. That's not at all becoming. If you are tired or overheated, stop dancing and drink water. The fruit sherbet will be very good, everything else is to be avoided. Do not dance with the same person all evening, however much you may like them, unless it is Sir Richard, who will not want to dance with you, I think, or Mr James, who may. If one of the family asks you to dance, always accept at once, even if you are engaged for the next dance by a servant. Don't laugh too much, it's vulgar, but smile and look cheerful all the time. Exhibit your good manners always, show you are well brought-up. Don't go into a corner with the other girls and giggle. That is what common girls do. I think that is all.'

Ellen was alarmed. 'Why do I have to be so careful?'

'I want everyone to see you are a refined young lady, even though temporary you are working as a housemaid. That must be clear to everybody, the Markhams or the simple country people. Do you understand me?'

'Yes.'

'Good. Now sit down and wait. I will fetch you when the time comes. I am going down to see everything is in order. But first there is one thing I must do . . .' She sat down at a table in the corner of the room, which held a silver-framed mirror and several phials and bottles. 'I want to look my best too, you know,' she said, and laughed. 'Though you, no doubt, think of me as your old cousin aged over a hundred, I have my vanities too you know.' She lifted one of the phials, shiny and black with a silver top, and showed it to the girl. 'Do you know what this is, my dear? I imagine not. An innocent country girl like you would not be familiar with such things. This is tincture of bella donna, and those of us who want our eyes to sparkle find bella donna is what we need.' She threw back her head, and let several drops fall into each eye. She laughed again, seeing Ellen gaze at her curiously. 'I would not allow anyone else to see my secrets,' she said, 'but I don't mind you seeing them.'

'Bella donna, what is bella donna?' asked Ellen.

'Bella donna is deadly nightshade, a poison, my dear, which is why I keep this phial in the still room where no one can chance upon it – except Lucy, I suppose, and she has little enough reason to want it. But when it is made into a tincture by an apothecary, it makes a lady's eyes glitter. You may wonder why I need to make my eyes sparkle – you'll see, one day.'

She dabbed at her eyes and looked at herself in the mirror, apparently with approval. The little clock on the mantelpiece chimed six in little bell-like tones, a very feminine clock it was, just as the whole room was very feminine in its way.

'It's six o'clock,' said Ellen. 'May I go down now, Cousin Rundell? I shall miss all the fun.'

'You shall go down when I tell you. You will have plenty of fun, and more, if you play your cards right. You need to make an entrance, and it needs to be properly timed. I will tell you when to come down. Sit quietly, don't fidget.'

Many years later, looking back on that evening, Ellen remembered a series of impressions. Even going downstairs was memorable because they walked down the main staircase, lit by candles on every newel post. She recalled the moment before they went into the Great Hall, Mrs Rundell straightening Ellen's back, holding her by the upper arm, then opening the door and launching her forward – finding the room brightly lit, filled with noise and chat, hearing the noise subsiding into a brief silence and realising that she was the reason – the looks of the people around her, astonished, admiring, envious, suspicious, affectionate, Mrs Wentworth gazing at her with a strange expression, Miss Emily perplexed, Jem (very handsome in his evening coat) looking at her with approving interest, Billy beseechingly adoring, Beth open-mouthed and almost shocked, a mass of other men's faces, and somewhere Harry, though she could not see him – a glass being pressed into her hand and someone patting her encouragingly on the back, Mrs Rundell with her hand behind Ellen, pushing her gently forward – the arrival of the band, amid applause, the floor being cleared, Sir Richard taking first place in the row of dancers with Mrs Rundell, the family all pairing off with the senior servants, Mrs Wentworth with Jem, Miss Emily with the gamekeeper, Mr Dykes with Agnes, Miss Fisher with the rector, nobody asking her to dance until Mr James, anxious, dark, flushed, was bowing before her – the music striking up, Sir Richard and Mrs Rundell leading off, the line of dancers following, Mr James dancing rather well, and looking into her eyes from time to time, it was not unpleasant that he should look at her like this, the exhilaration of the dance, down the length of the hall and back again to the sound of the fiddles – could anything ever be more pleasurable? – a sudden view of Harry among the spectators, looking at her morosely, a spasm in her heart but on they swept, and when she passed the same spot Harry was there no longer, the dance ending, everyone laughing and applauding, Mr James bowing and asking for the pleasure of the next dance – she could not say no, she knew she was not allowed to say no – more exhilaration but also anxiety: what was Harry doing and would he mind and when would she have the chance to dance with him?

When the music stopped again, Mr James and Ellen were in the middle of the hall. A space formed around them, since Mr James was standing quite still and merely looking at Ellen, and she was so pleasurably exhausted she could hardly stir. The dress felt like part of her body; it was a delicious sensation. 'Thank you, Ellen,' said Mr James, 'that was a pleasure, a great pleasure,' and he bowed again, deeply. 'Might I claim the next dance?'

As she smiled at him to say yes (was this not what Mrs Rundell had instructed her to do?), someone intruded upon them, urgently and angrily. 'The next dance is mine,' he said. Mr James looked in surprise rather than anger at his rival, a very young boy, tousle-haired, in a not very well-fitting suit, a servant he recognised but could not put a name to. Harry met his gaze defiantly. They both turned towards Ellen, who was confused and embarrassed, not knowing what to do, aware, beyond the circle of her suitors, of curious eyes, of Mrs Wentworth staring at them with disgust, of Mrs Rundell, leaning on Sir Richard's arm and surveying them intently. The musicians tuned up again, and the couples began to form, but more slowly this time as though circling around this little confrontation. At that hectic moment Harry seized Ellen's hand and raised it as though to proclaim possession, while Mr James hesitated, smiled, bowed, muttered, 'Thank you,' to Ellen, and moved into the crowd. The dance began again. Ellen was enchanted to be dancing with her young man but at the same time felt sorry for Mr James, dimly aware of his good manners.

'Ellen, you look so beautiful,' Harry whispered, 'I couldn't not dance with you, I couldn't wait one more minute. You're mine, Ellen, you're mine,' he said, grasping her as firmly as he possibly could. Dance with her he did, dance after dance, never letting her out of his sight all evening, holding her hand even when they were not dancing in a way that suggested she was his, sliding his arm round her waist after a while, sitting out with her in a corner of the Great Hall, in a remote corner but not so remote that they were not observed and, above all, not letting anyone else speak a single word to her. At the end of the evening, when the band had stopped playing and a toast had been drunk to Sir Richard, and the family had gone and there was no more to drink, he pulled Ellen by the hand into the dark corridor that led to the smoking room and put his arms round her, pressing her hard against the wall. 'Oh, Harry,' she said, feeling the warmth of his body against her and his questing tongue exploring her lips, 'Harry my darling . . .' And then she noticed that there was a light under the door of the smoking room, and who would this be but Mr James, who might come out at any moment, and she thought that Harry was indeed about to be carried away, and she pulled herself away from him, kissed him firmly, but only once, and hurried back into the Great Hall.

There were her sister and Beth and Jem and a few others, sitting on the settles and chairs as they never normally did, and chatting. Mrs Rundell was not to be seen. When she came in they all stopped talking and looked at her.

'Ah, it's my little sister!' remarked Agnes. Her tone was not friendly.

'Yes,' said Ellen.

'You've been making a spectacle of yourself.'

'Have I?' she asked tremulously.

'At a ball, you never dance all evening with one man, even if he's your intended.'

'I didn't.'

'You as good as did. Saying no, you wouldn't dance, to Mr James like that, in front of everybody! And dancing with that little boy instead of Mr James, what were you thinking of there?'

'I didn't say no to Mr James, it just happened.' She was going to say, 'I love Harry,' but decided it would not be a good idea.

'You silly child, embarrassing Mr James and all the family like that. And you've maddened Mrs Rundell. She left a while ago looking like a winter gale.'

'Don't be cruel to the girl,' said Jem.

Beth had not yet spoken. She did not look very pleased either. 'No, it was no way to behave,' she said. 'You at your first servants' ball, flouncing around like a princess and treating the family with such rudeness. Poor Mr James, left alone in the middle of the room. Miss Lavinia and Miss Emily, they weren't pleased at all, I could see.

'And where did that dress come from?' her sister insisted. 'And the necklace? Where did they come from? Was it Cousin Rundell gave them to you?'

But Ellen only shook her head.

'Very pretty, you looked,' said Jem, 'quite a picture——' but he was interrupted.

'You'd best be going to bed. We've seen quite enough of you,' said Agnes.

Ellen moved towards the door and burst into tears.

'Don't be too hard on her, she's very young,' said Jem, but Agnes and Beth sat stony-faced and unforgiving. Ellen stumbled up the stairs to her room, wishing she had never seen these beautiful clothes, and fell sobbing on to her bed, still wearing the necklace, as though it were a chain.

Ellen woke in the cold dark morning and found her pillow smeared with powder and the necklace lying in a hard little heap beside her. When she looked in the mirror she saw her face was still made up, though splotchily now, her hair was tangled and full of hanging pins. She was late, she knew, but when she ran downstairs she found the house completely quiet. No one had told her (why not? she wondered later) that the morning after the servants' ball they could lie abed till eight or so when it was no longer decent to be in bed. The Great Hall was in chaos, and since nobody else was there and she did not feel energetic she sat on a bench and recalled the evening before. From what the others had said last night, she must have been very rude to Mr James. What would he think of her? Would he no longer want her to serve his meals?

During breakfast Lucy came into the servants' hall and made

her way towards Ellen, scowling even more than usual. 'You're wanted,' she said.

Ellen did not need to ask where she was wanted. Amid complete silence, she set off to fetch the white dress, the petticoats, the shawl and, above all, the necklace. The clothes looked rumpled and there were one or two marks on the dress, but they were not too bad.

She was sure Mrs Rundell would be furious, but to her surprise she was merely businesslike and cool.

'Have you brought everything?' she said. 'The dress, the petticoats, the shawl, the stockings, the shoes and the necklace? Good. Fold up the dress as best you can for the moment. The shawl, put that over there. The petticoats you must fold. Hmm. You can keep the shoes and the stockings, I see no harm, though I am not quite sure that you have deserved them.' And as Ellen — by now practised in such things — tidied the clothes and put them in their boxes, Mrs Rundell talked.

'Did you enjoy yourself last night?'

'Yes, Mrs Rundell.'

'Good. You certainly appeared to. Indeed, I would say you were quite transported with pleasure. You made quite an impression, one way or another. You realise, I suppose, that you need to be careful — a young girl in your position needs to play her cards sensibly. Just as I do, even though I am hardly a young girl. An attractive woman has many advantages, but sometimes she must be wary of how she uses them. Above all, she must guard the precious gift that only she possesses, until it is the moment to use that gift to best advantage. You understand me, I suppose.' Ellen nodded obediently. 'Last night you were a little carried away.

Remember that if you want to succeed, you must let your head rule your heart – which is not what happened last night. You're young, you have time. But don't forget my advice.' She surveyed Ellen once again, with that peculiar mixture of assessment and approval Ellen was familiar with. 'However, you made an impression on everybody present, and that is perhaps the most important thing. Just be careful not to be led into temptation – or, at any rate, temptation of a sort that won't be good for you.'

'Yes,' said Ellen.

'By the way, last thing, when I wanted you to help me off with my clothes, you were not to be seen. I had to tell Lucy to help me. Very clumsy and stupid she is with clothes, and very bad tempered, these days. One would almost think she was annoyed with me, or jealous of someone, I can't imagine why.' She gave a gurgling sound in her throat, then looked at Ellen sharply. 'I hope you were sensible.'

'Oh, yes, Mrs Rundell, I was sensible.'

'I thought you would be. A sensible girl, essentially, you are. But passion is a very strange thing. Or so they say, they who experiment it.' Again she gave her gurgling laugh. 'Passion is a very strange thing.'

The dress and the petticoats were tidied away. Ellen curtsied. 'Will that be all, Mrs Rundell?'

'Yes. Now, let me take a look at you. Ah! Your face is clean enough, but your hair – what have you done with your hair? Come here.'

And holding Ellen's little body against her strong bosom, she twisted the girl's head round and pulled out the hairpins that still lingered there, combed the hair vigorously, brushed it, tweaked and smacked it, until it was back in its usual straight lines.

'Oh,' she said, 'and you may as well keep the scarf, though take good care of it, and don't tell the others I've given it to you.'

It snowed the night after that one, for the first time that winter. When the servants woke up, the snow was still falling. They at once felt the stillness outside, and the cold seeping through the thin ceilings. When they looked out of their windows, the snowflakes were drifting down to settle on the roof and window-ledges and on the lawns beyond. A few hours later when the gentry awoke, the snow had stopped and was piled over the house and the garden. A few rays of sunshine crept apologetically over the horizon, then disappeared behind the high trees in Keeper's Wood.

In the afternoon the family and their friends sallied out, laughing and shouting, built a snowman on the front lawn and decorated him with holly, and tobogganed down the hill. The maids were supposed to be at work in the sewing room but reckoning this was still holiday time they slipped out to the garden beyond the stables where they would not be seen, and there they, too, threw snowballs and laughed loudly amid the white quietness, broken only by the patter of the snow falling from the branches.

Ellen thought she might see Harry in the garden, but he was not there. None of the gardeners was outside. They must be indoors, working at something or other, mending their tools. They appeared in time for dinner but Harry was not among them. She could not ask the other boys where he was, only steal little glances at them from time to time. He never came.

The house resumed its ways, except for Harry. He was not to be seen. Ellen asked Beth where he might be, but Beth could not find out at first: her father would not tell her. Then, after a day or two, she kept Ellen behind in the sewing room when the others left.

'Harry has left Markham Thorpe,' she said. 'He's been offered another position, up in Northumberland, and he has taken it. He left yesterday.'

'Taken it? Left? Without telling me?'

'They needed someone at once, it seems. Nothing my father said would stop his father sending him off. His dad said he must go at once.'

'But couldn't he come and say goodbye? Harry? Couldn't he come and say goodbye?'

Beth looked at her blankly. 'No, it seems not. He had to go, they wanted him at once. We can't do as we want, us servants, we do as we're told. If they offer us a good opening, we take it. Our convenience is not to the point.'

'But I don't understand. Why didn't he come and say goodbye?'

She sat on her little hard chair gazing at the flowered table-cloth, but Beth did not respond to her silence, though above all Ellen wanted Beth to say something. But she said nothing. She merely folded up her sewing things and said, 'It's time for tea,' and left the room. Ellen sat by herself for a long time and tears poured silently from her eyes until the front of her dress was quite soaked. She cried because of Harry and she cried a little, too, because of Beth.

The daughters and Mr Wentworth and Mr Dykes left the house soon afterwards, with their servants. Late on the evening before they were going, Agnes found Ellen in her room, preparing for bed. Agnes had not spoken much to her sister in the past few days and at this point was not wearing a very friendly expression.

'A real muddle you've landed yourself in,' she began.

'Why?' asked Ellen.

'First of all, the ball. You let Cousin Rundell dress you up like a prize chicken ready for the slaughter, didn't you? She tried that on me a year or two ago, and I said, no, I didn't need her fine clothes, I didn't want to be her slave, no, thank you very much, I didn't want to be beholden to her. What she's looking for is someone who will be her spy, who'll tell her what is going on in the servants' hall, who'll let her know who's saying what about her or about anyone else in the house. That's what she wants.'

'I don't believe you,' said Ellen.

'You're an innocent,' said her sister. 'Just a little girl who doesn't understand anything. What's more, our cousin Rundell, she doesn't like being a servant, she thinks it's not good enough for her. I can understand that, indeed I can, but I don't agree with the way she deals with it. My life will be quite different. I see another way out of domestic service, and I intend to take it. You're too young to understand.'

'You're always lecturing me,' said Ellen, crossly.

'And did you see her own dress? Purple silk, *décolleté*, quite fashionable in a Leeds sort of way, though folks would smile in London, think she looked like a housekeeper dressing herself up. Yes, Cousin Rundell plans to be a lady, though if you ask me she looks like something quite else.' She shot a look at Ellen and bit her lip. 'She's vulgar, that's what she is, in a way you and I will never be, my dear.'

Ellen was too depressed by life generally and particularly by the departure of Harry to reply. She was tired of hearing criticisms of Mrs Rundell from everybody around. Mrs Rundell had been very kind to her.

'If you are going to accept her presents, you have to follow the rules,' her sister went on. 'And you need to ask yourself why she gave you those presents. I suppose you wouldn't imagine it might be to attract the attention of a certain important unmarried gentleman?'

Ellen did not listen to all this closely. Only later did she think about it. She was hating this lecture by her sister.

'But instead, how d'you think the family felt,' Agnes went on, 'seeing Mr James looking so foolish?'

'He didn't look foolish, he smiled so politely and then he danced with Beth and with you and with – I don't know who . . .'

'Yes, because he's a gentleman and he knows the rules – even though he may not always obey them . . . Just make sure you are not in a lonely part of the house with him of an evening. In any case, you wasted your time, silly girl. I understand young Harry has gone off to Northumberland.'

Agnes looked at Ellen coldly.

'You might consider that maybe it's no accident he went off so fast. He may have been sent off, you know, and the offer of a fine job may have meant more to him even than your pretty eyes . . .'

Ellen burst into violent sobs.

Her sister looked at her consideringly. 'Yes, cry, my little girl, cry, you'll need to learn to. Being pretty puts temptations in your way that are hard to resist, particularly when you're on your own. Now you'll be on your own here, no elder sister to look after you, and even in a quiet place like this, there are more temptations than ever you might expect. Cry, and one day you may learn good sense.'

She looked at Ellen and her face softened. She took her little sister in her arms and kissed her. 'I'll have to see if I can find you a life somewhere else, but not just yet, not just yet. Anyway, I'm off early. We'll be back soon, no doubt. Good night, little one.' Out of the room she went with her candle, leaving Ellen in the darkness.

Ellen crawled into bed. It was cold in her room, and her breath sent little puffs into the air. It was cold in bed, too, even though she piled on top of it the blankets her parents had sent her from home. She screwed herself up into a ball to make herself warmer. In a while she realised it was not totally dark outside. Faint moon light crept through the little panes of her window and made a pattern on her floor, but so indistinct that it disappeared from time to time, she supposed whenever a cloud passed across the moon. She heard animals running across the roof, squirrels they must be, and the house itself was not inhabited only by humans. Once the humans were asleep, the other inhabitants could play, the mice particularly. She could hear them scrabbling behind her wall – though she hardly minded mice, she thought, as she drifted into sleep. She did not like rats, but her sister had told her there were hardly any rats here, only in the barns, and Harry had said the same. She had still not heard anything from Harry. Why had he gone so suddenly? She could not understand it. Had she offended him in some way? He had seemed so fond of her at the servants' ball, and then he disappeared, and it was hard to bear. What had Agnes meant about it being no accident that he had gone off so fast . . . ?

A sudden thought made her sit bolt upright in bed. About Harry, and that he had not written. As she knew, all the post that arrived for the family was collected by the butler from the back door. Any post for the servants (not that there was much of it) was taken to the housekeeper's room, and distributed by her. Suppose Harry had written – it was quite possible, wasn't it? – that his letter had been seen by Mrs Rundell, who had certainly not liked Ellen's behaviour, and that she had kept it, or even destroyed it. Was this possible? Could she find out?

She worried about this for hours, as it seemed, and was hardly aware that at some point she fell asleep.

The house went back to its old ways, though the thought of the wedding three months away, and then only two months, ran constantly through everyone's mind. The dining room was closed again, the drawing room too, and the governess retired upstairs. In the kitchen Mrs Saunders showed signs of discontent. She had so little cooking to do for the family: it seemed to annoy her. She spoke of looking for a new situation where her skills would be appreciated. Katherine was ill a good deal, stayed in her room, spoke very little when she did appear, found her cleaning duties difficult so that Beth and Ellen worked harder. Mrs Rundell became rather quiet again, hardly interfering in the business of the house, overseeing activities in a detached way as though they were beneath her notice. She spent a good deal of time in her room, entertaining Sir Richard, and when he was away on business, which happened from time to time, Mr James.

It was noticeable, to the eager pairs of eyes that followed everything that went on in the house, that the housekeeper and Mr

James were becoming very good friends. She who could be so disagreeable and defiant also knew how to charm, particularly how to charm men. Mr James was often to be seen making his way to the housekeeper's room, or leaving, looking contented as though he had been well fed, and no doubt he had since the still room was known to be stocked with tasty cakes and biscuits that no one saw who was not a friend of the housekeeper. Lucy, who could sometimes be prevailed on to gossip about her patroness, let it be known that they talked about money sometimes, and that Mr James, who was supposed to have the running of parts of the estate, would ask Mrs Rundell for advice. And there was some secret between them, clearly – Lucy would sometimes overhear them making sly references to a third person, though she was never sure who this third party might be, though sometimes Ellen wondered, from the way Lucy looked in her direction, whether it might be her.

Ellen had less to do than before. She became used to having an hour or two in the afternoon to spend on her own, reading and studying her French primer. The French lessons continued. Often when Ellen went up to the schoolroom she would find the governess gazing out of the window or sitting at her table, her books in front of her, not doing much. She would look up with a questioning but not unfriendly air when Ellen came into the room – after all, as she once said in an unguarded moment, Ellen was one of the most intelligent young people she had ever taught.

The servants teased her about the French lessons and said, '*Bonjour*, Madame,' when she came into the room. When she once said, 'They may be useful to me, I may not be a housemaid for ever,' they all laughed, and someone said, 'No, you'll be marrying one day, no doubt, and what help will French be to you then, when you've eight children and washday every Monday?'

She was not summoned very often to see Mrs Rundell, and when they did meet the housekeeper hardly spoke to her. She did one day ask whether a letter had arrived for her lately, and the housekeeper looked surprised and not very interested and said that any letter would be passed on to Ellen, if that was required. She spoke in a slightly distant and defiant sort of way, which made Ellen mistrust her, but she did not dare to ask more directly — how could she accuse her cousin of concealing or destroying her correspondence? In any case, Mrs Rundell had other things to think about, most particularly making Sir Richard comfortable.

Ellen did not much enjoy visiting that part of the house at this period. If ever she found herself close to Mrs Rundell's rooms, she always seemed to encounter Lucy in the passages, scurrying to and fro with trays, pushing past Ellen as though she were in the way even though she might merely be sweeping the carpet. In the servants' hall, Lucy would fix her with a hostile stare. It made her uncomfortable.

One day, meeting Lucy by chance in the maids' passage outside their rooms, she asked her whether she had offended her. Lucy, who kept her face averted when she saw Ellen, looked at her for a moment, raised her eyebrows and twisted her mouth. Then she snorted, loudly and aggressively. 'Don't you try to please me, you little minx,' she said. 'I understand you and your ways well enough.'

Perplexed and upset, Ellen decided she must talk to Beth about this behaviour. It was true Beth was not so much her friend now: she spent so much of her time with Jem, and never invited Ellen to visit the head gardener's house any more. But they were surely still good enough friends for such a question. One afternoon when they were together in the sewing room, Ellen asked about Lucy. Beth frowned and looked at Ellen consideringly.

'Well, if you must know – yes, I suppose you must. When Mrs Rundell came here, after the death of her ladyship, she brought a maid with her, who had worked with her in her previous position and in the position before that too, I believe. That was Lucy. I was just a little girl then but, of course, people talk, and they said Lucy had been a charity child. The people in the Union are always trying to settle workhouse children in service, and Mrs Rundell gave her a job in the house where she was housekeeper. Lucy became devoted to her, I suppose she had been kind in her way. No doubt Mrs R is glad to have someone to work for her for almost nothing . . . So Lucy's been here ever since. She may be called the still-room maid but she's more like a personal maid to Mrs R, looks after her clothes – and she has a good many of them, Lord knows how she pays for them   and runs around doing what Mrs R requires.'

'But why does she hate me? Because I think she does. She looks at me in such an evil way.'

Beth sighed. 'Don't you understand?' she said. 'Mrs Rundell is Lucy's life. She adores her because Mrs R saved her from the Union. Mrs R is like a mother to her. If you ask me, it's the fact that Mrs Rundell tells her what to do that makes the poor little thing like her so much. She wants someone to tell her what to do and think and what sort of person to be. She's no kind of a person on her own. And Mrs Rundell – as you know – loves telling others what they should do.'

Ellen considered all this. 'Yes,' she said, 'but why does that mean she hates me?'

'You silly girl, because now you are Mrs Rundell's favourite. You're the one she gives dresses to and gets better wages for, not Lucy. Maybe she has special plans for you – there's no saying what goes on in her mind. Some of us think she has special plans. So how should Lucy feel, when she's no longer Mrs R's favourite but Miss Ellen is?'

'I'm not her favourite, am I?' said Ellen, with the faintest sensation of pleasure.

'That's what everyone thinks. You must know, if anyone does. Why do you get yourself invited up to her room, where some of us never go year in year out, and why did she dress you up for the servants' ball? Everyone knows everyone's business in a place like this. You can't keep a secret for more than five minutes. They all think you're Mrs Rundell's pot of cream, and that you like her – you like being pampered by her, you're glad of it. Your sister never was her favourite, whatever else she may have done.'

'So what should I do then, Beth, what should I do?'

'Do? What is there for you to do? Gain promotion, I suppose. When I leave, I wouldn't be surprised if you became head housemaid in place of Katherine. I'm sure Mrs Rundell has a plan for you.'

'I don't want to be everyone's enemy,' said Ellen, drearily. 'I don't want to be anyone's.'

'Enemies are easily come by in a place like this, and friends can be lost, too.'

'When I see her we just talk and she gives me some . . .

something to drink. Perhaps I should refuse to see Mrs R when she invites me. Should I do that, Beth?'

'No, I shouldn't do that, that would be the end of all of us. She would think the servants' hall had told you not to go. You should just keep your eyes out. I suppose you think Harry left of his own free will, do you? Mrs R didn't want him hanging about, did she, being sweet on her little cousin, and so publicly too?' What was this? Did they all know something she did not?

Beth twisted her ring reflectively, and Ellen realised it was her engagement ring, which Beth had never shown her. 'Well, I shall be leaving Markham Thorpe quite soon, and I'm not sorry. This is not the house it was, not by a long way. Once Miss Emily is safely married and out of the way, Heaven knows what will become of it.'

Ellen looked at her tremulously. 'But you are still my friend, Beth, aren't you? You are still my friend?'

But Beth would not smile at her or reassure her. She merely looked away. 'With Mrs Rundell for your friend, Ellen, you don't need others, do you?'

She remembered Harry especially when she went into the garden during the afternoon, along the paths where they had walked together and in the grove behind the walled garden where they'd met most often. Sometimes tears welled in her eyes, unexpected tears she tried to resist. On other days she felt quite calm, and was able, pacing along the paths where the leaves, yellow and brown and black, were gathering into rough piles, to feel she resembled the heroine – Lady Alice, was it? – of *Houghton Towers*, Lady Alice who had been abandoned by the man she loved but who through her good-natured sweetness and patience finally won him back.

One warm afternoon, encouraged by the sun, she sat in her grove, quite confident she would not give way to tears, and thought about her future. Did she have to stay any longer at Markham Thorpe, a place that was much less easy to deal with than she'd imagined? It was true her parents said she must stay at least two years in her first position, and that Mrs Rundell could help her in all sorts of ways, but what did they understand about life here? In the midst of these thoughts, she glanced up and saw one of the gun dogs running past her and pausing with a wag of the tail to acknowledge her presence, something dogs had a habit of doing even when their masters preferred not to. She looked along the path, and there, walking hurriedly, was a man, dressed in brown, with a gun under his arm. It was Mr James.

Ellen wondered whether she could escape, but he was so close that if she moved she would be noticed, she knew she would. She pulled herself into the shadow of the tree she was sitting under and sat still. It was not that she disliked Mr James, not at all. After all, had she not danced with him? On the other hand he might dislike her, that is if the Quality noticed servants sufficiently to go to the trouble of disliking them. In any case it was so awkward meeting one of the family like this, out of doors, when there was no reason for you to meet, when in a curious way you both felt like ordinary human beings, not like master and servant. What were you to say to them when there were no rules to obey? And what would he say – what could he possibly say to her, meeting like this?

It seemed he had not noticed her. He was interested in rabbits, not people. But then he stopped and looked round, and saw her. He lowered the gun he had just raised. 'Oh, I'm sorry,' he said, 'I didn't see you. I hope I didn't frighten you.' Then, rather tentatively, he added, 'Ellen.'

'Oh, no,' said Ellen. Actually he had frightened her but she was not going to admit it. 'I didn't think you were going to shoot me, Mr James.' Then she remembered she ought to stand up, so she stood up and bobbed a curtsy, though in a way it seemed more natural to stay just where she was while he stood.

'Sit down,' he said, 'please. There's no need for you to stand. We're not on duty here. Neither of us is on duty.'

She sat down. He leant his gun against a tree, and came a little closer to her, lifting his cap politely. 'I thought you might be afraid of the gun,' he said.

'No, I'm not afraid of the gun. Should I be? They say you are a very good shot.'

'No, I'm nothing special,' he replied. He had very dark eyebrows, and his moustache was very dark too, but not well cut. She knew that he looked after it himself, and it had disappointed her for a long time that he did not do it better. If it were tidier, she thought, he would look less shaggy – indeed, he would be quite good looking, even, though at first she had not thought him good looking at all . . .

He smiled. Unlike her, he did not seem ill at ease, perhaps a little shy but, that was not the same thing, probably. 'Thank you for looking after my rooms so well. They've never been tidier,' he said.

She was not really listening, but studying him without knowing that that was what she was doing. 'You should take more care of your moustache. You should cut it more attentively,' she said abruptly, then realised this was no remark for her to be making, and clasped her hands in alarm. How could she have been so indiscreet? How could she have said such a thing?

But he did not seem to mind, rather the contrary: he laughed. 'Oh, I should, should I? Well, I will take your advice, Miss Ellen. I enjoyed our dances at the ball at New Year. You dance very well, I wanted to tell you that.'

She could think of nothing to say to this, and looked at him silently. The sun had gone in, and he seemed to grow larger in the dim light of the little grove.

'I must be going,' he said. 'It will be dark in an hour or so. I must catch the light.'

'Yes,' she replied. He lifted his cap again, and was gone.

She sat for a long time in the grove after he had gone, though she knew she should be back at the house. Through her mind went all the warnings her sister had given her about Mr James. She felt sorry for him. She wanted to comfort him, though quite why or for what, she could not say.

Two days later she was surprised, going into Mr James's dressing room, to find on the marble-topped table where his jug and basin stood, in place of his old shabby shaving equipment, an unfamiliar shaving brush with an ivory handle and soft brown bristles, a gleaming razor, with a brown leather case, and new lathering soap from a maker in Leeds.

She thought about those purchases a good deal. Mr James never usually bought anything very much; one wondered if he had any money. It was strange that he should make these purchases, almost as though they were a compliment to her. It was stranger still that, a few days later, Mrs Rundell, chuckling and in high good humour, remarked to her, 'I am told you have persuaded Mr James to purchase a beautiful new razor. What an influence you have over him, my dear.'

How on earth did she know such a thing? Could he have told her? It was true that Mr James seemed to like Mrs Rundell more than anyone else in the house did, apart from Sir Richard. A day or two before when she had gone to deliver a package to Mrs Rundell she had found Mr James seated at her table, the two of them drinking tea and something else, it seemed. He looked embarrassed, though pleased, when she came in, and there was a furtive rustling of papers on the table. But Mrs Rundell seemed unperturbed and went on with her sentence which ended, '. . . no date at all, Mr James, we do not need to worry about any dates. It can all be settled easily one of these days.' Ellen wondered what on earth they could be talking about – she thought it must be money.

'Dear Sister,' Ellen wrote to Agnes. 'Why did you give me so many warnings about Mr James? I don't quite understand it. He is so thoughtful to me, so polite . . . and he never troubles me when I am doing his rooms. What did you mean about not being alone with him in an empty part of the house?'

Her sister replied quite soon, sooner than was her way.

. . . I would not say Mr James is a bad man, not to say bad. But he is shy of real ladies, I would say, and what he likes is maidservants. The history is this, as I discovered soon after

I arrived at Markham Thorpe. Nine or ten years ago, just after her ladyship died, he put one of the maids at the house in the family way. Her pa worked on the estate, they'd known each other all their lives, she tried to hide it but of course she couldn't. Nothing was said in public but everyone knew it was Mr James was the father. He always liked servant girls best, that's what they said. She went back to her family and had the child, and Sir Richard paid for the boy to be brought up. I'm told that he and Mr James had a terrible quarrel over it all, Sir Richard disapproves so much of such things, the Markhams believe they have a duty to the people on the estate . . . The boy must be twelve or so now, still lives nearby, and his mother is married. That's why I said you must be careful of Mr James.

The letter went on:

We are having a fine old time here, going to parties and the theatres, and in and out of the shops, buying Miss Emily's trousseau. She's spending and spending, not like her, really, she being so careful usually, it's as though she wants to spend as much as she can. I am learning a good deal, in particular which are the best retailing establishments, which treat their young ladies well, and which make the finest clothes. I would not mind being employed in such a place, I can tell you. You would be your own mistress in the evenings and able to lead your own life, not obliged to stay up till two in the morning and be all smiling when your lady comes home — instead you are able to have a pleasant time yourself and meet all

146

sorts of people (and I don't mean other ladies). Well, we'll see. Miss Emily is very excited about her wedding. She adores her Mr William but somehow she's not completely happy. I find her sometimes sitting in her room, brooding, her head on her hand, but if I ask her how she is doing she won't answer me. She hates to talk about Markham Thorpe, won't speak about it unless she has to. She's not looking forward to staying a whole month at the house before the wedding . . .

Part Four

The cathedral was filled, to the last chair. The bishop presided, attended by the rector of Markham and other men of the cloth. The bride wore an ivory-coloured dress (following the example of the young queen, married a few years before), rich in blond lace, and on her head a chaplet of orange blossom and a veil. The dress, the orange blossom and the lace impressed the good people of Ripon, assembled in force in the narrow square in front of the cathedral to watch this great event. When the bride left the cathedral and stepped with her husband into the square, crowded with carriages and onlookers, she released her veil, and it floated for a moment into the air five feet behind her. The crowd (many of whom had known her since she was a child) agreed that she was prettier than she had ever been, and that her husband was a fine-looking man, and quite worthy of her. There were plenty more people to gawp at. The county was there in force, the Carlisles and the Fauconbergs, the Winns and the Lascelles, the Constables and the Robinsons, the Gascoignes and the Worsleys, and many more, from all over Yorkshire and beyond, from high aristocracy to modest gentry, though many of them hardly saw the Markhams except at great events. Emily, who could still usually coax her father into doing what she chose, had had her way. Not only the whole of Yorkshire, but friends from London and elsewhere, including several from the little boarding-school in Kew where she had been sent aged fifteen, had been invited and apparently had all accepted.

People were curious about the family, no doubt of that. There had been a good deal of gossip about the Markhams lately in Yorkshire society, among men chuckling over their port and women gossiping in the corners of drawing rooms. The Markham girls were quite the thing, it was agreed, and Lavinia had made a most respectable match (even though there was no title, but there might be, one of these days) and now Emily was making a better one. But what on earth, people wondered, was going on at the house? Sir Richard had disappeared, one never saw him, he had not been hunting all last season though he was a passionate huntsman; last year he was not even seen at York Races, which he had attended for over fifty years. Was he ill? Was there some other reason? (And here the half-smiles and the innuendoes began.) He had withdrawn his subscription from various societies, and one wondered if there were financial problems, though there was no reason why there should be: it was a perfectly respectable estate, more than six thousand acres. A few people suggested that someone was deliberately holding back money, for reasons of their own, though at this point the conversation would sink into whispers. As for James – James was so silent, so reserved, blushed as soon as you looked at him – the only place he was at ease was in all-male company. But he must be thirty-five, why did he not marry, was there something wrong with him?

And they went on chattering. It was said, at least one had heard it was said, that is to say several people had heard the story from their servants who knew the servants at Markham Thorpe, that Sir Richard had gone the way of many elderly widowers, and become entangled with the housekeeper. Of course, quite a few thought, though they did not say so publicly, that as long as the children could keep her in check, and prevent a marriage that would make it impossible to see the family, it really didn't matter who kept Sir Richard warm in bed. People who had seen the housekeeper said she was not ill looking, considerably younger than Sir Richard, dressed expensively and just within the limits of her position – vulgar, of course, though she tried to be refined. It was all embarrassing but one couldn't blame the man, after all he was widowed ten years ago . . . and so the tongues wagged . . . Where did she find the money for those dresses? they wondered. Could there be a clue there?

The wedding invitation was irresistible. Who could refuse the chance to admire young Emily, so pretty, so gay, and so like her dear mother? Who could not want to pay their respects to one of the oldest Yorkshire families, baronets since 1638? Who would not wish to see what state of repair Sir Richard was in, and how James comported himself? And, above all, to be honest (though nobody was), how entertaining to glimpse the housekeeper, and see whether she was seated close to the family and how she dressed at an event where, properly speaking, she should scarcely be visible.

Anybody hoping for scandal was disappointed. Mrs Rundell kept in the background and never went near Sir Richard. She had dressed carefully, in a lilac dress, rich but plain, with a pearl necklace and earrings, and a large hat, a hat with feathers, but perfectly discreet feathers. She sat near the back of the nave next to Mr Fellows, among the more important tenant farmers. At the end of the ceremony, when the congregation was pouring into the square, she curtsied to the family in the most decorous manner, and hurried back to the house in the carriage waiting for her and the butler. Nothing could have been more proper.

Nothing could have been more proper, either, than the behaviour of the family as they received their guests. Mr and Mrs William Dykes and Sir Richard lined up outside the front door at Markham Thorpe in the spring sunshine, smiling, shaking hands, remembering names, exclaiming with pleasure at the sight of friends and neighbours they had not seen for a long while. To the guests' relief, the house seemed to be still the shrine to hospitality it had always been. Sir Richard was a little pale and had to lean on Lavinia's arm, but he stayed at his post until the last carriage deposited its passengers on the gravel and the family made their way into the Great Hall.

The wedding breakfast for two hundred people was an even larger party than the one given for Lavinia (who, marrying soon after her mother's death, had not wanted too grand an event). With tables laid in the Great Hall and the dining room and the drawing room, and with the buffet – the roast meats, the lobster, the salads, the sandwiches, the petits fours – arranged all the way along one side of the Hall, the party fitted in pretty neatly. The afternoon passed exactly as planned, and very convivial it was, and nobody could fault the caterers. The only mishap occurred just before the cake was to be cut. The old butler, a fixture of the house whom many of the guests had known for years and years, was carrying a tray with a decanter and some glasses towards Sir Richard, whom he chose, as always, to serve himself. The mishap was crueller in that Mr Fellows was evidently so pleased about Emily's marriage. As he bustled towards his master, he tripped on the edge of a rug and fell to the ground, the decanter and glasses smashing around him and the wine shooting round the room. In the appalled silence that ensued Emily and her husband and Sir Richard stood up, Sir Richard crying, 'Fellows, Fellows, are you all right?' as the butler crawled about on the floor, trying to pick up the glass and himself at the same time. As the baronet, not altogether secure in his walk, began to move towards his old servant, another male servant crossed the room and helped Mr Fellows gently to his feet. But the butler did not want to be helped, shook off the young man's hand, bowed in his master's direction and bent down again. It was a sad sight, the dear old man, so embarrassed and confused, shaking his head while he tried to pick up the pieces of broken glass. Though Sir Richard said, 'You go and rest, Fellows, you go and sit down until you feel better, it's of no consequence, no consequence at all,' he refused to leave, still feeling for splinters of glass, although the young manservant tried to pull him away. Only when the house-keeper – the famous housekeeper – tugged the butler by the arm (very sharply, though only those sitting close by could see this) did he let himself be taken away.

The glass was swept up, the talk resumed, the meringues and the ice-creams were handed round, the guests gave themselves up to conversation. But not Sir Richard. He returned unhappily to his chair, shaking his head, muttering to the noble lady on his left, 'Fifty years Fellows has worked for me and my father, fifty years, and such a thing has never happened in all those years. The poor man, and at Emily's wedding too, the poor man.'

On his right Emily was talking to her husband. 'Poor Mr Fellows,' she said, 'what a disaster. He was so pleased about my marriage. I was his favourite when I was a child; he always had time for me, would find ways to amuse me when the others wouldn't include me in their games, let me help him wind the clocks and lay the table, though no doubt I was in the way.'

'I'm sure he will recover very soon,' he replied.

'I don't know,' she said, 'that he will. I'm sure Mrs Rundell will want him to retire, it would suit her.' They noticed that Ellen was close behind them, and changed the subject. Mrs Dykes shivered. 'I'd always heard,' she said, 'that broken glass was unlucky, particularly at a wedding. What d'you think, is it a bad omen, William?'

'Don't be absurd, my love,' he replied. 'How could Mr Fellows tripping up be a bad omen?'

As the breakfast drew to its close, the cake was cut, the speeches were made and the toasts drunk. Mr and Mrs Dykes emerged into the afternoon sun, glowing with happiness. Many of the male guests also noticed her maid, demure and not exactly pretty, and yet – to the connoisseur – particularly well turned out and worthy of a second look. The guests cheered and threw confetti at the carriage, which was taking the young couple to Ripon before they caught the train to London and then their three-month honeymoon in Italy.

According to custom, the servants, clustered to the side of the house, waved goodbye too. 'How is Mr Fellows?' they asked Jem.

'Mr Fellows is doing all right,' Jem replied. 'He's gone home.

He's shaken, but I'm sure he will be back in a day or two.' Though the servants were not supposed to be too animated, they waved their handkerchiefs and joined in the shouts as the carriage drew away. Mrs Rundell stood a little distance from the others, her hands clasped in front of her after she had waved, once, in a dignified manner. Then she turned and looked intently towards the house. The other servants fell silent, for on her face was a strange expression, which none of them forgot. It was a look of greed and triumph, like a cat's when it stretches out its paw towards a mouse it knows it is about to kill.

Shortly after the Wentworths and the other relations had left Mrs Rundell summoned the household, including the gardeners, the grooms and the gamekeepers, to the servants' hall. She announced that Mr Fellows had retired and would no longer be working in the house, even occasionally. He was not well enough – they would not see him unless they chose to visit him in his house, and for the time being he was too weak to receive visitors. Since the family was obliged to make economies, no butler would be appointed in his place. Since Jem and Beth were leaving, Mrs Rundell would be looking for a parlour-maid to take the butler's place. 'Yes, a parlour-maid,' she said. 'You may not know the term. It means a woman who does the work of the butler and the footman. Quite a new thing, but very practical. This person may be someone from the house,' she said, 'or we may be looking outside.' It was clear to all that, without a butler, Mrs Rundell's authority would be unchallenged.

Mrs Rundell had more to tell them. It had been decided – she never said by whom – that as much of the house as possible would be closed. It was necessary, she continued, to reduce the number of gardeners and grooms, as well as the house servants, and this would happen shortly. The numbers leaving depended on Sir Richard's deliberations with the family lawyer. 'There will have to be economies in the kitchen, too,' she went on. 'We are no longer living in the old days. If visitors arrive unexpected, it will no longer be possible to entertain them, as in the past. This also means that if the family are ever away, you will all be on board wages. In the future this will truly mean board wages, as it has not done previous. At these times you will arrange for your own meals or you may pay the cook or the kitchenmaid to provide them for you. We are also obliged to close as many bedrooms as possible, so I am instructing Katherine to put the young ladies' bedrooms under dust sheets and the same for all the guest rooms.'

All this was greeted with silent apprehension. The servants gaped at her, as at some unpleasant apparition. She made a striking impression, her bosom rising and falling under her silk front, her black eyes larger and more protuberant than ever. She exuded power, and the enjoyment of power. 'There is something else to tell you. We have had a visit from the doctor. I am sorry to say that Sir Richard's health is not as strong as we would all wish. He needs regular nursing. The best solution, Dr Rowntree feels and I am in agreement, is that I should act as nurse to Sir Richard, and as far as possible relieve him of cares. I am glad to undertake this task.' Her gaze swept round her listeners, as though challenging them to dispute her words. 'My task is to look after him in every way I can. He will be happier being looked after by somebody he knows.' She paused, as an actress might before her best lines. 'This means that I shall be moving out of the housekeeper's room and into the boudoir. In the future the boudoir will become my sitting room. It will be still be known as the boudoir, not the housekeeper's room. I hope you understand.'

There was a gasp. The boudoir, the finest room on the first floor, had been Lady Markham's, and Sir Richard had never wanted anything changed there. No doubt noting their reaction, Mrs Rundell surveyed them with satisfaction. 'That will be all. We will naturally explain to those who are dismissed the conditions of their departure. It is Sir Richard's wish to be as generous as possible. Do you have any questions?'

They had no questions. They merely stared. Some wondered how soon they could find another position. Others wondered whether they would be dismissed at once.

'No questions?' she said. 'Excellent. You may go about your duties, as usual. If you do have any questions, come to me, not to Sir Richard or Mr James. They do not wish to be disturbed with domestic issues. Speak to me.'

'I consider that you would be suitable for the position of parlour-maid.'

'Me, Mrs Rundell? I couldn't be parlour maid, could I?'

'There's nobody else here who could perform these duties. Beth is leaving the house, Katherine is not strong enough, Lucy is not to be considered. We could look for somebody from outside but I do not wish to employ additional servants at this junction.'

'But I have no experience, I wouldn't know what to do . . .'

'Oh, we will soon train you, my girl. In any case, you have good manners, you have common sense, you know how to behave yourself. And you now know how to serve at table.'

'But I don't know how to manage at dinner parties . . .'

'There will be no call for you to manage at dinner parties. There will be no dinner parties, at least for the time being. You will not attend Sir Richard at dinner because he will be taking his meals with me, and Lucy will look after us, to the best of her abilities – at least she does not spill things. You will serve Mr James, that is all. That's not difficult, is it?'

'But Katherine, poor Katherine, how will she manage all on her own? Unless you want me to continue with my housemaid's duties.'

'I do not want you to continue with those duties, certainly not. You are quite wasted in such work. We will have someone in from the village. Now that there are fewer rooms to clean, Katherine will manage perfectly well.'

She looked at Ellen closely and patted her cheek. 'You have no need to be anxious, child, I am always thinking of what is best for you. So – it is settled then. Oh, and you will be paid an extra three pounds a year. I have written to your parents and they have been good enough to express their satisfaction. They are very grateful, they tell me, for the money you send them. Poor things, they have so many children to look after, we must do everything we can to help them, must we not?' And since Ellen still looked doubtful, she went on, 'Don't you understand, child? You are much too good to be a housemaid, much too well educated, and our family is not suitable employed in such work. We come of better stock. Why, our common forebear Mr Braithwaite of Malton was an attorney and quite the gentleman, with a place in the country as well as his residence in Malton – my mother often spoke of him. He was no servant, he had servants of his own, at least six, as I understand. You and I are on our way back to that status. Indeed, who knows? We may surpass it, and I am doing everything I can, everything in my humble powers, to assist you. So now you are being promoted. It's the first step to becoming a housekeeper like your cousin Rundell.' She nodded at Ellen impatiently, stood, rustled her skirts, cast a swift glance at herself in the glass. 'Don't look so fearful, girl, go about your duties. I will tell the servants' hall tomorrow.'

'But suppose I don't want to—'

'None of that, Ellen. While you're in this house, you do as I tell you. You should be grateful I take so much interest in you.'

'Yes, Mrs Rundell, I am grateful, Mrs Rundell, but—'

'No more buts. I tried my best for that sister of yours but she would have none of it, proud obstinate girl, wanted to make her own way in the world. As for you, Ellen, you are less proud than Agnes and twice as pretty, you are a girl after my own heart. I would have liked a girl like you for my own daughter, had I been fortunate enough.' She was looking out of the window as she said these words, and did not turn round as Ellen curtsied and left the room.

'I must congratulate you, Ellen.'

Katherine did not speak in a friendly tone, and Ellen was not sure how to reply. They were standing in the maids' corridor, on their way to bed. It was chilly there, and Ellen wanted to escape into her own room where there would be no one to tell her what to do, as everyone in the house seemed to want to.

'Thank you,' she tried.

'I hope you will be happy in your new duties.'

'I did not ask to become parlour-maid, you know. I never asked Mrs Rundell if I might become it. She said I must.'

'Is that so? I am sure you are telling the truth. Meanwhile, with Beth leaving, I will be looking after the whole house on my own, with a little help from Lucy.'

'I will help you as much as I can, Katherine.'

'You will be too busy to do that, Ellen, too busy curtsying and carrying trays and making yourself agreeable to the Quality, not least Mr James. In any case, I don't want your help.'

'I'm sorry, Katherine, I'm truly sorry—'

'This is not the house I came to all those years ago. It's the fault of your aunt. She's not a good woman, always scheming, always criticising. It doesn't matter if you tell her what I say, she can't kill me, not even she. The worst she can do is send me away.' Though she spoke with bravado she looked briefly terrified at the thought.

'I won't tell her anything, only I don't like to hear this—' began Ellen, but Katherine did not want to listen to her.

'Do you think it's easy for me, when I am not strong, to do so much work – work, work, work, that's what my life is – and what does she do but sneer at me, hurt my feelings, try to make me feel I am nothing?' In the light of their candles, which threw vast shadows on the walls and made the passage stretch endlessly into the distance, Katherine's face rose into the light and disappeared again.

'Katherine—'

'Don't you Katherine me. You are her niece, she likes you, you're no friend of mine.' And Katherine raised her candle close to her face so that for a second Ellen saw it as she had never seen it before, tight and hard and fierce, the mouth clenched, eyes black.

Katherine sighed harshly. 'How should I be feeling, living out my days in this house where I'm despised, shuffling into old age, while you, Miss Ellen, as I should no doubt be calling you, are groomed for higher service?' She turned away and went into her own room, slamming the door – something she had never done in all the months Ellen had worked with her.

Beth and Jem were married at the parish church, and they invited all their families   very numerous they were – and quite a number of the household, and Sir Richard, who attended and sat in the front pew alongside the father of the bride, with Mr James in the row behind next to Miss Fisher. Mrs Rundell had announced that she would be away in Leeds for a few days at just this moment, so it was not necessary to decide whether to invite her or not – nothing was said on the subject. They had their wedding breakfast in the servants' hall, over eighty people, and a very cheerful occasion it was, Jem being the most affable of men and his wife the sweetest of women, the best of the old household as people said to one another. Everyone drank to the health of bride and groom and to the health of Sir Richard and Mr James and to Markham Thorpe, and Jem made a long and entertaining speech in which he explained that he was going to become steward to a family in the south to which he had been recommended by his brother, who worked on the neighbouring estate, and that he would miss all his friends in Yorkshire but hoped they would visit him and Beth regularly. It had been a grand time working at Markham Thorpe, he said, but now that he was a family man he had to look for a better position and he thought he had found a very good one. And since Sir Richard had left the room by this time he added darkly, 'And the prospects for employment at Markham Thorpe do not look promising, as we all know, unless, that is, you are related to a certain lady,' a sally that was greeted with bitter laughter and thumping of the table, particularly from the bride's father, who had seen half of his gardeners dismissed the week before. The party stayed a long time in the servants' hall, and after the breakfast they danced to the fiddles of the village choir.

Ellen was not there. She had not been invited. She stayed upstairs in her room and cried for a long time. Then she told herself she must be strong, and that Beth was leaving and not worth thinking about. She did not quite convince herself, since she'd thought Beth was her best friend, but she told herself that she was becoming a little more mature.

She never properly said goodbye to Beth, and she never saw her or Jem again. Now she really was alone, she thought, with no friends, unless she found comfort from someone new, but she had no idea of who this new someone might be.

Ellen knocked at Miss Fisher's door. There was no response.

She knocked again. Again, no response.

Hesitant and anxious, she turned the handle and opened the door. Though it was a bright afternoon, the room was almost dark. Miss Fisher was sitting at her desk (as she liked to call it), the old schoolroom table, where she and Ellen had spent many happy times. Usually when Ellen knocked she would be greeted by a warm 'Come in' and Miss Fisher would rise to greet her, ask her in French how she was, pull forward a chair, offer her some fruit or a little cake. Not today. Today she sat at her desk, her face in her hands, motionless. The curtains were closed. There was a faint, unpleasant smell of dampness.

'Miss Fisher?' said Ellen, trembling a little. She noticed things out of order in the room. The floor was scattered with fragments of glass. She recognised the remains of a vase, which always stood on the table, filled with flowers brought to her by the head gardener. It was a vase the governess was particularly fond of — it had been given to her by her mother. Indeed, as she had told Ellen more than once, it was almost the only thing of her mother's she had. Around the spikes of glass lay the flowers Ellen had seen the day before, as though the vase had been hurled to the ground.

'Miss Fisher, are you all right? It's me, it's Ellen, I've come for my lesson. Are you unwell?'

Still no reply. Ellen noticed something else. On the floor by the window lay some books, twisted, with their pages torn.

By now Ellen was not only puzzled but frightened. She thought of leaving, it was not pleasant to be in this room with someone who refused to acknowledge she was there. But Ellen was a brave girl, and was learning not to mind being unpopular. She made her way to the table and knelt in front of the governess, touching her arm. Miss Fisher looked up, but stared into the distance. She was dishevelled, as though her hair had slipped to one side in some curious way.

'Go,' she said. 'Leave my room.'

'But why? What's happened?'

'You know what's happened. Don't mock me. You are part of her family, part of Mrs Rundell's family. Of course you know what's been planned.'

'But I don't, Miss Fisher, I don't know at all.'

Miss Fisher straightened herself and, for the first time, looked Ellen in the face. Her eyes were red.

'I promise you,' Ellen said, 'I don't know what has happened. Please tell me, please tell me. Can I help you at all?'

Slowly and unsurely, as though she still did not wholly believe the girl, Miss Fisher spoke: 'Very well. I have been told to leave. Did you know that? By the autumn. Mrs Rundell told me, not Sir Richard. She said Sir Richard was too tired to see me, not well enough, it would distress him, but he sent me best wishes. I am to move to Scarborough or wherever I choose to go – as Mrs Rundell put it. I should find a place where I will have the company of other old governesses. Filey, she kindly suggested, which she said is genteel but not as expensive as Scarborough. Did you know that?'

'No,' said Ellen. 'I can promise you, with all my heart, I did not know that. I am very sorry. You have lived here so long, Miss Fisher.'

'Thirty years I have been here. This was my second situation, my second and last. I came here when we had just beaten Boney. Have you heard of Napoleon Bonaparte, Ellen? That was a great man, a tragic hero I consider him.' She shook her head, remembering that she had more important things to think about than Bonaparte. 'Mrs Rundell has a plan, you know, I'm sure she has a plan. She wants to empty the house of everyone who could be an enemy to her, and fill it entirely with her friends. She wants to rule at Markham Thorpe, after all.'

'But it's not her house. How can she rule at Markham Thorpe?'

'It could be her house, child. Can't you see how it could be her house? Sir Richard trusts her, Sir Richard likes her, don't ask me why. Poor deluded man, such a good man, but not well now – clearly he is not well, if he can be deceived by a woman like that. But I shouldn't be speaking to you. I can't trust you either.'

'You can trust me,' said Ellen. 'I won't say anything to Mrs Rundell. I don't tell her stories about the house, that I don't, I can promise you, Miss Fisher.' She had found Miss Fisher peculiar on first meeting but had become used to her. This afternoon she again seemed alarmingly odd.

'Yes, well, perhaps I believe you.' She looked round the room and gave a strangled laugh. 'She told me this morning. She came to see me – I don't think she has ever been in this room before, at least not when I have been here. I dare say she looks around in my absence. I had the pleasure of not offering her a seat, and she did not venture to take one. It was Sir Richard's decision, she said. In the interests of economy the household has to be reduced. At least my pension will be paid to me as promised. I have some savings, of course, since I have lived here all these years for nothing and very comfortably on the whole until I was banished to the attic and not allowed to dine downstairs.' She looked into the distance. 'I have never quite understood why the family has these financial difficulties now. There was no shortage of money when her ladyship was alive, none at all, they were very generous. It's only in the past two years we've kept hearing about money, money, money . . . As far as I know there's been no disaster with the funds. It's very mysterious, and what is more mysterious is that when money needs to be found, as for Emily's wedding, it always is. My belief is, Rundell is managing the money in her own way, to her own advantage, stealing it, I dare say. Ah, well . . . Sit down, child, sit down. The housekeeper woman ventured to hope that I would visit Markham Thorpe once a year, the family would not want to lose my friendship. And then she went on, "Nor would I want to lose your friendship," and then she sneered, no other word for it, sneered. Lose my friendship indeed! It's not something she's ever enjoyed, or wanted.' She snorted. 'When she went I was so angry I threw my vase across the room, my mother's vase – ah, well, I shall be dead soon, and then no one would value it. It matters very little what happens to such things.'

'If it's true what you say, can nobody stop Mrs Rundell?' asked Ellen. But she felt uncomfortable, as though she were betraying her flesh and blood.

'And you, Ellen, I was so angry with you, I tore up our books and threw them on the ground. I have never damaged a book, never in my life. But I was wrong, I suppose, I don't think you're a bad girl . . .' She went on as though talking to herself. 'The only people who can stop Mrs Rundell now are the children. The girls, I should say. Not James. What does James ever do, poor fellow? As long as he has enough wine and the chance to go shooting, what more does he need? And he likes Mrs R, don't ask me why, he likes her, and he seems to be indebted to her in some way . . .'

Ellen was so startled by this remark that she felt she had to hide her face. She bent down as though to pick up the pieces of glass but Miss Fisher stopped her. 'Don't you be doing that, Ellen, don't you be doing that. You sweep it up, you don't pick it up. Surely that's the first thing they teach you as a housemaid, though you're not that any more, are you? No, the girls . . . and Mr Dykes, too, perhaps could take a stand. I doubt the other son-in-law would be much use – Mr Wentworth, more noise than sense, a fine gentleman but that's all there is to be said for him.'

Miss Fisher had never spoken to Ellen in such a way. During their talks she had always remained scrupulously correct on the subject of the family.

'Yes, I should write to the girls, that is what I should do. I would speak to Mr Richardson, the lawyer, but I don't trust him, too friendly with Mrs Rundell: he sips his tea in her parlour much too often.'

Miss Fisher seemed to be more herself. She wiped her eyes and her nose and pulled down her cuffs.

'Fetch me my writing box, Ellen. I shall write at once. I shall have to make sure the letters do not go by the normal post. Mrs Rundell controls that, you know, and reads everything that comes in or goes out, and no doubt she removes anything she doesn't like. Ah, well, there are means of avoiding that. It's not so far to Ripon, after all. Yes,' and she frowned in the direction of her papers, 'I must word this carefully, so that they come at once . . .'

'No French, then, today?' said Ellen.

'No, no French today.' She looked ruefully at the floor. 'Besides, I have torn the books. It would be hard to teach you.'

'So no more French lessons at all?'

'Well, I suppose we might continue them one of these days. We shall see. But I shall only be here for a few more months, and I need to be making visits to Filey or wherever it is I go, unless – that is – unless things change. I will write to the girls this afternoon. It's a pity Emily is away for so long on her honeymoon, three months, they say. Not a word, mind, not a word, to anyone at all. This house is so full of prattle and backbiting!'

'No, Miss Fisher.'

'I suppose I can trust you. You'd better go.'

The French lessons never did resume, as it turned out. During one of her little chats with Ellen, Mrs Rundell remarked that she saw no good in the lessons continuing. 'You can learn French, if you wish, it is a polite accomplishment for a young lady. But I do not wish you to spend any more time with that old woman upstairs, do you hear me?'

Ellen protested, but she knew that there was no arguing with Mrs Rundell. No more lessons, that was the rule. She wrote a little message for Miss Fisher, not having the strength to tell her in person, and pushed it under the governess's door one afternoon when she knew she was out with her dog. Miss Fisher never replied, and whenever she saw Ellen would look straight through her.

Three times a day Ellen served a meal to Mr James. Not always – sometimes he would disappear to see his sporting friends at the Unicorn Hotel in Ripon, or dine upstairs with his father and Mrs Rundell. Mrs Rundell tried to persuade him to do this often, telling him that his father liked to see him, but the suspicion between them was still so great that he would only dine upstairs once a week or so. For these occasions Mrs Saunders would be instructed by Mrs Rundell to produce a particularly good pudding, since Mr James was well known to be partial to puddings. How was Mrs Rundell to know that Mrs Saunders, who was very attached to Mr James, provided him (but not the upstairs party) every day with something specially nice in the pudding line, which would also be served in the servants' hall if she was in a good humour? But generally he consumed his meals alone in the smoking room, looking through *The Times* and the sporting press before leaving them in a crumpled heap on the floor. He would argue with his father about the newspapers, too: Sir Richard liked to see them first even though he never read them and they remained in a neat pile on his desk. Usually Mrs Rundell, who liked to control everything in the house, made sure that the papers went first to Mr James before being taken upstairs.

It fell to Ellen to set his table. She did this with scrupulous attention. As she laid out the knife and the fork she would feel sorry that so often this was a table for only one. His guests were rare, though when they did come they stayed long and drank deep. At dinner time Ellen would hurry through the Great Hall and down the long passage with the soup, say, 'Good evening, sir,' to which he would reply, 'Good evening, Ellen,' and deposit the tureen. Fifteen minutes later she would return with a tray bearing silver dishes (in spite of his carelessness over many things, he insisted on silver dishes – 'I must have the dishes my mother used,' he would say, if anything else were offered) and set these out on the table, with the pudding and the cheese on the side table. The portions looked so small and lonely, she wished there were someone else to share them. He dealt with his wine himself (he kept the key to the wine cellar, now that Mr Fellows had gone – there had been a dispute over this with his father, but Mrs Rundell had insisted that Mr James must have the keys, and she had prevailed, even though Sir Richard wanted the keys himself) but when he drank beer she would fetch it from the kitchen in his very own glass, with his initials on it. And a good deal of it, four or five or six glasses, would be consumed.

They did not speak much during these meals, at least not to start with. He would thank her each time she brought something new. Whenever she said, 'Will that be all, sir?' he would reply, always in the same words, 'Yes, thank you, Ellen, that will be all.' He would ask her if she had had a pleasant day. She would say yes. Then she would make the same enquiry of him, having discovered that this was permissible. Sometimes she would glance up from her task and see him looking at her as though wondering whether to speak. But he seldom said anything of consequence.

Naturally, employed so many hours in his service, Ellen thought about him a good deal. She liked him, she realised. He was always polite. He would apologise if anything had been spilt, he would ask her to tell the cook how much he had enjoyed his dinner. And she worried about him. He was often so melancholy, withdrawn. He could not like sitting in this gloomy room, particularly in the summer when there was no fire and the light penetrated only dimly through the windows overhung with ivy. Surely he could not enjoy drinking his wine, and then his port, on his own, clouding his head with no one to talk to. She would sometimes come upon him, when she entered the room quietly and he did not know she was there, looking so sad that she longed to comfort him. ('You don't need to knock at dinner time, just come in. You can't carry all that food and knock, there's no sense in it,' he had said to her one evening early on.) He would be sitting with his shoulders hunched, his paper clenched in one hand, staring into the distance. With the light fading outside and only the cawing of the rooks to break the silence, the room seemed to Ellen filled with sadness.

A sense of intimacy grew between them, even though they

spoke so little. She came to know what he liked to eat (he was a man of regular habit) and how much, which dishes she should serve him and which he preferred to take himself, how long he spent on each course. At first she thought she should try to make no noise but soon realised he liked some bustle. Was this what matrimony would be like, she wondered once, the woman knowing exactly what her husband wanted and providing it? It was certainly not like her own family where her mother made all the decisions, but perhaps other families behaved like this . . . And she shook herself, amazed at such foolish thoughts.

One evening, though, he seemed resolved on conversation. As she was arranging a dish on his table, he emptied his glass in a determined way and said, 'Ellen.'

She was surprised and turned her head suddenly. He was looking at her intently.

'Won't you talk to me?' he said.

'What should I talk to you about, sir?'

'Oh, anything, Ellen.' He seemed to like pronouncing her name. As he had told her once, it was so gentle, like her. 'Anything you like, Ellen.'

'I don't know what you would be interested in, sir. I don't have anything interesting to say, I'm only a housemaid. That is to say, a parlour maid.' She hesitated and almost smiled. 'But being a parlour maid hasn't given me any more things interesting to say, sir.'

'Are you happy here at Markham Thorpe, Ellen?' He poured himself another glass of wine.

What answer could she give? 'It's a beautiful house, sir. I'm glad to have the chance to live here.'

'It was more beautiful in my mother's time, you know, more cared for, more cheerful . . .'

'If you say so, sir,' she said.

'Would you not like to be a lady, Ellen? And live in a house like Markham Thorpe?'

'Oh, I'm no lady, sir, I'm only a maidservant. Maidservants can never be ladies.'

'That's not true,' he said. 'They can become ladies if they marry gentlemen. I suppose if they have good manners and speak well, that helps. But, then, you do.'

'Is that all it needs to be a lady, sir? It's surely birth that counts, isn't it?' And after this speculation she hurried on to fill the silence, 'Will you not be eating your meat, sir? It will get cold, and you won't like it, and Mrs Saunders is so disappointed when you don't eat your dinner. Sir,' she added, thinking she might have been presumptuous.

'So tell me, wouldn't you like to be a lady, Ellen? After all, as I'm told, your father's grandfather was a gentleman, and lived a grand life with a house in the country.'

'How do you know that?' she asked.

'And if he had not spent too much and ruined himself, his son would have lived a life of ease, and no doubt his grandson and all the rest of you. Being a gentleman or a lady is not a question of divine right, Ellen. When I go round the farms here I see people who are just as good as me, who could be squire of Markham just as well as I could, probably better, only they . . .' He stopped and looked gloomily at his plate. 'I am sure they would manage the estate better than I do, at the very least, though that would not be hard.'

'Won't you eat your dinner, sir? I wish you would eat your dinner.' He said nothing. She made an effort to escape. 'Will that be all, sir?'

'No, Ellen, that will not be all.'

'They will be expecting me in the kitchen, sir.'

'Let them expect you. You must tell them I wanted to talk to you. I am the master here, after all. Sit down, won't you?'

'Sit down, sir? How can I sit down in front of you, sir?'

'If I tell you to sit down, you sit down, d'you hear me? Your cousin Rundell sits down all the time in front of my father, and that's not the only thing she does either.' And he laughed, rather coarsely.

Looking round anxiously, Ellen spied a chair in the furthest possible corner of the room from his table and sat on the very edge.

He said, 'No, you don't need to sit right over there. Come closer. Sit on this chair beside the table.' And as she still hesitated, staring at him in fear, he went on, 'Don't be frightened, Ellen, I won't hurt you. I may seem a bear but I'm not really one. I'd just like your company while I eat my dinner. It's my mother's birthday today, you see, it's sad to be dining on one's own. Come and sit closer.' His manner had changed once more: in the eyes of this man she did not understand at all, she saw a glance of gentleness, even entreaty, that was new to her. How could she say no? As she walked uncertainly towards the table she felt she was doing him a kindness of some sort, though she hardly knew what.

'Will you have a glass of wine with me, Ellen? Don't say you can't.' There was a mixture of authority and kindness in his voice.

She found it impossible to resist him. 'Look, here is a glass for you, I brought it out on purpose.'

A glass of wine was being pushed towards her.

'I've hardly ever drunk wine,' she said. 'I don't think Mrs Rundell would like me to be drinking wine, sir.'

'Oh, is that what you suppose? You might be wrong. In any case, today would be my mother's birthday, and I like to remember it, one way or another. Raise your glass, will you, and help me drink to the memory of my dear mother?'

They drank. He emptied his glass, she drank only a little. She did not like the wine at all, she thought, but for the sake of politeness she tried a second sip and liked it a little better, and then a third sip, and it was really quite pleasant.

'Tell me about your family,' he said. 'Tell me about how you grew up, and about your sister Agnes, and about your other sisters and brothers, I know you have several of them. And while you tell me I will be good and eat up my dinner.'

So she talked, and with the encouragement of a sip or two of wine she forgot her fears. She told him about her father and the Literary and Philosophical Society, and how her mother had to sew or take in laundry to keep the family going, and that she had not seen them since she arrived at Markham Thorpe since it was too far to go for a day, but she would have some holiday later in the summer and would be visiting them, and how Agnes had been a bold girl even when she was at school, always showing herself off and dancing around with the boys, and how she had four little sisters and three little brothers, all of them at school because the vicar of the parish knew her father through the society and let them attend the school out of kindness, and on she went, carried away at the thought of all these people she hardly ever saw, happy to think of them and yet missing them, until the clock struck the hour and she cried, 'Oh, sir, here I am running on and running on, and there's a cream pudding for you in the kitchen, which Mrs Saunders is ever so particular about, and I must go and fetch it instantly, and you must be so tired of me prattling away . . . Have you finished your dinner? Sir?'

'Yes, and I'm quite ready for my cream pudding. And thank you for the stories, Ellen, I enjoyed them very much.' And indeed he did look cheerful, as she had not seen him for a long time.

In the kitchen she was met with a quizzical look from Mrs Saunders. 'You've been a long while,' said the cook. 'You look flushed, my girl.'

'Is the pudding ready for Mr James, Mrs Saunders?' For once, she did not feel like saying sorry, as she seemed to do so often.

'Fully ready, Ellen, and I'll put it on the plate for you, and if you delay a minute longer it will be spoilt.'

When she took the pudding back to Mr James she put the plate in front of him, curtsied, said, 'Will that be all, sir?' and left the room before he could ask her to sit down again. She felt – what did she feel? – she felt confused. She did not know what she was thinking, really she did not. She felt like someone in a book, now who could this be? And she realised, with alarm, that she felt like the maidservant Pamela, in the old book she had read when she first arrived at the house.

The following morning, quite early, there was a loud pealing at the front-door bell. This was unexpected, since few callers came to the hall without announcing their arrival beforehand, and most of those who did come, such as Mr Richardson the lawyer or Mr James's friends, went to the side door. The front-door bell was only used for great events, or by the gentry paying formal calls. In general it was kept locked and barred.

Ellen ran to the Great Hall and with some difficulty unbolted the door, to the sound of blows on the outside. It opened on Mr and Mrs Wentworth, both red with exasperation, he with a walking-stick with which he was about to strike the door again.

'Ah, there you are – why are the doors all locked? Does the bell not work? We tried the side door, we tried this one. Is this a fortress? What is this?' cried Mrs Wentworth, as they pushed their way into the house. Behind them were two servants, carrying luggage.

Ellen curtsied. 'I'm sorry,' she said, 'but we did not expect you, ma'am.'

'Not expect us! I belong here, this is my house, must I request permission to visit? And why are you opening the door, may I ask? What's your name? Ellen, is it? Why are you opening the door, and not the butler?' Her manner was haughty and disagreeable, very different from the way she had been when she wanted Ellen to become her lady's maid. He, on the other hand, looked her up and down and smiled at her in a way she found disconcerting.

'I am the parlour maid now, ma'am,' said Ellen, meekly. 'Mr Fellows was not so well, he had to stop working.'

'Oh, yes, poor Fellows, I had forgotten that.' She looked around the Great Hall impatiently. 'It's very sad in here, I can't think what has been going on . . . Does no one clean the house any longer?'

'The Great Hall is not used very much at the moment, ma'am.'

The Wentworths were alarming: both of them were so angry, Mrs Wentworth to the fore, supported from behind by her husband who was wearing a fashionable travelling coat and a vacant expression. The London servants, whom she did not know, were bored and disdainful, their eyes moving lazily around the room as though they found everything in it beneath their attention. Used by now to the workings of the house, Ellen wondered about practical questions. Where were they all to sleep? Mrs Wentworth's room was closed and under dust sheets and had not been aired since they left after the wedding. And where would they sit? The drawing room was closed too. Would they have to go into the smoking room with Mr James? Would they be having their meals in the boudoir (and she almost laughed at the thought of this, since she did not much like Mrs Wentworth)?

'We've had a long and very tiring journey,' said the lady. 'Tell the cook to make us some breakfast and my servants where our room is, and where they will be sleeping. They don't know the house. Don't stand and stare at me, girl.' She strode across the hall to the drawing-room door and turned the handle. The door would not open.

'What is this?' she said.

'The drawing room is closed and the door is locked, ma'am. I could open it for you, of course, but everything is under dust sheets. You would not be very comfortable at all, ma'am.'

'Why? Why on earth? We will have to sit in the dining room, I suppose.'

'The dining room is closed too, ma'am.'

'Is the whole house locked up? Charles, it's worse than I thought. This is disgraceful. You – whatever your name is – go and find Mr James, quick as you can. At least he should be able to explain. And I want to see Miss Fisher at once. Go, girl, go . . .' But as Ellen was running out of the room – she was not sure which direction to go in, or which order to obey – the big door at the end of the Great Hall opened, and in walked Mrs Rundell.

There was a silence. Mrs Wentworth looked Mrs Rundell up and down. Mrs Rundell did the same to Mrs Wentworth. Then, very slowly, Mrs Rundell curtsied. 'Welcome to Markham Thorpe, ma'am.'

'Ah, Rundell, there you are,' said Mrs Wentworth. She sounded, at the same time, hostile and just the least bit nervous. 'We were wondering if anyone was here at all. We have come to visit Papa, we are worried about him.'

'Is that so, ma'am?' said Mrs Rundell. 'I am sorry to hear it. There is no reason to be worried, let me insure you.'

'Arrange for some breakfast at once, will you? And have our bags taken to our rooms.'

'Of course, ma'am, of course. Only, if you will forgive me, ma'am, there is one difficulty. We were not expecting you and your usual room is not prepared for visitors, ma'am. We will have to see where you can best be placed.'

'I want my own room,' cried Mrs Wentworth.

'Well, that is not easy, ma'am. Indeed, to be honest, it is not possible. The old mattresses have been taken out of your room. They needed to be renewed and the new ones are not yet ready. I will see what can be done but it cannot be arranged for tonight. We shall have to find another room that can accommodate you.' She coughed. 'I am not sure how long you will be staying, ma'am?'

'As long as is necessary, I suppose.' She clenched her fist as she said this. It was possible – was it possible? – that she was afraid of Mrs Rundell.

'It would be helpful, ma'am, to know how long that might be.'

'I don't know, do I, until I have seen how things are?'

'If you were able to tell me, necessary for what, ma'am, I could perhaps elucidate you.'

'That is no business of yours, Rundell.'

'Very well, ma'am. If you will permit, ma'am, I will give the necessary instructions following your unexpected arrival. I assume you will be lunching and dining at home, ma'am?'

She said 'ma'am' in a soft voice, which sounded as though it were meant to be highly respectful, but it did not seem to make a favourable impression on Mrs Wentworth.

'Yes, I am not here to pay calls, thank you. We will be taking our meals at home.'

'In the house, ma'am? Yes, of course.' And executing another deep, indeed exaggerated curtsy, she turned towards Ellen, who had listened with interest. She thought that Mrs Rundell was being at the same time polite and insulting. It was clear that the Wentworths were furious.

Facing Ellen, Mrs Rundell reverted to her housekeeper manner. 'Ellen, go to the kitchen and speak to Mrs Saunders. Breakfast for two, to be served in here. Then you will show Mrs Wentworth's people to two of the rooms for visiting servants, and tell Katherine to air the beds.' She turned back to Mrs Wentworth, and her voice changed again. 'Sadly, ma'am, we have had to close a good deal of the house, as you know, in order to make the necessary economies, but you are very welcome to sit in my room should you wish to do so. Sir Richard is generally there.'

'In the housekeeper's room? Why does he choose to sit there?'

'He likes it, I understand, ma'am. And, after all, he is very used to sitting there, ma'am. The housekeeper's room is very pleasant. You would know it as the boudoir. I believe it was your mother's room, was it not?' And having spoken till then in a subdued, respectful voice she added, loudly and viciously, 'Ma'am,' shooting at her listener a look that was neither subdued nor respectful.

Mrs Wentworth looked at her with horror. 'The boudoir, your room? How dare you – how dare you? I . . . I . . .' She seemed about to sob.

Her husband put his hand on her arm and murmured, 'Lavinia,' and visibly she pulled herself together. 'We would like to see Sir Richard as soon as possible,' said her husband, in as authoritative a voice as he could muster.

'Of course. I will prepare him for your arrival.'

'No,' Mrs Wentworth interrupted. 'We would like to see him now.'

'Sir Richard must not be surprised too suddenly. He is not well, he is resting. I will need to prepare him. He may not be fully dressed as yet.'

'You don't dress him, do you? I mean, surely Mr Fellows . . .'

Mrs Rundell bobbed a little curtsy, as though to say yes, she did. 'Perhaps you would like to sit here for a little while or would you prefer the smoking room, which is kept heated for Mr James?' she asked, pointing to the uncomfortable settles that lined the room. 'I will attend to the necessary arrangements occasioned by your unexpected arrival.' Gesturing imperiously to the visiting servants to follow her but without waiting to find out whether the Great Hall would suit the new arrivals, she turned on her heel, then pretended to recall herself and faced the Wentworths again to deliver a deep, sarcastic curtsy.

There followed three uncomfortable days. Mrs Wentworth spent a good deal of time in the governess's room. She went walking in the garden with her brother and could be seen from the house, gesticulating and clenching her fists. She refused to dine in the housekeeper's room but would visit her father there. Though she tried to persuade him to see her on her own, he would not agree, and they did no more than walk the length of the lawn together. Ellen and Billy served the Wentworths their meals in the smoking room with Mr James, and Miss Fisher, who gladly came downstairs from the schoolroom. Whenever Ellen entered the room she would interrupt a heated conversation, which was immediately hushed, the voices breaking out again as soon as she closed the door.

What was going on was clear to everyone below stairs. In the servants' hall guarded discussions took place, guarded, Ellen thought, because of what she might say to her cousin. It was agreed that Miss Lavinia had come up to Yorkshire to persuade her father to dismiss Mrs Rundell, that Miss Fisher was supplying Miss Lavinia with stories against the housekeeper, that Miss Lavinia was trying to enlist her brother on her side. It was evident that Mrs Rundell was determined to keep Miss Lavinia from being alone with her father, and to make the visitors feel as unwelcome as possible. The Wentworths were assigned a small guest room, down a long corridor, with a view of the back courtyard. It was decreed by Mrs Rundell that Mrs Wentworth's room (the Chinese

Room, as Mrs Rundell described it, though it was 'Miss Lavinia's room' to everyone else) was not usable – at least a full day's cleaning was needed to make it ready, and they no longer had enough servants to work so rapidly. 'Of course, if we had had more notice . . .' she would remark, each time the subject was broached. Meanwhile Mr Wentworth lounged around the house and the garden, spending much of his time in the smoking room and trying, without success, to engage Ellen in talk.

Meals in the servants' hall were not what they had been: there were so few people around the table, for one thing, and the food was sparser. 'I am sorry,' the cook would say, putting down a dish on the table, 'that this is not better, but someone I could mention is very tight with the money these days, you know. Meat only twice a week . . . When I think of how it used to be, meat every day, and good meat too!' She remarked more than once that she was looking for a new situation, and had heard of a family nearby who wanted a good plain cook. 'The difficulty,' she said one afternoon, in a confidential mood, though she seemed not to care who knew about her plans, 'is who to ask for a character. Should I be asking Sir Richard, if I can reach him, get past the dragon? Or Mr James? Or Miss Lavinia? The only thing that's certain is that, come Christmas, Mrs Saunders will not be at Markham Thorpe.'

On the morning of the fourth day after their arrival, Mrs Rundell and Mrs Wentworth, encountering each other in the Great Hall, repeated an exchange that had become almost a habit. Mrs Wentworth demanded to see her father. He was not ready to see anyone. She asked when he would be ready. He would not be ready for some time, he was particularly tired this morning, he had been tired ever since his daughter arrived. Besides this, he did not wish to speak to his daughter about the matters they had already discussed and he had asked Mrs Rundell to make this clear. Demanding again in a yet louder voice to see him and being refused, the daughter of the house lost her temper and tried to push past Mrs Rundell. The housekeeper, stretching her arms out to either side to bar the way, raised her chin in the air and allowed herself the indulgence of an insolent smile. 'How dare you block my way?' demanded Mrs Wentworth. 'How dare you?'

'I am carrying out orders, ma'am,' replied the housekeeper.

'Get out of my way, you old witch! I must see my father — I must make him see sense,' cried Mrs Wentworth. Abandoning fashionable manners and forgetting propriety, she thrust the housekeeper, as hard as she could, against the wall.

Mrs Rundell, who was stronger, recovered her balance, seized Mrs Wentworth's wrists and pushed her away. Drawing herself up, she remarked, without losing her calm, 'I think we are forgetting ourselves, Mrs Wentworth.'

The door to the smoking room opened and out came Mrs Wentworth's husband and brother. 'What on earth . . . ?' they said, and 'What is this noise?' and 'Lavinia, come away from here.'

But as she cried, in a paroxysm of anger and frustration, 'No, no, no! I will not leave, I want to see my father, I want to see my father,' the door to the staircase hall opened. There, leaning on a stick, wearing an old gown, stooping and not looking well, was Sir Richard.

'Yes?' he said. 'What is this? What is this shouting and yelling? Lavinia, you are beside yourself.'

'No, Papa, I am not beside myself. I need to explain, I need to tell you the truth.'

'The truth is that you want me to do as you please, not as I please. So as long as I have the power to do so, I prefer to do as I choose, thank you. Mrs Rundell has been very good to me, that is what matters. I am not concerned with your point of view.'

'I am only thinking of your best interests, Papa. This woman—'

'Please do not refer to Mrs Rundell in that manner. Mrs Rundell comes from an excellent family. She is no less a lady than you are,' and he gave a little bow in the direction of the housekeeper. This lady stood, arms folded and face impassive, in an attitude of patient superiority.

Mrs Wentworth snorted loudly.

'I would ask you, Lavinia, to show Mrs Rundell the respect you would show to a member of our family.'

When Sir Richard had his seizure Mrs Rundell, for once, was not in the house. She had gone to Ripon to visit the tradesmen who supplied Markham Thorpe, and the coachman reported that she made regular visits to the family lawyer. When she went to Ripon she was driven in the ancient family carriage by the groom, who acted as coachman on the rare occasions a carriage was needed. Since they barely spoke to one another, she would write her instructions on a piece of paper and hand this to him in advance. For these expeditions the housekeeper dressed herself in a richly adorned bonnet and a silk pelisse (of which she had several) and a dress with full skirts. Very handsome she looked too, with her hair neatly pinned, though not so neatly that a few raven tresses could not escape. Her gloves on this particular afternoon were long and white, a lady's gloves. The maids clustered at a window to observe her progress, and it was noticed that the waiting carriage was stationed at the front of the house rather than at the side as would have been usual, and that she went out through the front door, something she had not done before. The groom was sitting on the box with an air of disgust, and as she approached he remained immobile. 'I am ready,' she said, and stood still. After a long pause he climbed off the box, very slowly, as slowly as anyone possibly could, and opened the carriage door. Ignoring him, she placed herself comfortably inside.

'Well,' said Mrs Saunders, 'and is she not completely the fine lady?'

'Where, I want to know,' said Katherine,' did she find those gloves? Such beautiful gloves, more for Court than Ripon, but I suppose she thinks she has to dress up when the opportunity arises. But where does she find the money for her rich clothes, or to refurnish the house? We're always being told there is no money at all . . .'

'I can tell you where the gloves come from,' said Lucy. 'Mrs R has not just taken over Lady Markham's boudoir, she has taken over her wardrobe. You know Sir Richard wanted nothing of his wife's thrown away? Well, there are cupboardsful of dresses and shawls, cupboards full, and what of late has our Mrs R been doing but going through them and taking out things that might suit her?'

'Has she, indeed? The impudence of the woman! But she's larger than old Lady Markham, isn't she, by a long way?' answered Katherine.

'No doubt she is, but it's not the dresses she's after — they would be out of fashion after all and our Mrs Rundell is mighty keen on fashion. No, what she is after is the trimmings, the shawls, the laces, the gloves. The girls never had these things, their father did not want it. He preferred them to be kept in memory of his wife. But now he wants Mrs Rundell to enjoy them – you should have heard the way she coaxed him into giving her the key to her ladyship's cupboards.'

They began to disperse. They were not so busy, now that the Wentworths had fled back to London, and Mrs Rundell did not seem to care whether the house was kept very clean or not. But this afternoon they were certainly needed. As they walked down the passage they heard a cry and a thump from the Great Hall. There on the floor lay Sir Richard, near the open front door, which he must have been trying to close. His body was a little twisted, and he could hardly speak or move.

They summoned the doctor from Ripon, they carried Sir Richard upstairs, they put him to bed, they filled his bed with hot bottles, though it was a warm day; they lit the fire. 'Bad, very bad,' asserted Katherine, miserably. 'Will he live?'

The doctor arrived within the hour and made an inspection. 'It is a seizure,' he said to the maids, clustering anxiously outside the bedroom, 'but not, I think, very severe. He should be better soon. He must be nursed carefully. Who will do that?'

'Mrs Rundell will nurse him,' they replied. The doctor gave them some instructions, and left.

When Mrs Rundell, with several packages under her arm, followed by the disgruntled groom with more packages, rang at the front door, Ellen was there to meet her. 'Sir Richard, it's Sir Richard . . .' she said.

'What's happened to Sir Richard?' cried Mrs Rundell. 'Where is he?' and up the stairs she sprang, two steps at a time, her face contorted.

The doctor was right. Sir Richard was not very ill. Within a few days he was out of his room, using a stick. He was supported by Mrs Rundell at all times. Certainly he was not as strong as he had been, and spoke a little more slowly, but nothing worse than that. What changed was that Mrs Rundell hardly let him from her sight, accompanied him on his walks across the lawn, smothered him in blankets, told him he must go early to bed. She came into the kitchen every day to supervise the dishes that Mrs Saunders made for him, little delicate dishes of chicken and eggs, and sometimes she insisted on cooking these dishes herself for him in the still room, to which nobody else but Lucy was admitted. No one could deny that she nursed him admirably.

After a few days of this, there was a further development. Mrs Rundell summoned the household to the servants' hall. 'Sir Richard is still not as well as I would like him to be. What the doctor recommends is sea air, and I intend to take him to Scarborough for a few weeks. This means that the house will be closed except for the rooms used by Mr James. Lucy will accompany me – I must have a little help. Katherine, you may go home and visit your mother, about whose sufferings we have heard so much over the years. You will be on board wages. We expect you back within three weeks, but no sooner, do you understand? I am sure your mother needs you. Mrs Saunders – what will you be doing, Mrs Saunders? Mr James must have his meals prepared but there is very little else for you to do. I suggest you go on leave too. I'm sure there must be someone who will be pleased to see you.'

Mrs Saunders drew herself up. 'Thank you, Mrs Rundell, but I think this is the moment to inform you that I have been offered a situation, a very good situation, with another family, and I am herewith giving a month's notice.'

'Ha, is that so?' was the reply. 'In that case, Mrs Saunders, I suggest that you do not work out your full month's notice but leave when we do, at the end of the week.'

'And who is to cook Mr James's meals, if I may ask?' enquired the cook, piqued by the readiness with which her resignation was accepted.

'Joan can cook them.'

'Joan? The kitchenmaid?'

'She must have learnt how to cook by now – she has been here for almost three years. Have you not taught her your tricks?'

'My tricks, Mrs Rundell, is not a suitable way to describe my skills as a cook.'

'Call them what you like, Mrs Saunders, there is really no need to make a great mystery out of roasting mutton.' She laughed harshly. 'I'm sure the girl will produce passable meals, and Mr James is not very particular. I can consider how best to fill the position when we come back from Scarborough. I suppose you will need a character, I will be happy to supply that.'

Mrs Saunders, idly fingering a knife that lay beside her, eyed Mrs Rundell. 'Thank you, Mrs Rundell, I'm most obliged, but in the household to which I am going a character from a house-keeper would not be regarded as acceptable. Mrs Wentworth has kindly agreed to write to Lady Osborne on my behalf.'

'Lady Osborne, eh?' For a moment Mrs Rundell looked discon-certed. Lady Osborne was the wife of a viscount, and her house was a good deal larger than Markham Thorpe. 'So you are rising in the social order?' she remarked.

'That seems to be the habit in this house, Mrs Rundell,' replied the cook, smiling broadly.

Mrs Rundell, gripping her dress, decided to be gracious. 'I'm sure we shall miss you, Mrs Saunders, and we wish you all possible good luck in your new situation. So that seems to be all settled.'

There was a pause. They shuffled their feet and looked at the floor, wondering about the full meaning of Mrs Rundell's arrangements. No one imagined she was acting straightforwardly. The plans seemed to have been made so carefully – except for one thing.

'And me, Mrs Rundell, what shall I be doing?' It was Ellen, small and agitated in the corner.

'Ah, you, Ellen. In my absence you will be in charge of the household, though you are due a holiday and this will be the moment to take it. We cannot do without you, can we, our little Ellen? You will look after the house. You will order the meals, serve Mr James, make sure everything is in good order. What you will not do is clean the house, that is beneath you, beyond keeping Mr James's rooms comfortable. Let the dust gather until Katherine returns, and then she can be as busy as we know she likes to be. In my absence, consider yourself the housekeeper.'

A shudder ran through the room.

'How long do you and Sir Richard expect to be away, Mrs Rundell?' asked Katherine.

'As long as necessary,' she replied. 'How long that will be I cannot say.'

Ellen had never learnt how to cook. At home her mother prepared meals, helped by the little maid who came in by the day. At

Markham Thorpe, cooking was not her province, and there was no opportunity to learn since Mrs Saunders did not welcome enquiries into her methods. Ellen had no ambitions in roasting or basting. But now she found herself in charge, with Mr James (and indeed herself) to feed and no one to cook but the poor oppressed kitchenmaid, whom Mrs Saunders had always treated as a half-wit. Joan could, it emerged, more or less manage to keep a fire hot, and could place a piece of meat in front of the fire on a spit and turn it, but the result – burnt on the outside, raw on the inside, and accompanied by vegetables boiled so long you could hardly tell what they were – was hard to eat. At first Mr James did not complain when she served up these sorry examples of Joan's craft, merely looked surprised, but after a while he began to say, 'Oh, no, she's burnt it again,' or 'Is there anything she can cook?' or 'Would it be better just to eat bread and cheese?' Ellen, who liked to do whatever she did as well as possible, felt ashamed of her lack of skill, and looked in the library for books on cookery. She found a few, mostly written by housekeepers and cooks in noble houses in the last century. They were not very helpful, but, determined to be determined, she tried some of the recipes. Soup, she found, was not too difficult.

If it had not been summer, living in the house almost alone would have been unbearable. Joan was no company: she hardly opened her mouth except to ask what to do next. At least there was little Billy. Though his way of following Ellen everywhere with his eyes could be annoying, he was a pleasant lad, and occasionally, knowing one was adored could be reassuring. He was a country boy and, when permitted, would accompany Ellen on walks in the park, pointing out the birds and telling her which plants were healthy or otherwise useful. There were only a few gardeners now – and, after all, the one she loved had gone away, and never been heard from – and Mr Hurst tended to be distant. 'Ah, it's the housekeeper, come to give me my orders,' he would say, with a swallowed laugh, when he saw her. On the whole she thought this was not meant to be friendly. In the stables, there was only one groom left, who looked after Mr James's horses. He was only too interested in showing Ellen the stables, and she avoided him.

And there was the village, of course, but what was she to do there? She knew nobody except the laundrywomen who came up to the big house two days a week, and they showed no signs of friendliness. When she did venture into the village she saw nobody she knew: people tended to stare, not even say, 'Good day'. Ellen had been told when she joined the household that the servants from the big house belonged to another world, and it was true – they certainly did not belong in the village. Occasionally she would go into Ripon but did not feel at home, either, in those busy streets. Markham Thorpe was her life.

As the days went by, the house became drearier. All the furniture in the downstairs rooms and most of the bedrooms was covered with dust sheets, and many of the doors were locked. The blinds were pulled down along the passages and even in the Great Hall. Where once Miss Emily had arranged flowers, there was nothing to be seen but empty surfaces, and when flies died they lay for days on the floor. The place was tumbling into an uneasy sleep. Joan and Ellen and Billy abandoned the servants' hall, and ate their meals at the kitchen table. On a rainy day – and there were many, that summer – it was miserable to look out of the windows on to the lawn and the park beyond, acres of empty greenness, not a person in sight, just the melancholy trees and the straggling flowerbeds in the pale milky light of a damp summer evening. Ellen longed for the doorbell to ring and for someone to arrive, but no carriage ever came up the drive. She felt that she was confined perpetually to this life of solitary inaction.

Letters arrived occasionally. Two came from Mrs Rundell, telling her that Sir Richard was responding well to the sea air in Scarborough and was mending but was not well enough to come home yet. She asked Ellen for a full account of what was going on at Markham Thorpe. 'Nothing,' she said to herself, frowning crossly. More interestingly, a letter arrived from Agnes, saying that she was planning to leave Miss Emily's service. At the hotel in Naples where the honeymoon couple were staying, Agnes had made the acquaintance of a most charming gentleman, 'English, I hasten to add,' she wrote, 'who has become very friendly and has asked me to join him on a number of excursions. When I said this was difficult because of my duties in service, he said, "Damn domestic service, a girl like you should do as she pleases."' He had paid one of the Italian hotel maids to do the work that Agnes should have been doing. After two or three of these excursions, which had been very pleasant but entirely decorous, he had suggested that Agnes should become his permanent companion. She would, he proposed, accompany him on his travels in Europe before returning with him to London where he would settle her in a charming little house ('my own house, Ellen, just imagine that!') and set her up in her own millinery business.

'He is not young, but very distinguished, indeed he is an Honourable, and money is nothing to him, I mean he has such a great amount of it, and he is very kind, and seems to like me. So when I leave him (I should say, dear sister, that I do nothing with him at all untoward) after a pleasant walk and conversation and a little light refreshment in a café, it is dispiriting to go back to the suite occupied by the happy couple whose slave I am and have to pick up and fold their clothes and think about what they want all the time, rather than, even for a tiny moment, what might interest me. I believe I can trust him, so I think I may agree to his requests, though I certainly will not give him that prize a woman holds but which once lost is never recovered – before I am settled in London with the house and the business secure. It's important to keep a man waiting, you know, to heighten his interest, test his resolve, as you will learn one day if you do not remain enslaved by domestic service. You may be shocked by what I am telling you, dear little mouse, but don't you see, for girls like us who know we are better than many of those who are more privileged than we are, what other poss- ibilities are there? And you, do you want to stay in that dreary place all your life, even if you are elevated to the rank of parlour maid or housekeeper? No, you don't – and if you do you deserve the worst. I mean if some nice gentleman, as it might be Mr James, were to make you an offer, are you sure you should say No? Think about it care- fully.'

Ellen was dismayed by this letter, so contrary to all she had been brought up to believe was proper. What would Mother and Father think? Would they ever speak to Agnes again, fond of their children though they were? She wrote back a letter of entreaty, to the *poste restante* that Agnes had given as her address, but no answer came.

Ellen was alarmed not only by what Agnes said about herself, but by her remarks about Mr James. She could not help being constantly aware of his interest in her. When she came into the smoking room, he would look at her and yet not look at her, talk to her in a desultory way and then drop into silence, hum and haw and ask how she was doing, give her little shy smiles and then become morose. When she went walking in the afternoon, she would encounter him, unexpectedly as it were, sometimes on foot, sometimes on horseback. He would smile, bow, raise his hat, remark on the weather, hesitate, while she would curtsy and, as soon as she decently could, hurry on. She looked after his rooms as carefully as ever but no longer included the gentle gestures of the past. There was no more solicitous tidying of his mantelpiece.

She knew, she knew perfectly well, that there was more to come. At mealtimes he was constrained by the etiquette of service, by the knives and forks and the silver dishes containing his unappetising victuals. Sometimes she would send in Billy in her place, to avoid spending too much time under his sombre gaze. Out of doors it was different. Though she tried to avoid him, it was hard in such a complicated garden with its alleys and herbaceous borders. It was in the walled garden, where she liked to sit on the bench beside Lady Markham's Pond, that he caught her by surprise one afternoon, when she was gazing into the water. 'A penny for your thoughts,' he said, and she jumped.

She was actually thinking about her sister and what might happen to her – how she might be abandoned by a heartless lover like Rosalind in *Love Forlorn*. This she did not explain: all she said was, 'I was thinking about my sister, Mr James.'

He sat down on the bench beside her. Instinctively she rose to her feet.

'No, sit down,' he said commandingly.

She sat, though she did not want to, but he sounded for a moment like his father and her instinct was to do as she was told.

'You always call me Mr James,' he said, 'even when there is no one here to hear us. Will you not call me James?'

'I couldn't do that, sir.'

'Why not? It is my name, after all.'

'But you're my master, sir. I can't call you by your Christian name, it wouldn't be right.'

'If I'm your master you should do as I tell you, shouldn't you?'

'Yes, sir, of course, sir. But no servant calls their master by their Christian name.'

'Your cousin is a servant, isn't she? And she calls Sir Richard – I mean my father – Richard. I've heard her do it often. She likes to say "Richard" when we are having meals together. I hated it at first, but now – now it seems quite acceptable.'

'I can't speak for Mrs Rundell and Sir Richard, sir. For me it would not be right.' She looked at him defiantly. Almost to her surprise, she realised that she did not feel any fear of him. She knew he would not make any violent attempt on her. He knew her too well, was that it? She tried again to leave, but he still wanted to keep her.

'People wonder,' he said, 'well, I myself wonder – whether my father and Mrs Rundell might be married. What would you think of that?'

'I have no thoughts about it, sir, it is not my business.'

'What do they say in the servants' hall?'

'We hardly have a servants' hall these days, Mr James.'

'If they were to marry, that would make us relations, would it not?'

'No, sir, hardly.' She wished this conversation would end.

'Oh, yes, certainly it would. That means it is quite suitable, at least it might become quite suitable, for you to call me James, just as I call you Ellen. God made us equal after all. It's only man who has given us a different position in society. Should we not listen to the word of God rather than of man?'

She could not help smiling at this argument.

'Ah, Ellen, a smile, a smile at last. Though I'm quite serious. And I am serious too, when I say I know you cannot like me, because I am older than you and ugly and stupid, and good for nothing, but I have to tell you, Ellen, that . . .' and he stopped.

She tried to look straight ahead, but could not prevent herself stealing a look at him.

'I have to tell you that for me you are the most beautiful woman I've ever seen, both in face and in character. Ellen – Ellen, I love you.'

What was she to say to this? She almost laughed, it was so unexpected and somehow absurd. But she felt his hand, his unexpectedly small and fine hand – which she had so often seen holding knife and fork and which had surprised her by its delicacy – she felt his hand touching hers, then closing around it. She did not pull hers away, but withdrew it steadily. As she did so she looked fully into his eyes. Dark and luminous, they were fixed upon her.

'Don't say that, sir,' she said.

'It's true.'

What could she say to that? She did not want to hurt his feelings but she could not say she loved him. At most she felt sorry for him, would have liked to comfort him, knew (as never before) that he was lonely. For the first time the thought of becoming mistress of Markham Thorpe ran through her mind, with all its pleasures and satisfactions, not least not being a servant any longer – but this was an unworthy thought, an absurd and impossible thought, and she suppressed it firmly.

'I will have to think,' was all she could bring herself to say. She was very conscious of his body close to hers, his large and clumsy body, his great head with its wild hair, the smell of tobacco and soap – she knew all too well that the soap was the finest lavender soap from a shop in St James's Street in London. But she was still not afraid.

'Won't you let me hold your hand?' he said.

'How can I? If I do, you will think I am saying yes. I can't say yes.'

'Then are you saying no? Ellen, are you saying no?'

'No,' she answered.

'What do you mean, no? Do you mean you are not saying no?'

She turned towards him again, looking into his intently pleading eyes. She felt a strange stirring inside her, almost as she had with Harry. 'I don't know what I think,' she said. 'I must go.'

But she did not go. Mr James took her in his arms, his extremely strong arms, and kissed her. For a moment, taken by surprise, she felt herself give way. Then she twisted out of his embrace and ran, gasping and aroused, out of the walled garden. She sent Billy in to serve him his dinner that evening.

Two days later Ellen was collected by her father for her long two-week holiday in Malton. She was delighted to be at home, not having been there since she left for Markham Thorpe the previous summer. She was so happy to see her family again, her brothers and sisters all bigger than when she had said goodbye to them, all delighted to see her after the first moment or two of shyness, her youngest brother Robert hurling himself into her skirts like a cannonball.

Malton seemed very busy after the silence of Markham Thorpe, what with the market thronged with farmers on Fridays, the shops lit up at night and filled with people, the big market-place on either side of the church busy with people bustling in and out of the King's Head. From her parents' house she could walk in a few minutes past St Leonard's Church and down to Wheelgate to her father's shop. Here she felt she belonged, which she never did in Ripon. Whenever she walked through the streets she saw people she knew, who greeted her warmly and asked how she was – though she noticed that when she told them she was in service they looked away and changed the subject. None of them wanted to hear about her new life.

As soon as she had arrived in Malton, she knew she never wanted to go back to Markham Thorpe. Seen from a distance the house seemed strange and sad, as though all colour were drained from it, and its life were ebbing away. Now that she was at home, she could not imagine returning to that house and eating her dinners in the kitchen with dull little Joan and silly Billy and listening to the wood-pigeons only because there was no other sound to be heard. What sort of life was that?

On the third evening of her holiday she told her parents she did not want to go back to Markham Thorpe. They greeted this remark with stony silence. She suggested that she might work out her notice, then leave.

They stayed silent for a while, staring into the distance. Then her father coughed and looked at her mother. Her mother looked at her father. 'You must go back, my dear,' said her mother.

'Why?' said Ellen. 'If I work out my notice that's enough, isn't it?'

'No,' said her father, 'that's not enough. You must stay for a while longer. You must remain for two years at least. You will need a character.' He looked down at his hands and shifted in his chair. 'Besides, Cousin Rundell has been so good to you, and you have risen so rapidly in the household, you have excellent prospects.' He seemed uneasy as he said this, avoiding her eye.

She thought it best not to tell him quite how excellent her prospects might be, if she chose. What would they say if they knew what Mr James had said to her? She felt she respected her parents as much as she had in the past.

'She came to see us one day from Scarborough, all the way from Scarborough, she came in a carriage and a very elegant one too. She said that the new train was really not for her, she is such a lady, you see. Very gracious, she was. She says,' continued her mother, 'that you are a true help to her, that you know exactly what to do, that you are everything a good servant should be. She is so proud that she was able to leave you in charge of the house.'

'Is she? Well, that's very kind. But I don't want to be everything a servant should be,' said Ellen, crossly.

'She told us her news,' said her father, 'that she is to become the companion and nurse of Sir Richard. We understand that in that case you would be considered for the position of permanent housekeeper yourself, and what a promotion that would be, for a girl who's not yet twenty. You could do anything after that, she says.'

'And not just any housekeeper, but a lady housekeeper, with special privileges and the right never to have meals in the servants' hall with the common servants,' added her mother, expectant and proud.

'She never told me all this,' said Ellen, hotly. 'And what does it mean, that I could do anything afterwards? Be a housekeeper in a larger house? Anyway, they've sent away most of the servants at Markham Thorpe. There's hardly anyone left to look after that great place.'

Her parents looked at one another and hesitated.

'We'd heard,' said her father, 'that the numbers in the household had been reduced, but Cousin Rundell says that in future all that will change. She says that she has taken the management of the family finances into her own control, and has made them more regular. Indeed, she expressed interest in employing Harriet at the house, in the most genteel capacity, of course.' Harriet was Ellen's next sister. 'That would be a great thing, you know. We need to settle our girls.'

'Harriet! Why should poor Harriet want to work there? There's no genteel capacity available, only being a housemaid. She will not like that, any more than I did, having to wear those horrible clothes and work and work and work. Anyway, the place is so unsettled at the moment, there's no saying what will happen.'

But it was no good. Her mother was as firm as her father. In their eyes she could see an unfamiliar determination. 'Yes,' continued her mother. 'Cousin Rundell tells us that the financial position will improve within the household, and she will generously contribute some of her own resources. If she can resolve the family affairs with the lawyer, which she thinks she will be able to do, there will be enough money to put everything on a proper footing. There will be a full household again, and you will find yourself in a situation you will welcome.'

Ellen pursed her mouth and did not speak. The thought of going back to Markham Thorpe, now that she had escaped, was depressing, even frightening. She was worried, she had to admit it, about Mr James. Was he really in love with her? She knew she could not be in love with him: he was too strange, and bearish, and then he was a gentleman, and it was not right for a plain girl like herself to fall for a gentleman. Somehow, though, she could not quite forget him. Even when she was at home with her brothers and sisters and cousins, playing games with them in the garden or eating dinner or walking in the fields by the river, the thought of Mr James kept returning to her.

Her parents were looking at her impatiently, as though expecting her to reply. Mrs Rundell's visit had evidently impressed them hugely. In the past they had always been so gentle with Ellen, so anxious she should be happy, even if they had made her go into service a long way from home. Now they only seemed anxious about themselves.

Her mother spoke. It was her mother who seemed particularly determined she should stay at Markham Thorpe. 'You must go back,

Ellen, and stay at least another year. You will not be going back to being a housemaid, after all. And we think — we have good reason to think — that at the end of a year you will want to stay longer.'

There was no shifting them. She did not say yes, she did not say no, but she knew she had lost. They would not let her stay at home, and where else was there for her to go? She could hardly follow Agnes's example.

Her parents had said very little about Agnes, merely remarking how fortunate she was to have such a good employer as Mrs Dykes. So it was a surprise for all of them when one afternoon, after a loud knock, the front door burst open to admit Agnes. She was even more elegantly dressed than usual, in a silk dress and a bonnet in a style they had never seen before. When they enquired, timidly — 'Oh, it was made for me in Italy,' she said. 'Clothes are so charming there and, if you can find a dressmaker you trust, so inexpensive.' She was in Scarborough with Mrs Dykes, just for a few days, and thought she would visit her family, had just come over on the new train, and would spend the afternoon with them if they liked. What an adventure this was, to have a visitor arriving by train. The Braithwaites had waved at the train (which had only started to function that summer) but had not yet travelled in it.

Agnes talked a great deal, in a lively but genteel way and in a voice that gave no indication that she had once come from anywhere as provincial as Yorkshire (as she clearly considered it). She called her mother 'Mamma', she called her sister 'Ellen darling', she strolled around the house, saying, 'Oh, how it all comes back to one, it's so charming to live in a cottage,' and 'You dear old things, it is so good the way you keep everything as it always has been.' The effect was patronising but not without affection. On the whole they were pleased to see her, if a little alarmed.

Agnes told them all about Scarborough and how Mrs Dykes had been received by her father, who was installed in a handsome rented house with a view of the Cliff Bridge. 'She was written to, you know, by the governess, and she thought it was her duty to come up and find out what was happening. Well, of course Sir Richard always liked her best of all his children, she reminds him of her mother, but what a time she's had. Cousin Rundell hardly lets her near him without being there too, and goes walking with them along the front (with me nicely in the rear), and is always there at meals, and fusses over him when Mrs D tries to talk to him and keeps sending Mrs D away, saying he's tired. I don't think he is usually as tired as all that, to be truthful, but she wants Mrs Dykes out of the house. Even at church, you know, there are difficulties. We went to church on Sunday, to St Mary's, Scarborough, which is the church where the best people go. There is a good deal of display. Mrs Rundell always likes to be there, in one of her best dresses, she has quite a few, and one of her finest bonnets, and she sits beside him in his pew at the front of the church, and when we all went to church Mrs D had to sit on the other side of Cousin Rundell away from her father. And we can't go to the house when we like, we are only invited now and again, there's no question of calling when we feel disposed. Of course, while I am having tea at Sir Richard's house, I talk to the servants. Lucy is there and a couple of Scarborough people I didn't know, but they tell me a good deal. They don't know whether to address Mrs R as the housekeeper or the mistress of the house, she never makes it clear. Lucy, you know, she's no longer loyal to Mrs R, no, not at all, something has happened . . . Anyway, they say that Cousin R won't let Sir Richard out of her sight, she looks after him as well as can be, nothing but the best is good enough, and there seems to be no shortage of money at all, but as for company – well, he is not allowed to go up to any public place without her being there, and he never walks out on the front without her beside him, and when people call she insists on sitting there too.

'I don't know at all what is being planned, but Mr Richardson the lawyer from Ripon is in and out of the house all the time, having long meetings with Cousin Rundell and then short meetings with Sir Richard. But,' she went on, 'we won't be up in Yorkshire much longer. It looks as though Mrs Dykes is going to go home. So Mrs R will have her way.' She wriggled in her chair and examined her beautiful white glove. 'Well, I for one am very glad I'm no longer working at Markham Thorpe.'

This last remark was not well received. 'You'll be wanting to go for a walk, no doubt,' said her mother. 'Why don't you take your sister out for a stroll, Ellen? But no more talk about Markham Thorpe, if you please, Agnes.'

Out they went, arm in arm, Ellen pleased after all to see her sister. When they had walked down the hill, Agnes said, 'No, let's not go to the market-place just for the moment, let's walk to the corn mill and down by the river, where we won't see anyone we know. I want to talk to you, Ellen.' And as they stood and looked at the river, she told Ellen her plans – that she was waiting for her admirer, whom she had met in Italy, to come back to London, that he had made the acquaintance of Mr and Mrs Dykes at the hotel and had been given a pressing invitation to call in London, so that one way or another she would see him, that he was as keen as ever, wrote to her every day, and was investigating the purchase of a house in St John's Wood for her, which should be the very thing. As soon as this was all settled, she would be away, and no more domestic service for her . . . 'Cheer up, my dear,' she said, to her sister. 'It may not suit you, Ellen, and no doubt they will try to stop you coming to see me, but we'll always be friends, won't we?, and I'm sure we will meet often, even though I shall be a fallen woman.' She laughed and twirled her parasol. 'And while you are carrying trays and pulling up blinds in that dreary old house, just think of your sister who will have her own cook and her own maid to carry trays for her and will dine with a courteous gentleman at a table covered with silver and a linen cloth and go shopping in Regent Street in her own carriage, and ask yourself whether virtue is indeed its own reward. Personally, Ellen, I'd be glad to give up virtue in favour of comfort and pleasure – you know you will enjoy yourself in this life, and as for the next . . .'

She peered at Ellen, laughed again at her anxious face, and squeezed Ellen's chin between her finger and thumb. 'You sensible little thing,' she said. 'Well, perhaps Cousin Rundell has something very special planned for you. That would not surprise me at all. Tell me, how do you like being mistress at Markham Thorpe while they are away? And how do you like Mr James? You could do very much worse, you know, than Mr James, but you must make sure that he marries you before anything else happens.'

What on earth had made Agnes say that? Did she suspect something? And then they were off to the market-place, and round the shops, and back home, and in a little while Agnes had gone, leaving her sister more confused than ever.

*　　*　　*

A day or two later Ellen's mother took her aside. 'Ellen, we did not tell you this, but Cousin Rundell has been very good to us, you know. Every quarter she sends us a cheque. It really is so kind, and the cheques are not negligible and they make all the difference between survival and – well, you know, my dear . . . Without this assistance we would not be in a happy position at all. Your father has allowed his debts to rise and rise and there would be no way of paying them, and then what would happen to us? It would be . . . well, it might be the debtors' prison.' She squeezed her daughter's arm. 'Cousin Rundell means so much to our family, and she is so fond of you, she speaks of you so warmly. Whatever we do, we cannot afford to lose her friendship. You may think you are not completely happy at the Hall, but you must remember our interests, and your brothers' and sisters'.' She paused importantly. 'And we have reason to understand that when she becomes Lady Markham, she will have occasion to be very good to us indeed, and to you too.' And she smiled in a knowing, intimate way at Ellen.

Ellen knew she could not escape. She would not know how to escape, to start with, and if she did, Mrs Rundell's cheques would stop at once. That night, and during later nights, she dreamt about Markham Thorpe and its inhabitants, dreaming that the trees had grown higher and higher around the house and were close to overwhelming it, so that the rooms – oddly shrunk, in her sleeping vision – were so dark you could hardly see the far walls. In the morning she would wake in her own room at home, with her sister Harriet beside her, but with the realisation that only six days, or five days, or three days, remained between the moment of waking and her dreaded return to the house.

Part Five

After her two happy weeks at home Ellen returned to Markham Thorpe. Markham Thorpe – the very name depressed her. During the holidays she had come to dread going back, though there was no reason for fear, as she thought. Although unexplained things happened there, they did not seem threatening. On the contrary, the house enveloped one, it gave one a sense of security when one lived there. Its inhabitants seemed so far from the rest of the world, with the park wall stretching round and shielding them, but also keeping them in. Events that outside would have seemed of minor importance came to be full of meaning. All the details of domestic life became very important – who held which position in the household, and who was in or out of favour. To the servants, that house was everything. They almost forgot there was a life outside.

This life had become natural to Ellen while she was at the house. But back in Malton, she felt she was part of the world again, doing what she wanted and wearing the clothes she chose (though she had precious little money), not compelled to think all day about Mrs Rundell's moods, or Mr James, or the cooking, or all the other things they had to worry about, particularly if they were conscientious, as Ellen was. From a distance, Markham Thorpe could seem like a prison.

It felt like autumn when she returned. As her father drove her up the back drive he remarked that the place had changed: the fences were sagging, the grass growing wild. When they turned the corner the house was no longer welcoming, but a grey, looming mass. You could see no lights, though it was growing dark; no smoke was rising from the chimney. Even the stable clock had stopped.

Mr Braithwaite looked round him in surprise. 'What's amiss?' he said. 'Are they not looking after the place? Ellen, child, what's amiss?'

'Not many people work here any more,' she told him.

'Cousin Rundell said they had had to reduce the establishment, but she did not tell me the place had become so neglected,' he said. He looked thoughtful as he spoke. 'Will you be all right here, Ellen, my dear?'

Yes, she would be all right, she told him.

It did seem strange to go indoors. The back door was locked, as it never had been, with so many people going in and out. When she pulled the bell they heard it echoing inside the empty house, but nobody came. They knocked and knocked, and at last little Billy appeared, looking rather wan. 'Oh,' he said, 'Ellen, it's you. I'm sorry, I was at the top of the house. I'm so glad you're back, it's been so quiet.' He took them into the servants' hall but it was cold and damp, and they went into the kitchen. The kitchen was warmer but no more welcoming. It was in a state of chaos, with piles of dirty plates and dishes of unfinished food. 'Will you make

me some tea, Ellen? I suppose there is some tea in the house?'
said Ellen's father. She had the key to the tea chest, which had
been entrusted to her by the housekeeper, and there she found
some of the precious tea leaves kept for Mrs Rundell. Out of
curiosity, she thought she would make some tea with them, even
though she knew that the housekeeper guarded it jealously.

'How have you been, Billy?' Ellen asked him, as they drank
their tea. It was very strange tea, heavily smoked. After one cup
they all decided that they did not care for it, and she made another
pot of tea from the servants' hall supply (though there was almost
none of that left).

'Oh, it's been miserable,' he said. 'Joan has hardly cooked at
all. I've been eating bread and cheese and there's hardly any bread
left since no one bakes any more, and I've had to go asking for
meals from Mrs Hurst. Joan just sits and looks out of the window,
in a trance, like. And the house is so empty and there's nobody
but me in the men's dormitory and to tell you the truth, Ellen,
I've been mortally afraid sometimes in the night, all those beds
stretching away into the darkness, and knowing there's no one
else in the place but little Joan, and I've dreamt that there were
people in those beds after all, and woken up shivering.'

'Mr James?' she asked. 'Surely Mr James has been in the house?'

'Now and again, but not very much. He's been away visiting
– he left as soon as you did. And when he is at home he takes all
his meals at the Unicorn in Ripon. He's here today. He asked this
morning when you were coming back.'

'And where is Joan?' she asked.

'Joan, I don't know where Joan ever is, she's hardly to be seen.
She comes in and makes porridge sometimes, that's all she eats,

but otherwise she stays in her room and for all I know she keeps in bed. Oh, I'm so pleased you're back, Ellen,' and he gave her a happy smile. He was always a sweet boy, that Billy, Ellen thought. She hadn't set much store by him at first, didn't like him staring at her, but he was a good boy.

Her father had to be given something to eat. There was no sign of Joan, though Ellen knocked on her door, so she explored the larder. She found some cheese and a knuckle of ham, which looked not too old, and she sent Billy to ask Mr Hurst for some salad. She did not go and tell Mr James she was back, she did not like to, but the minute she put the food on the table the bell from the smoking room rang.

Ellen sent Billy to answer it but she knew she would only get a moment's relief. Back came Billy. 'He would like to see you, Ellen. He doesn't need anything, he just would like to see you. He says you're not to hurry your dinner, but when you have finished would you go along to the smoking room. And your father too. Mr James would like to see your father.'

So they finished their dinner, such as it was – Ellen was ashamed of Markham Thorpe, knowing what the hospitality had been in the past – and off they went through the shadows, carrying their candles, since no lamps were lit along the passage. There was Mr James in the smoking room, and the room had no fire and there was only one lamp, and he was sitting in the elbow chair where he liked to sit, with a bottle of wine open on the table beside him and three glasses.

When she saw him, Ellen felt what she supposed came naturally to women: she felt maternal even though she was so much younger than him, she wanted to look after him and make him happy. He looked so miserable, all on his own in that dreary room, like a bear in his lair – not a frightening one, but sad.

He cheered up as soon as they came in. He stood up to greet them and put out his hand and bade them be seated. 'Some wine, Mr Braithwaite?' he said, and 'Some wine, Ellen?' She said no, but he smiled and poured her a glass all the same, and she drank it, one way or another.

'You'll stay the night, won't you, Mr Braithwaite? There's a bed made up for you, I believe. We can't have you driving home through the night.' Ellen's father nodded and smiled in assent. 'Now, Ellen tells me you are a leading member of the Malton Literary and Philosophical Society. Tell me what you have been debating lately.'

And so they talked. Ellen's father was delighted with him and she could see why. Mr James spoke very clearly that evening, much more so than he ever managed to do with Ellen, with whom he had a way of speaking to the ground or the far wall. He expressed great interest in the Literary and Philosophical Society – which cannot have been of any concern to him, in reality – and he was so kind that Mr Braithwaite, usually a reserved man in company, glowed and hummed and smiled, flattered by all this attention from a gentleman. Ellen sat very quiet and listened – though what did she care about the vicars of Old Malton church in the Middle Ages, about whom her father talked at length, while Mr James nodded and asked questions? After a while, since they were set on stopping there, she lit the fire. She could see no reason why they should ever cease, especially when Mr James opened a second bottle of wine, so she stood up and curtsied and made to leave. Mr James said, 'Ellen, are you going? Where are you going?' and tried to stop her, but she said that she must see to her father's bedroom, and left. She might be his servant but that did not mean she had to listen to long, tedious conversations.

At last her father came to the kitchen where they were sitting. Joan had appeared by now and was crying because Ellen had been sharp with her. Nobody could have been in a better humour than Mr Braithwaite. What a serious man Mr Markham was, and how well informed, and what a kind host, how fortunate she was to work for such a family, and so he went on, rejoicing in the evening, and hardly weary at all, though they had spent all day travelling. In the midst of all this she saw his eyes resting on her, speculatively, in a way she did not care for.

While she had been half listening to her father talking about Roman excavations, her mind had been running on her duties at Markham Thorpe. She had been left in charge, and while she had been away, the house had become a disgrace, a place any good housewife would wring her hands over. Whatever she thought about domestic service she could not let Mrs Rundell and Sir Richard return to such confusion. And it made her sad that Mr James should be living in disorder, though he never complained. Perhaps, Ellen thought, the confusion suited his state of mind.

She put her father to bed in the steward's room, one of the few rooms that was kept prepared for visitors at the time – though, as she reflected, she would have liked to put him in one of the best bedrooms, and who was to stop her? It was late by this time, and a moonless night, and she set off through the dark and almost empty house to the housekeeper's room, which was now hers. The passages and staircases were lit only by her one candle, which threw great shadows against the walls as she passed the closed doors of the uninhabited rooms. The house was quiet. She was not afraid, she told herself, not afraid at all, there had never been any ghosts recorded at Markham Thorpe, and she was looking forward to the comfort of the bed that Mrs Rundell had bought for herself in Leeds. Ellen tried singing a little song but her voice sounded so tiny in the echoing space of the Great Hall that she abandoned it.

She walked up the great stairs – it was not allowed, but who was to know that she was doing such a thing? – to the first-floor landing. Then she screamed. It was a hopeless little scream in that huge space, with the portraits of long-dead Markhams staring down upon her as she could see in the trembling light of her candle. They looked ironic and amused, she had time to think, at the sight of a little maid screaming on the great staircase they had known so well.

'Don't scream, Ellen, it's only me.' And, indeed, it was only him. But why did he have to stand in the dark, in the corner of the staircase, waiting for her to see him, what sort of a trick was that?

'You frightened me,' she said, 'you frightened me, you . . . you . . .' What was she to call him, this man who was her master, but somehow more than that?

'I didn't mean to frighten you,' he said. 'I was on my way to bed – I did not trouble to bring a candle, I know the way so well.'

She held her candle up high and peered at him. Now that she could see him, he did not look menacing at all. On the contrary, he was smiling at her. She realised that, in spite of everything she had told herself in Malton, she was pleased to see him.

He took the candlestick from her and placed it on the newel post. It reminded her of a moment at the servants' ball, when the house had been so full of people and activity. He took her in his arms and kissed her long and hard. This seemed quite natural. More than that, it seemed wonderful. They stood for a long time on the landing in each other's arms. She wondered wildly what his ancestors would think about all this. And then he gently took her hand and led her along the shadowy passage to the house-keeper's room. He opened the door for her, in his politest manner, and followed her into the room. It was cold, but she had aired the bed during the evening, and someone had placed a vase of flowers on the big table. The room was not unpleasant at all, she told herself, her mind racing rather, trying to think about ordinary things and not knowing what was going to happen.

Then Mr James closed the door, and they were alone together.

The next day, Ellen woke from a heavy sleep, aware that it was quite late. She had realised at some point during her sleep that the large mass of man beside her, holding his arms round her, had kissed her and then gone, but she was too fast asleep to awake. She lay for a moment thinking about what had happened, remembering the sensations of the night, all at the same time agitated, happy, fearful. Then she told herself abruptly that she could not allow herself to think about such things, she must be up and about. She threw on her clothes and hurried downstairs, to find her father waiting for her with a look of impatience, watched nervously by Joan and Billy, children as they now seemed to her.

As soon as her father had gone, she made her dispositions. She spoke first to Joan. She told her she should not try to cook anything she found difficult but that there were certain things she must be ready to prepare when told to. There was no reason why she should not prepare three tolerable meals a day, and do such easy things as bake the bread. And she must keep the kitchen clean, starting this very day. 'I will be back presently,' Ellen said, 'and when I return, I expect the kitchen to be a different place.' Then, taking Billy with her by way of company, since in any case he was always following her, she walked round every room in the house, even to the bachelors' wing, and the upper maids' passage beyond the one where she had lived when she first came to the house, which was reached by a flight of stairs, and then through a door, which was usually kept locked. She made a list of everything that had to be done, in each room. It took her all morning. It was depressing at first, but underneath the dust and the flies you could see that this was a house that had been cared for properly for many years and there was not as much to do as you thought at first.

While she and Billy were in the Great Hall, they encountered Mr James, on the way out to see his horses, no doubt. He looked, she thought, particularly cheerful. She was glad of that. She and Mr James stared at one another for a brief moment – which made her tremble, rather – and then they resumed their normal manner. We must always be like this with one another during the day, she told herself. She gave a sketchy curtsy, at which he smiled, and gave a little bow. She had an inclination to giggle, but suppressed it.

Within a moment she was all business. She told him her intentions, and asked for enough money to pay for a woman from the village to come and work in the house for a month, and for permission to ask help from the gardeners. He laughed, and said, 'So, you are taking the place in hand, Ellen, are you? You shall have as much money as you need, if I have it, that is. Fortunately I have some money from . . .' He blushed and stopped. Then he asked whether Mr Braithwaite (as he called him) was still in the house, and praised him, saying how lucky she was to have such a parent, and how lucky her father was in such a daughter. Ellen said nothing to that, merely curtsied again.

They started work the next morning. They dusted and swept and pulled the furniture out to see what might be lurking behind it and took down the ornaments and polished the brass and set the grand-father clock in the Great Hall ticking and aired the rooms that had grown damp and cleaned the windows. They worked everywhere, all over the house, even the further set of visiting servants' bedrooms that had not been used for years. The only rooms they did not touch were the boudoir and Mrs Rundell's bedroom, which were locked. Ellen had the key but she had been told strictly not to go into them unless directed to by the housekeeper.

Up and down the house they went, Billy and Joan, the two women from the village and Ellen, and now and again one of the gardeners when they had to lift heavy things. Ellen had never been much of a one for domestic work but she did enjoy herself on this campaign. It was a pleasure to run up and down the stairs and use the grand staircase as though it was her own, and to open the windows in the morning and smell the freshness of the autumn garden, and see the house coming to life again, and shining, and full of colour. It was strange, Ellen thought, how the character of a house could change, as though it had a life and its mood could be transformed.

Mr James was around a good deal during this activity. He stopped riding into Ripon for his meals, and ate his dinner at home, particularly since Ellen made sure he got what he fancied. His tastes were quite simple – a fowl, a fruit tart, would satisfy him. He would wander through the house, his hands in his pockets, as though he were looking for something. The others would remark, grinning, it was most likely Ellen he wanted – how did they know, she wondered, that he was interested in her?

For the first day or two of the house cleaning Mr James seemed uneasy, would stand and watch them at work, whistling, his hands in his pockets. Then after a while he surprised them – not because he was lazy but because he was the Quality and they all knew that the Quality do not care to soil their hands with work, except to kill things. He surprised the servants because he took to helping them. Not that he dusted or cleaned the floors, but one day when a picture had to be lifted off the wall and Ellen said to Billy, 'Go and fetch Matthew from the garden, you can't lift that, it's too heavy for you,' Mr James pushed Billy gently aside, took the picture in his hands and lifted it off the wall. He was graceful as he did it, Ellen could see; he was a big man and often clumsy, but moving that picture he was so delicate and skilful. She felt proud of him – she knew well, now, how thoughtful and tender he could be. She tried never to think about the night during the day, nor about the day during the night. The nights were pure pleasure and yet though he told her often that he loved her, she never quite understood what she felt about him, nor did she feel she knew what sort of a man he was.

'Where would you like it placed, Ellen?' he asked. He put it down where she indicated and their eyes met, and they must have

221

smiled at one another without knowing it, because after a moment he looked embarrassed and left the room. The others exchanged glances and rolled their eyes, Ellen knew they did. But he was back in a little while. 'When you want the picture back on the wall, just tell me,' he said, and for once the man looked happy. After that he was around a great deal of the time, and would lift and carry things for them – such a strong man, such shoulders and arms, like a blacksmith rather than a gentleman. Very useful he was, although, as the others remarked, he preferred to do these helpful things when Ellen was in the room. If she was elsewhere, they hardly saw him. She tried to speak about this gossip to him at night but he put his hand over her mouth and laughed and said, 'Why should we be ashamed of people knowing, Ellen?' He might not be anxious, Ellen thought, but what about her? Was it so easy for her?

He found Ellen one morning when she was working in the schoolroom on her own. She preferred to work there herself. After all, it was Miss Fisher's territory and, in her odd way, she had been kind to Ellen. She did not want curious eyes uncovering the governess's secrets, whatever they might be. It was an untidy place when you looked into it, such dust behind the books, such unexpected bits and pieces under the sofa.

When he came in Mr James was waving a letter in his hand and seemed disturbed. 'It's from Mrs Rundell,' he said. 'My father and she will be back at the end of October. They are bringing Lucy and Katherine with them but more people than that. I understand your sister Harriet will be coming too, and a cook they have found in Scarborough, and two new maids. Mrs R has asked me to tell you that everything must be in order.' He stopped, and looked at her in admiration, even though she was wearing an old pinafore and had her hair bound up in a scarf. Indeed, he seemed to like her dressed for work. But he went on: 'She has no idea, of course, what you have been doing – she will be surprised, won't she?' He put his arms round her but she pushed him away.

'I have work to do,' she said, but fondly.

He was right. They had only two weeks to finish their cleaning, but they made a pretty fine job of it. The day came for Sir Richard to return to Markham Thorpe – though not his daughters, who, it was said, had been told not to come home for the time being. Ellen discussed with Mr James how the servants should receive them, whether they should line themselves up in front of the house. She thought it would look so sad, the only servants now being herself and Billy and poor little Joan and one or two gardeners, but he said, yes, he thought it should be done. Ellen had got into the way of consulting him over everyday matters, and he consulted her too. It was odd: it seemed to happen naturally, even though he was so much older than she was and, of course, a gentleman, while Ellen, as she often reminded herself, was nothing at all. They would talk of such things when they met during the day, though when he came into her room at night, fully dressed but wearing his soft slippers, there was hardly any talk about the house.

On the morning of Sir Richard's return they stood in their line, and the carriages rolled up. Out on to the drive came Sir Richard – looking much better than when he had left, thinner and less purple in the face, and more cheerful – and Mrs Rundell. He handed her out of the carriage in a courtly way. Ellen was astonished to see how Mrs Rundell had changed. Her hair was arranged in a quite new way, which Ellen knew was fashionable because it was the style her sister affected, and the smartest of bonnets, and a pale blue dress cut so that it showed her form to the best advantage. She too looked well, as though the sea air had done her good. They gave the impression, in their walk and their glances at one another, that they were intimately acquainted.

So out they came, and Mr James greeted them. Then they turned towards the servants. It was strange to be first in the line. Sir Richard smiled kindly and said, 'And how have you been looking after the old place, Ellen?' This took her by surprise, since in the past he had hardly noticed her. Instead of taking her place with the servants Mrs Rundell followed him along the little line. But she did not follow him deferentially and far behind: on the contrary, she walked along with her head in the air like one of the Quality. She looked at the servants as though expecting them to curtsy or bow, and so they did, and once they had done so she nodded graciously, as though it was good of her to notice them. For the moment she did not say very much to Ellen, or even smile – it was as though she was waiting. Only as they went indoors did she signal to Ellen to follow them.

When they finally went into the Great Hall, Ellen's work over the last month was rewarded. It did look very fine – the floor had been scrubbed till it shone, and the brass polished till it glowed, and the picture frames had been dusted, and the long table in the middle was gleaming, and a fire was burning, and in the tall blue vases she had arranged flowers (obtained with some difficulty from Mr Hurst), as she had seen Miss Emily do. The room looked everything that was welcoming and cheerful. Sir Richard and the housekeeper stopped short as soon as they came in, and anyone could see how pleased they were. Mr James was watching them, and when he saw they were pleased, so was he.

'Well,' said Mrs Rundell, taking Sir Richard's arm, 'you can see, my dear Sir Richard, how the house flourishes in the hands of my cousin. I am sure we must reward her, don't you think so?'

And she smiled archly at the baronet and then at Mr James.

After their return, life settled down for a while, and it looked as though the house was going to be properly run again. There were more servants, to start with. The most important was the new cook, Mrs Lyons, not a very pleasant woman in the view of the others, cold and superior and inclined to complain about the kitchen and the old-fashioned range, and over-inclined to tell the other servants that she had worked in very good houses and was used only to the best. The food she prepared was full of French names and sauces and she certainly never provided extra portions for the servants' hall, but she understood what a good meal should be. Mrs Rundell made daily visits to the kitchen to confer with her, just as the lady of the house would do in the normal course of things. And though she was not extravagant, the old standards were again being applied.

Where did the money come from for all these expenses, Ellen wondered. James told her a little about it. Mrs Rundell had taken control of the finances, gradually, over the past two or three years, particularly for the running of the household. Now at last she felt she could spend more money on it, and fill it with people whom she had appointed and who would be loyal to her. James did not seem to mind these machinations, which Ellen found surprising

225

– but, then, she had noticed for a long time that James and her cousin seemed to understand one another very well.

Ellen's little sister Harriet had joined them as housemaid, and there were two other new maids who had been employed in Scarborough. Ellen was fond of her sister, who was very good humoured and obliging and would look at her – or at anyone else who spoke to her – with large, questioning eyes under her uncontrollable hair. It was good to have her there, because she was a dear child, and also because in comparison to Harriet Ellen felt so much older and more collected.

But Mrs Rundell wanted more changes. A day or two after they had come back, Ellen saw Katherine, who had returned from her old mother's house, giving her black looks. When Ellen asked her if anything was wrong, she sneered and would not reply. Then Ellen found out the new arrangements. She was to remain as assistant housekeeper, though this did not mean being the regular housekeeper: she took her instructions every day from Mrs Rundell, and did not even have a full set of keys – the key to the still room, for example, was missing. One of the new maids was to be head housemaid, with Katherine and Harriet and another girl under her. Katherine blamed Ellen for this demotion and hardly spoke to her – perhaps because Mrs Rundell had told her that the house was much better looked after in Ellen's care than in Katherine's.

It was worse with Lucy. Mrs Rundell had, it seemed, found out in Scarborough that she could dispense with Lucy's assistance – and it was generally recognised that Lucy had become most disagreeable, unfriendly, prone to banging doors and almost throwing trays on to the table. One evening she came into the servants' hall – they were using the hall again, with Ellen sitting at one end of the table, though there was no senior male servant to sit at the other end – Billy could hardly do that. She was scowling like a tiger. When she was asked why she was so angry, she gestured at Harriet and growled, 'Ask her – she'll tell you.' No one knew what this meant, not even Ellen, since Mrs R was not inclined to consult her, liking to surprise her with new decisions.

They all looked at Harriet, who blushed and said, 'I am to be Cousin Rundell's personal maid, I mean Mrs Rundell's. She told me that's what she's decided.' This was greeted with general silence. 'I did not ask, I promise I did not,' she went on, being a good girl and anxious to please, 'I am sorry to upset you, Miss Lucy.' But Lucy was not to be mollified.

Poor Lucy! She took it hard, very hard. After all, she had been working for Mrs Rundell for more than twenty years, all her adult life. Though she often complained, there was no doubting whom she wanted to please. It was said that Mrs Rundell had been very hard to Lucy, telling her she was worn out and no longer any use, and would be better off in the workhouse she had come from.

That same evening, Lucy disappeared. This had happened before and at first they were not overly concerned. But late at night there was still no sign of her, and none the next morning, and after twenty-four hours they began to worry.

Two more days passed, and no news. Ellen did not tell Mrs Rundell that Lucy had gone, she thought it would only irritate her, and for the time being Mrs R was too pleased with her pretty new maid to notice. Then a messenger arrived with a note for

Katherine. Katherine read it and asked Ellen, in that way she had of speaking as though resenting every word she uttered, whether she might have three hours' leave to go into Ripon, and whether the groom might take her on one of the horses.

When Katherine returned she told Ellen what she had found. Lucy had been discovered half fainting in one of the snickets (as they called the little lanes in Ripon) in the early morning. They had taken her to the workhouse and there she had been delirious for a while, but they knew from her clothing where she came from. The matron of the workhouse had sent to Katherine, at Lucy's request, to ask her to bring all her possessions to her at the Union.

Mrs Rundell had to be consulted. It was she who had brought Lucy to Markham Thorpe and doubtless she would have views. She did, rebuking Ellen for not having told her sooner. 'Send the carriage for her,' she said. 'She must come back at once. She can't escape so easily!' and she gave a grim chuckle. Lucy returned, but a quiet, chastened Lucy. She hardly spoke, least of all to Ellen. But after this she no longer worked for Mrs Rundell at all: she was a housemaid from that day on, on reduced wages. Though in Ellen's view she had always been difficult, now she became odder than ever, like a wounded animal. She kept to herself, would never speak at meals, would hardly even look at anyone. Only to Katherine would she talk, in the cold corner of the servants' hall away from the fire, glancing around her the while to see if anyone was listening.

Lucy and Katherine were now the only indoor servants left from the old days, apart from Mrs Rundell herself. It seemed, from the rumours that spread so readily around the house, that Mrs R

228

had been harsh to Katherine also. The poor woman had not wanted to come back to Markham Thorpe from her mother's house, but she had had no choice. Her mother had no money other than what her daughter sent her, and at Katherine's age – she was close to fifty, and not strong – she would have difficulty finding another position. But having to be at Markham Thorpe did not mean she welcomed being there. Her friendship with Lucy created a good deal of awkwardness in the servants' hall. As Mrs Lyons remarked, she had never known a household so divided.

During these weeks Miss Fisher reappeared. One day, with no prior announcement, she was back at the house again, as they discovered when her bell rang. Ellen went upstairs, to ask if she could assist her. She received her as coldly as ever, and told Ellen she would be staying until the New Year, while her place in Filey was made ready. 'I see that my rooms have been tidied,' she said. 'They have not looked so clean for years.'

'No,' Ellen said.

'I will be taking my meals upstairs as usual,' she went on, and turned back to her writing. Ellen was dismissed, as rudely as could be. But she hardly minded – she was becoming less sensitive, one way or another. It just made her glad that Miss Fisher was going. Ellen relished her position, and appreciated the comfort of the housekeeper's room. The only thing that made her uneasy, at first, was having one of the maids tidy it and bring her a cup of tea, first thing in the morning, but even this she came to enjoy.

Seeing James was not as easy for Ellen as it had been when the house was almost empty. But see him she did, sometimes in his rooms, which it was still her duty to look after and valet. They would arrange times, he would be waiting for her there, he would take her into his arms. As a result the rooms were not cleaned or tidied very much – there was no time for that. Now and again he would visit her in her bedroom. She protested at first, saying that Mrs Rundell might see him, that there would be all sorts of trouble, but he did not seem concerned. 'Oh, I don't think Mrs Rundell would mind at all,' he said carelessly, one day. She fell to thinking about what this might mean.

Then Mrs Rundell made another announcement. She liked these announcements, Mrs R, she enjoyed assembling the staff in the servants' hall, with everyone curtsying or bowing when she arrived. But this time she was planning something special, and she told Ellen first. One morning she was summoned to the boudoir. Very comfortable it was, too, the fire roaring in the grate, the room filled with the smell of flowers in the blue and white bowls and the vases all around the room, the sofas covered with silk cushions, and everywhere little ornaments that had come – Ellen had helped to clean them – from the store cupboards where they had been put after Lady Markham's death. There had been nothing like this in her ladyship's time, Katherine said. It had been pretty but quite plain, but Mrs Rundell had richer tastes. She liked to be pampered. She liked people to see that she was being pampered.

Mrs Rundell was seated at her desk, the desk Lady Markham had used, in the midst of all this splendour, wearing one of her new dresses. Sir Richard, in his slippers, dozed beside the fire. He woke up when Ellen came in, smiled at her, nodded, and settled down to doze again. But she thought he must be listening to the conversation.

Mrs Rundell was in expansive form. She invited Ellen to sit down. She usually did this but not always. Ellen thought this must be so that she understood it was a privilege. She told her there was to be a change in the regulation of the household: family prayers were to be reintroduced. There had been no prayers since Ellen had been at Markham Thorpe, though in far-off days they had taken place daily. Mrs Rundell announced that in her opinion they were essential to a decent household, as did Sir Richard. Daily family prayers were to commence the following morning in the Great Hall, at nine o'clock, and the rector would be present on this first day since it was an important occasion. On this day not only the indoor servants but the grooms (they were back to two, and another was expected) and the gardeners would be present, since Sir Richard had something important to say. 'I know I can trust you, Ellen, to make sure everything is well ordered,' said Mrs Rundell. 'I want no jostling, no unseemly crush, no unsuitable behaviour. The servants will sit on the settles at either side of the long table in order of seniority, women on one side, men on the other. You will tell the men to set out four dining-room chairs at the drawing-room end of the hall, away from the front door, for Sir Richard, Mr James, Mr Walters, and myself, and servants' hall chairs will be placed further down for yourself, Mrs Lyons, Mr Hurst and Mr Andrews. All must be orderly, as in the best houses – and Markham Thorpe is, once again, one of those. Above all, I require that everybody should be present. I want no absences, no nonsense from Katherine or Lucy. If anyone is seen to be absent, they will be dismissed. I hope that is clear. And send a message, would you, to Miss Fisher. She is required to be present, even though, most sadly, she will not be with us much longer as she moves so soon into retirement.'

Sir Richard intervened here: 'I have a note for Miss Fisher,' he said. 'Will you make sure it reaches her, Ellen? And, Alice –' Ellen found it strange to hear the Christian name used; Agnes and she sometimes referred to her as Alice behind her back as a joke but otherwise she had never heard it '– Alice, my dear, I think we should have a chair put out for Miss Fisher, a drawing-room chair. After all, she is not a servant.'

'Leave me to make the arrangements, Richard, if you will,' she said. 'I'm sure I know what should be done.'

'Yes, my dear, of course you know best, but there must be a proper chair for Miss Fisher.'

'Very well, Miss Fisher shall have a proper chair. And Mrs Braithwaite and I' (she liked to refer to Ellen as Mrs Braithwaite, it was a joke in a way since she was only eighteen, but it was not altogether a joke) 'will arrange things as they should be arranged.'

Quite a business it all was, too. It meant a message to Mr Hurst (who sent a message back, complaining), and a message to the stables, and words to all the indoor servants first thing in the morning. Ellen was no longer nervous about speaking to them all – she knew them well enough. They seemed surprised but things were always changing in that household and there was nothing unusual about family prayers. Mrs Lyons was positively pleased, remarking that this was as it should be and that Markham Thorpe was the only house she had worked in where prayers were not a matter of course.

The last person Ellen had to speak to was Miss Fisher. She was not often seen around the house since she stayed mostly in her rooms, apart from her walks in the park with her dog. Miss Fisher had not melted towards Ellen, she never spoke to her unless it was essential, but Ellen knew she had to brave the governess's coldness and deliver the note. Up she went to the top of the house and knocked on her door. To her surprise, she thought she heard voices inside. Miss Fisher hardly ever had visitors – she could hardly receive the servants, and Sir Richard never ventured there, and she had only one or two acquaintances in the neigh-bourhood, even though she had lived there so many years. She led a lonely life when the dining room was not functioning.

When Ellen knocked, there was a creaking, sudden silence inside. Then Miss Fisher said, 'Come in.'

The room was quite dark. It was late afternoon and no lamps had been lit. Through the low, narrow windows Ellen could see the red light of the autumn sunset behind the trees, dimly reflected in the room. There were three people sitting there. They remained silent and unmoving as she entered. These people were arranged in a little half-circle, on the upright chairs Ellen had come to know so well during her French lessons. They had their backs to the windows. In the twilight she could not see who they were.

Ellen had never felt so unwelcome in all her life. The room was cold and hostile. The three figures did not move. Nobody greeted her or even spoke. They just sat there, as though inter-rupted in the midst of a rite. She was frightened.

'Miss Fisher?' she said, a little tremulously, not sure which of these figures was she.

The figure in the middle spoke. 'Yes?'

'It's Ellen.' Nothing was said in response, not even 'What do you want?' So Ellen had to go on. 'I have messages for you, Miss Fisher, from Sir Richard, and from Mrs Rundell.'

Further silence. Ellen was still frightened but she was beginning to lose her temper. What business did they have to sit there, like three old witches, treating her with such contempt?

'The message from Mrs Rundell is that family prayers will be held in the Great Hall tomorrow and every morning after that, at nine o'clock, and you are — you are —' she had trouble finding the right word '— all members of the household are invited to attend. Indeed, it is expected that they will.'

There was no response to this, either. Ellen held out her hand with the letter from Sir Richard, and after a moment Miss Fisher took it.

It was time for Ellen to go. But before she did, she could not prevent herself saying, as firmly as she could, 'I think you would be foolish not to attend, Miss Fisher, truly I do.' She said it partly because she was worried for Miss Fisher's sake about the danger of defying Mrs Rundell, and partly because she was annoyed at the governess's behaviour, and wanted to assert herself.

Out she went. The sunset was fast fading, and as she left the room it was almost completely dark.

She resisted the temptation to listen outside the door. She had guessed who the other women were. What she could not understand was why they were sitting in the schoolroom.

The next morning, just before nine, they assembled in the Great Hall. What with the new people and the outside men, the array of servants looked quite impressive: there were twenty of them at least. Miss Fisher came in last, looking stranger than ever, in black. She looked round the room anxiously, not knowing where to sit, before someone pointed out the chair that was waiting for her. When she noticed it, this chair perplexed Ellen. The previous evening she had put out for the governess a dining chair like the ones for the family, but it had been taken away and replaced with a little low chair, placed as far as possible from the family, at the lower end of the long table. There she had to sit next to the garden labourer and the junior housemaid, in a position of humiliating insignificance. While the prayers were being said, she sat motionless, looking not reverent but furious.

As nine o'clock struck the Quality appeared, in a little procession, Sir Richard at the front, supported by Mrs Rundell, then the rector, then Mr James. The servants all stood, with a good deal of shuffling from further down the table. The rector welcomed them, remarked that any place where two or three were gathered together in an act of worship was a sacred place, and expressed his happiness that prayers were being revived. They knelt on the floor, their faces pressed into the table or the bench, amid some stifled giggles and a loud snort from the lower end of the hall. The rector prayed and asked for a blessing on this house. Then they all stood. There was a silence, and Mrs Rundell was seen to give Sir Richard a mild push. He stepped forward. He said, 'Dear people, I wish to tell you all something. Mrs Rundell has been kind enough to accept my hand in marriage. We have decided that the ceremony will take place privately, on Christmas Eve, here in our church of Markham. I am very happy that Mrs Rundell has agreed to become Lady Markham.'

Mrs Rundell looked demurely at the floor, her hands folded

neatly in front of her. The rector beamed, as was his duty. Mr James smiled in a nervous sort of way. Sir Richard took Mrs Rundell's arm, and they faced the servants for a moment.

If they had hoped for cheers or handclaps, they were disappointed. There was total silence. Even the grooms, who were not quiet fellows on the whole, kept mum. The couple looked at the servants, the servants looked at them. Then Mr Hurst stepped forward.

'On behalf of us all, Sir Richard, I would like to express our best wishes for your future happiness and for the well-being of Markham Thorpe.'

Then the servants clapped and one or two of the men said, 'Hurrah,' in an uncertain sort of way. Though Mrs Rundell had not personally been offered any good wishes, she bowed her head graciously and nodded around the hall. The two of them moved slowly out of the room, followed by Mr James and the rector. Still in silence, and subdued, the rest dispersed – though as soon as the servants at the front had left the room, the murmur of voices rose into a hullabaloo of laughter and even, Ellen thought, humorous imitations of Sir Richard and Mrs Rundell. She hurried after them to hush the noise, but they had dispersed in all directions and she was left standing foolishly in the servants' passage. There Mr Hurst found her.

'A new Lady Markham, eh?' he said. 'Good news for the old house, d'you think? And what about a new Mrs James Markham, isn't that something we're needing too, to secure an heir for the good Markham name?' He bowed and left her standing alone, wondering what his words were supposed to mean, and why he had said them. What did she think about this announcement, something she had long suspected might happen? She supposed if it made Sir Richard happy . . . and yet she was not sure she could trust her cousin, altogether . . .

As the days crept towards Christmas, there was much speculation on the form the festivities would take. It was known the daughters would not be there — their father had written telling them they were not invited this year but he hoped that they would come in the future to pay their respects to their new stepmother. It became apparent that Mrs Rundell had very ambitious plans for Christmas, which was to become a sort of extended celebration of her nuptials. She gave Ellen instructions that the house was to be decorated in the usual manner but even better, with the Great Hall fuller than ever of holly and ivy. An innovation which excited all of them was that, following the example of the Royal Family, a Christmas Tree was to be set up in the Great Hall. In the days before Christmas, box after box arrived from London containing (as Mrs Rundell showed Ellen and Harriet) silver and gold tinsel and little glass balls and tiny toys, candleholders and coloured candles, and the most delicious silver fairy to go at the very top of the tree.

The wedding was to be a quiet affair. It would take place in Markham church, with the Reverend Mr Walters presiding. No guests, only two witnesses. Every morning Ellen visited Mrs Rundell to tell her what was going on and receive instructions, though as the days passed these meetings became more like conversations. She was told during one of these talks Mrs Rundell's version of why there was now so much money at Markham Thorpe. She was, she said, generously spending her own money on the house — she did not tell Ellen where it came from, merely remarking that she had received 'a very kind legacy'. She even suggested that one day it might be Ellen's. Another morning she told Ellen that Sir Richard and she would be very pleased if she would act as a witness at their wedding, along with Mr James. It was a request that certainly did not expect a 'no', so she said, 'Yes,' but nervously. She already knew that the other servants saw her as the housekeeper's ally, and this would identify Ellen even more strongly with her cause – though it was true that the new servants did not dislike Mrs R as the old ones did. Afterwards there was to be a little dinner, just for the newly married couple, the two witnesses, the rector and his wife. Ellen was to have a new dress, she was told, made by the very best dressmaker in Leeds – her Christmas present. Mrs Rundell had already checked, in her usual thorough way, that Ellen's measurements had not changed from the time of the servants' ball.

It all took place as planned, at least the wedding did. Christmas Eve was perishing cold, with snow in the air, and it was a struggle even to walk across the lawn and through the gate and down the lane to the church. But walk they did, Mr James and Ellen. He offered her his arm and squeezed it tenderly. He seemed happy about the day, she thought, the only member of the family who was, but then he was the only one who treated Mrs Rundell like a human being and not an upstart domestic servant. Arm in arm they walked through the scurrying snowflakes, the two of them alone, since the carriage had been ordered to carry Sir Richard, and then Mrs Rundell, to the church. She was aware as they walked of curious eyes watching them from the house – she could not see anyone looking but she knew too well from her own experience that the servants loved to spy on such events. As they walked down the path Mr James said, in a conversational sort of way, 'Ellen, I would like another wedding service to take place in this church, yours and mine. Will you marry me, Ellen?'

She thought he was joking and looked at him laughingly but, no, he was quite serious. 'I will have to think,' she said, altogether taken aback.

'Think hard, my love,' he said. 'I mean what I say.'

The church was extraordinarily cold, heated only by a little stove close to the altar, and inside it was suffused with dead white light from the snow. The rector read the service rapidly; no one responded to the banns (no doubt the daughters would have liked to claim that Mrs Rundell's social status was a just and lawful impediment), and they were out in twenty minutes, a little group huddling under the porch until the rector joined them. Then they all entered the carriage.

They had been away for only forty minutes but as they approached the house they noticed something peculiar. The whole length and height of the house, the blinds had been pulled down, as though it were empty. It looked completely blank, like a face with no eyes, and very sinister the effect was, when the wedding party might have expected welcoming firelight and candlelight from the windows. Nothing was said – perhaps the newly married couple, bound up with one another, simply did not notice anything. Once they were inside in the Great Hall they found the fire blazing and the Christmas decorations sparkling in the candlelight.

Then they had dinner. The dining room looked magnificent, with festoons of holly and ivy, all tied with scarlet ribbon, round the walls and in the middle of the table an enormous silver candelabrum, with curling branches covered with silver vine leaves and bunches of grapes and six tall white candles. It was new to the house, their hostess told them, from Garrard of London. In spite of this splendour, the meal was somehow cheerless, though the new Lady Markham did her best to preside in a gracious manner (an art she had not quite fully acquired). There they sat, with an abundance of good food, with delicacies sent from London in addition to the best efforts of Mrs Lyons served by Billy and one of the new maids. They did their very best, as instructed by Ellen over the past few days, but it was not the most accomplished service Ellen had seen: Billy had a tendency to let his hand wobble when he was serving wine and he spilt some claret on the beautiful white damask cloth – it looked like blood. Ellen felt she was the one who should be serving, with a moment of regret for that humble function, but she knew that could not be. There she was, she who had so often served Mr James, newly promoted to the status of a lady, sitting at table in a genteel manner as though she were a member of the family (which she supposed she was, in a way) and wearing a beautiful blue silk dress, which had been delivered two days before. The dress matched the turquoise necklace she had worn at the servants' ball and had not seen since – the previous evening, Mrs Rundell, highly animated and as excited as a young girl had given them to Ellen, remarking that the necklace was her bride's present. But in all her elegance, Ellen still felt uncomfortable.

Mr and Mrs Walters drank and ate a great deal as usual and seemed quite merry, though no doubt, Ellen thought, they must find the situation as peculiar as she did. The weather, and the question of how much it would snow in the coming weeks, occupied a good deal of time, as did the local hunt, and the constant topic of the railways and how they were devastating the country, and by way of a more cheerful topic the Queen and her babies. Ellen said very little, because she was so shaken at having risen to the status of a lady, and because she did not know, in her heart of hearts, whether she believed that this marriage was a good one. They all drank a great deal of wine, some of them because they often did and Ellen because of her uneasiness. She wished, at times, that she was anywhere but there, even though she was glad to see her cousin so cheerful and the old baronet so content and so affectionate towards his bride and indeed towards Ellen (though not towards Mrs Walters). He kept proposing toasts to Ellen, as did Mr James. The new Lady Markham even encouraged it — 'Come on, James, why not another toast to my little cousin? No girl could deserve it more.'

That afternoon the ladies did not leave the gentlemen to drink their port. At four, when it was beginning to grow dark and the conversation had become completely stagnant, the Walterses rose, said thank you and merry Christmas, and left. A few minutes later, the happy couple went upstairs to drink tea in the boudoir. James and Ellen were invited to accompany them.

The boudoir was highly inviting, the flowers and plants richer and more heavily scented than ever. Something was smouldering in the perfume burner in the corner, filling the air with a soft, delicious smokiness.

'Sit down, my dears,' said the new Lady Markham. 'Ellen, why don't you sit on that sofa? It is so very comfortable, and close to the fire. James, sit there, too, won't you, and keep my little cousin company?' He did not demur, and there he was, his large and now familiar bulk close to Ellen on the ample cushions of the sofa.

Lady Markham had arranged a table with a little Christmas tree surrounded by presents wrapped in gold paper. The candles alight in the chandelier, on the mantelpiece and on the many small tables were reflected in the great glass over the fireplace and in the crimson silk curtains. It was a luxurious sight, that room, remarkably different from the rest of the house. Ellen's spirits rose, even though Lucy, grim-faced, was in attendance. When she left the room briefly Lady Markham remarked that Lucy had asked, as a special favour on this great day, to be allowed to serve them after dinner. 'I could hardly refuse the poor thing, could I?' she said. 'She has so few pleasures in life.'

Ellen became drowsy in the warmth and, no doubt, from having drunk so much wine, and must have dozed off a little. She hardly attended to the talk, except to notice that what the men said was rather fast, as though they could best communicate through such talk. Lady Markham several times reproved her new husband and stepson for their freedom, even while tittering and covering her mouth with her hand. During all this Lucy brought in the tea, which she had made in the still room some way away, and passed it round the room. She came back with Mrs Rundell's teapot containing her own special tea, and placed it carefully beside her plate.

Mrs Rundell poured herself a cup. She raised it to her lips, then put it down untasted. 'You may go, Lucy,' she said. 'Here is a present for you, for old times' sake.' And she handed Lucy a little gold package, which Lucy accepted with a curtsy and a rapid smile. She did not seem very interested in it. 'Merry Christmas.'

Still Lucy stayed. 'You may go,' said her mistress, rather sharply. Lucy still looked unwilling to depart, but curtsied and finally left the room.

'Why is it you are so fond of that tea Mrs – eh – Mamma?' asked James. He had not called her 'Mamma' before and, though it sounded awkward, he seemed to relish it.

'Oh, my tea is my tea,' she said. 'I was introduced to it by a naval captain I was once familiar with, who had spent a good deal of time in the East. But, you know, I've drunk so many nice things today I don't think I will be troubled with it.' She looked at her husband roguishly. 'It seems a pity to waste the tea, though. My dear, perhaps you should try it just for once, since you have always refused – as a sign of good will towards me? Will you not have a little taste?'

'And may I not try it too?' asked Mr James.

'No,' she said, 'I think it should be Sir Richard . . . I only have enough for one in this little pot.'

He nodded like a silly old man and held out his hand. She moved to sit next to him on his sofa, and held the cup to his lips. 'Can you like this?' he asked her. 'It has such a strange taste.'

'Yes,' she said. 'You know I drink no other.' She was sitting beside the baronet and leaning against him heavily, her hand resting on his knee. She giggled.

The room smelt heavily of the flowers and the burning pastilles and the scent Lady Markham was wearing, mixed with some other smell Ellen did not recognise.

Ellen should have left, but she could not. She felt as though she had been drugged and was quite unable to move. Though in a way she found it disagreeable to see her cousin on the sofa so close to Sir Richard, the sight somehow appealed to her too. And, then, she had James beside her and, after all, that was very pleasant.

In the unexpected silence that had fallen, James said, 'I think we should go, Ellen. It is time for us to go.'

He took Ellen's hand.

Mrs Rundell, ever attentive, noticed that they were stirring. 'Yes, James, time for you to go,' she said, 'time for you to go. Take your little wifie, your dear little wifie, and make her as happy as you can.'

What was this? Ellen asked herself.

'Come,' he said, and led her out. There was a little lobby outside the boudoir, like a small sitting room, furnished with a sofa. The room was lit only by the fire, and was warm and welcoming. Ellen did not feel like going further, and sat down in front of the fire. The room was completely quiet but for the hissing coal.

'I want to marry you,' he said. 'Ellen, I want to marry you.'

'What did she mean, James?' Ellen asked urgently. 'What did she mean when she said, "your little wifie"?'

James did not reply, merely reached for Ellen in the dark as though he owned her. She did not like this: she did not want him to think she belonged to him. And he had drunk too much. She pulled herself away and for the first time since they had become lovers, refused his advances. A truly unpleasant suspicion had dawned upon her. She pulled herself together and ran to her room. She locked herself in. Quite awake now, she sat on her bed and thought, over and over again, about what Mrs Rundell had said.

*　　*　　*

Ellen was woken very early the next morning by Maud, the junior housemaid. 'Miss Ellen,' she said, very agitated, 'you are to go to Mrs Rundell – that is, to Lady Markham – directly, in the boudoir. Directly, there's no time to be lost. She says you are not to dress, only put on a cloak over your nightdress.'

Ellen ran off. On the way she remembered, to her surprise, that it was Christmas Day.

Her cousin was alone in the boudoir, half dressed, trembling and staring, hair flowing wildly behind her on to her back. 'Ellen,' she said, 'Ellen, it is Richard, Sir Richard, my husband—' She choked, as though she could hardly speak. 'He is very ill. He vomited all night, terrible pains, the pupils of his eyes are dilated, his pulse horribly rapid. I can hardly understand what he is saying. He keeps grasping at imaginary objects, it is horrible to watch. He is very weak, I cannot picture what this can be. I don't want you to see him, he is too weak. He was so well and happy yesterday – what can this be? Send for the doctor – Dr Rowntree must come immediate. But I don't want any of the servants coming in here. Go and find Billy downstairs.'

Ellen sent Billy to the doctor's house in the village. Then she returned to her cousin.

'He is worse – even in these few moments he is worse,' she wailed. 'What can it be, what can it be? He is delirious, he is talking about his childhood and his first wife, he keeps saying her name, he wants to see her, he wants to see his children – he will not speak to me.'

Ellen asked how she could help. Fetch hot water from the kitchen, that was what she could do. Lady Markham did not want anyone else coming to her room, no one except Ellen or Harriet.

The kitchen was in uproar, the whole household assembled, most of them in their nightclothes – even Miss Fisher was there. Ellen had no idea how they knew there was anything wrong: it was as though there were invisible currents in a house like Markham Thorpe that could send messages round without anyone knowing how. They all fell on Ellen.

'Who is ill?' they cried. 'Maud says she thinks it is Sir Richard who is ill, or it may be Mrs Rundell. What is wrong? Why has Billy gone off for the doctor?' And on and on they went.

Ellen ordered the hot water; she told Harriet that she, too, was needed; she said that she could tell them nothing.

'Tell us who is ill, Ellen,' said Miss Fisher. She was looking, as Ellen thought, very peculiar, even more so than usual, until she realised the wig Miss Fisher normally wore (Ellen had never realised she wore a wig) was missing, and she was almost completely bald.

'It is Sir Richard who is ill,' Ellen answered, and upstairs she hurried, with Harriet behind her.

When the doctor arrived Sir Richard was still alive, but only just. Dr Rowntree looked extremely flustered when he came into the boudoir, having been hurried, no doubt, from his Christmas breakfast. He was a long time in Sir Richard's bedroom, and when he came out he looked heavily shocked.

'He is very ill, I do not know what it is – I do not recognise the symptoms. I think perhaps he may have been poisoned,' he said. 'At least, I think so, though we cannot know by what means. What did he eat yesterday?'

'He ate – he ate a great deal,' Lady Markham said, and choked.

'It was the wedding breakfast, you know,' Ellen intervened, since Lady Markham could hardly speak. 'I can tell you what we ate but there was nothing on the table that only Sir Richard ate. We all helped ourselves to all the dishes, I think.'

The doctor paused, as though realising the full irony of the situation. 'Death is likely, I fear. I cannot do anything but bleed him, and I am not sure how far that would help the patient, but I will do it if you want me to.'

'Anything to save him, anything!' cried Lady Markham.

'I will see how he is in a few hours. In the meantime, Mrs . . . Lady . . .' he could not bring himself to call her Lady Markham, it seemed, 'you must, of course, tend the patient, though I think your niece should be with you at all times. Nothing in the room must be moved unless it is essential for the patient's comfort.'

In the meantime Lady Markham had more or less composed herself, at least externally. Her hair was no longer streaming over her shoulders, she was almost dressed, she had dabbed at her face. Only her eyes, fiery red, betrayed her feelings. 'What else should we be doing?' she asked.

'You had better tell the household what has happened, that Sir Richard is very ill. Until then, you should remain here with the patient, with this young woman in attendance, I suggest. Everyone in the household must remain at Markham Thorpe. No one is to go away, you understand that, not even to see their families or to church.'

'Very well, Dr Rowntree,' she said. 'I will, of course, continue to nurse my husband, if I may.'

'Yes, so far as that's possible,' he said. 'But he is beyond nursing now.' He considered for a moment. 'The still room – where is the still room, and what do you keep there?'

He looked round the richly furnished room, still filled with cups and glasses from the previous evening, and asked, 'Is there anything here that he might have drunk by mistake, anything that could have poisoned him?'

'No,' she said. 'How could there be?'

'He might have been tired late last night, I suppose, he might have taken something in error . . .' He looked at her with a strange expression. 'I heard of a woman once, in York, who used tincture of bella donna to make her eyes sparkle and kept it in a pretty glass pot – and her child drank it by mistake, and died of atropine poisoning.'

She reddened. 'I have tincture of bella donna, I use it from time to time,' she said, 'but Sir Richard could not have drunk that. How could he have done? He is not a child.'

'Can I see it? We might at least discover how much of it remains.'

'Oh, yes,' she answered. 'I keep it in the still room. I will go and fetch it.'

Off she went, down the passage and through the door to the still room. After several minutes she returned, perturbed and defensive.

'The bella donna has gone,' she said. 'It has been taken.'

Sir Richard died at noon on Christmas Day, a fact announced by the wails that emerged suddenly and loudly from the bedroom he had shared (publicly, at least) for so short a time with his second wife.

The house was strange during those days after Sir Richard's death, still adorned with Christmas garlands and candles and the spangled Christmas tree, yet filled with whispers and fear and the presence of death. Beside the tree lay a pile of presents, many of them from Mrs Rundell to various members of the household, but nobody had the heart to touch them.

No one of the servants knew what was happening. They had the police officers from the Ripon Liberty in, and the coroner, and the lawyer. There could be no funeral until the coroner had made his decision, so the body was kept in Sir Richard's room for three days. Nobody cared to be in that part of the house. Mrs Lyons announced she could not stay in a house where there had been such happenings and she would be seeking other employment, and the new maids seemed inclined to follow her. Lucy and Katherine kept to themselves, pale, silent, cold. As for Miss Fisher, they never saw her – she stayed in her rooms. Everybody, in the house and out of it, thought and spoke, and probably dreamt, of nothing but Sir Richard's death.

As for Lady Markham, wife for only a day, her position was extremely uncomfortable. She could no longer sleep in the master bedroom, and the boudoir was locked up by order of the coroner. She told Ellen she would like to move into the old housekeeper's bedroom, and Ellen could not refuse. She would not let Ellen move out: she said she wanted her to stay. They slept together in the large bed, though she could never sleep until she took something from a little glass phial – laudanum it must be, Ellen thought – which despatched her into heavy, troubled slumber. It was unsettling, sleeping beside her: Ellen would have liked to be anywhere else, almost, and yet she felt sorry for her cousin. Lady Markham said she liked Ellen's company and, indeed, she depended on her. She was dull and heavy during those days, staring out of the window on to the icy lawn outside, and unable to do anything for herself – Ellen had to wash her, and bring her little meals, which she refused to eat. As for directing the affairs of the house, Lady Markham tried this once, but when she did issue an order to Lucy it met with such a blank stare that she gave up. She had no heart for it, or for anything else. She sat in the old housekeeper's sitting room, drinking tea – though not her favourite brew, which had been taken away – and hardly doing anything. For much of the time, she wept silently, the tears sliding down her cheeks. She did not speak to Ellen much, merely asked her now and again, politely, to fetch something. From time to time she would invite Ellen to sit beside her and would hold her hand, now gently, now quite firmly, according to her mood.

They searched her rooms. They found a great many papers, which they took away. The gentleman in charge of the inquiry talked to her at length. He talked to Ellen too, and to James, about what had occurred on the final evening. He seemed very puzzled, this gentleman, but nobody was arrested.

Ellen and James no longer met at night. He sent for her to see him in the smoking room, as though to discuss business. This was a little hard, she thought for a moment, but she could understand it – the house now was so full of suspicion, prying eyes, and people lingering in passages in case they might see or hear something of interest, that it was better to be straightforward and meet publicly. After all, he could not come to her bedroom any more. She approached the smoking-room door apprehensively, and knocked. She found him pacing back and forth and had no idea of what to do, though she had been thinking about this moment for hours. So she curtsied, and stood in front of him with her hands folded together, like a housekeeper.

'Ellen,' he said, 'Ellen. You don't need to curtsy, you know.'

He looked shocked and worn, as though he had hardly slept, but she did not think he had been crying. He did not seem particularly sad.

'Won't you sit down?' he said. He looked at her, as though wondering whether to kiss her, but did not move. Ellen felt she could hardly move, either, and did not sit. Their intimacy seemed far away, as though Sir Richard's death had created a barrier they could not shift.

'I am very sorry for your loss,' she said. She almost said 'sir' but stopped herself. But she did not say 'James', either.

'Thank you for your sympathy. How is Lady Markham doing?'

'Lady Markham weeps all day.'

'Will you give her my condolences?'

She bowed her head. It was strange, this exchange: their words hid quite other thoughts. In a way she wanted to comfort him from habit, was it? – but in this house of death, with the body of Sir Richard lying upstairs, she could not bring herself to touch him.

'We must be very careful,' he said. 'So many people will be watching me, and you too, more than ever.'

'Yes,' she said. There was a pause. She was not sure that she wanted to be part of a conspiracy with him. 'Now that you are Sir James, you are a different person.'

'I don't want to be known as Sir James.' She looked startled. 'At least, not until my father is buried. And what do you mean, I am a different person?'

'You are my master now,' she said.

'I have always been your master,' he said, with a sort of leer, and moved towards her, but she shrank away and he stopped. She felt ashamed of what had happened between them. For the first time, she felt guilty.

He looked at her oddly, as though unable to communicate. 'One day soon, all this will be resolved, and we can . . . we can . . .'

Go back to the way we were, no doubt he meant to say. But could they? Did she want to follow the pattern of her cousin Rundell (which must be what he and her cousin had planned)? And if he truly wanted to marry her, could she face everything that would mean – the hatred of his sisters, the contempt of the county, the sniggers of the servants?

'Will you have the beds made up in my sisters' rooms?' he said. 'Their own rooms, not the guest rooms. They will be arriving tomorrow.'

'Yes,' she said.

'And open the drawing room and the dining room, and there will be meals served there as in the past, I suppose,' he went on.

She did not say anything. She looked at him miserably.

He turned away and rifled through the papers on his desk. He was very agitated, she could tell, even though she could not see his face. She knew his body so well, she could tell every emotion from the way he held himself.

She curtsied to his back and left the room. She paused for a moment, knowing that many eyes would be watching her, particularly after a meeting with Sir James. To them, she must appear controlled, even though she had never felt so confused in her life.

She had another reason for concern, something she had thrust to the back of her mind. In the past few days she had sometimes felt low and heavy, and she had been sick once or twice. From watching her mother over the years, she knew too well what this might mean.

The next day, the other members of the family arrived. There was no line of servants to receive them, only Ellen opening the front door to a group of melancholy, agitated people in black, followed by their less agitated maids and men, also in black. The Wentworths hardly acknowledged her, though Mr and Mrs Dykes inclined their heads and she perhaps smiled, but it was hard to tell since the women wore veils. James emerged, embraced his sisters and led them into the drawing room. They all spoke in a muffled undertone, as though unwilling to interrupt the shadowy silence of the house.

The family settled into a meeting. It went on all day in the drawing room. They hardly stirred out. Various people arrived to see them and Ellen ushered them into the drawing room until James came out, alone, just after Ellen had shown in the police detective. He called her, looking embarrassed, and took her into a corner of the hall. 'Ellen, I must have a word. The thing is — my sisters feel it best that you do not attend the family personally, at the moment, because of your close connection with Mrs Rundell. I must ask you to tell one of the others to answer the bells, anyone except your sisters. I am very sorry.' He coughed. 'They are very hard on the new Lady Markham, you see.'

She curtsied and then, as she thought about all this, glowered at him. Why did he let his sisters dictate to him? It was his house

— he was the baronet now, after all — he should behave as the master. 'Will that be all, sir?' she asked, as flatly as she could.

'No, Ellen, that's not all. Ellen, I want to speak to you so much, but how can I here, surrounded by so many eyes? Watching both of us. I don't want you to leave Markham Thorpe, Ellen, I want you to stay, more than anything I want you to stay. It's terrible what has happened, but it should not spoil our feelings for one another. Understand, please understand, that what I said to you that evening I truly meant. I want you to marry me.' He looked agonised, saying this, but Ellen was not persuaded. She could not forgive him for conspiring with her cousin.

'Of course I am my own master,' he went on, 'but my sisters will not like anything to happen between us, and then there is this terrible business with my father . . . You must go now, Ellen, I will find you as soon as I can,' and he pressed her hand for a moment before she pulled herself away.

Ellen took this opportunity to find Agnes, who was sitting by the fire in the servants' hall, chattering to one of the visiting male servants. Like everyone else in the locality they were discussing the death.

'Ellen,' she cried, 'what an important person you have become here, first parlour maid and then, I hear, housekeeper. And are you still the housekeeper, and not demoted as a result of all these misfortunes? I am sure my mistress will have very few good words for anyone connected with Cousin Rundell, or Lady Markham as we must call her.' She laughed scornfully. 'Will you be dismissed, do you suppose?'

Mr Wentworth's valet, a big idle fellow who was lounging on a settle with his horn cup full of beer beside him, was listening keenly.

Ellen did not care for him. She felt the house had been invaded by alien inquisitive people, and he was one of the worst. 'Shall we go upstairs, Agnes?' she said. 'There is so much we need to talk about.'

In the housekeeper's room she could entertain her sister suitably, for the moment at least. Lady Markham was not there, fortunately. They drank tea (Agnes laughed at the choice of drink – she seemed to find recent events a source of entertainment, altogether) and Agnes remarked that since the announcement of Mrs Rundell's engagement to Sir Richard, Mrs Dykes, who had always been so easy, had become much less friendly. She had abandoned the chats during her *toilette* that had once been pleasurable to both of them. 'The Markhams are very suspicious of us, you know, particularly you, who are so much in Cousin Rundell's confidence. They even think – what could be more absurd? – that you are trying to gain the hand of Mr James.' She paused and smiled brightly at her sister. 'People believe Mrs Rundell has been plotting to bring the two of you together, wanting to create a dynasty of servants here at Markham Thorpe. Could that be true?'

Ellen gazed at her dumbly, wondering how much had been said about her without her guessing it, and refused to speak further.

'After all this,' Agnes went on, 'will you stay in the Markhams' service?'

'I don't know,' Ellen said to her. 'Mother and Father would want me to, I suppose . . .'

'I think you may be told to leave, my dear, and soon. As for me, I am finally quitting the service of Mrs Dykes, and I am sure she will be relieved. I am going to be housekeeper to a gentleman in London, and a very nice gentleman he is too, and my duties are to be quite elastic.'

'And the Italian gentleman?' Ellen asked.

'The Italian gentleman was not suitable. If I was you, Ellen, I would leave domestic service as soon as you can and find yourself another occupation – you can see that it doesn't lead to anything unless you aim very high, like our cousin Rundell. And where has that taken her? No, much better to follow my example. You lose your reputation, but you gain so much else . . .'

They heard the bell at the front door being rung, and rung again. Ellen had told one of the maids to answer it whenever it rang, but with the house in such confusion she was not surprised that the girl failed to do so. In spite of Mr James's orders, she ran downstairs to open the door, and there she found the police inspector from Ripon and two constables.

They asked for Mrs Rundell. When talking about her new ladyship, hardly anyone used the title she had wanted so much.

Ellen set off to fetch her, but before she had left the hall, the drawing-room door opened. Out came the family and their lawyer. 'What is this?' they demanded. 'Are you making further enquiries, Inspector?'

'If you will allow me, Sir James, ladies, gentlemen, I have some business to conduct. I will explain its nature later,' he said.

The sisters, not wishing to be troubled with such negotiations, walked on. Gathering their voluminous skirts in their hands, they set off up the grand staircase, whispering to one another. As they passed Ellen they frowned, as though the sight of her was unpleasant.

They had reached only the third step when a door opened on the first landing. Through it came the figure of a woman, an ample and imposing figure, in the deepest mourning, and veiled. She stopped at the top of the flight of steps and looked down on the advancing ladies. They stopped still as well. For a moment there was silence. She could not come down, they could not go up, without one or the other giving way. The sisters stared at her insolently. She looked down at them calmly, as though entirely confident of her position. Then she threw back her veil, and spoke. 'I take precedence, I think,' she said – and down the stairs she came, slowly, deliberately, inexorably. Mrs Wentworth and Mrs Dykes tried to hold their ground, but only for a moment or two was this possible. As she advanced upon them, it became clear that she was not going to stop. They made way for her, forced to press themselves against the wall as Lady Markham she looked like a Lady Markham now, every inch of her, Ellen thought – progressed downstairs. When she reached the bottom of the stairs she turned to Ellen, even though the staircase hall by now was filled with people.

'Yes, Ellen?' she said. 'Has somebody arrived at the house?'

Ellen admired her at that moment, she truly did. She felt her courage and strength, her determination, at a time when everyone around her despised and disliked her, except Ellen. Poor woman, she thought, she had tried to achieve so much – whatever bad things she might have done, however much she had tried to arrange other people's lives for them. Ellen wanted, one way or another, to show respect for her.

'Yes, my lady,' she said, and curtsied.

The inspector spoke. 'I must ask you to come with me.'

Lady Markham looked at him steadily. 'Why?' she said. 'Are you taking me away? Do you suppose I am guilty of my late husband's death?'

'I must ask you to accompany me, Lady Markham,' he repeated.

'Of course.' She spoke quietly but confidently. 'Are you arresting me on a charge of murder?' she asked.

'I would rather not discuss this here, madam . . .'

'I would ask you to tell us all so that everyone here knows whether or not I am being arrested, and what I am being charged with. I don't want false gossip. I am surrounded by enemies here. It is better they should know the truth.'

'If you insist, I will confirm that that is the case, madam. You are arrested on a charge of murder.'

'Yes,' she said, 'I thought so. But whatever your information seems to tell you, your case cannot stand. You have no evidence, there is no motive. Above all, I did not do it. Why on God's earth would I want to poison the husband I had just married, and I loved? Give me one reason, Inspector, why I would want him dead.'

She was surrounded by silence, as though they were all transfixed by her. In a different world, Ellen thought, she could have commanded armies or presided over councils of state. And she did not appear to be lying.

'Take me away, Inspector,' she said, 'from this wicked house – but remember, it is not just the Markham family you should listen to. I am sure they have told you I am guilty, but you should listen to me as well.'

And passing through the little crowd, which parted before her, she walked to the waiting carriage.

News of what had happened spread through the house in minutes. Ellen was surprised by the feeling in the servants' hall. Though some of the servants thought Lady Markham was guilty of murder, for the first time there was some sympathy for her, as though the family had arrayed themselves against her for their own purposes.

The next morning Ellen was summoned to the drawing room, to be confronted by the sisters with Sir James in the background. He looked unhappy and kept his eyes on the fire. The women sat at a table in the middle of the room, and did not invite her to be seated. Then they told her that she was dismissed from what Mrs Wentworth called her 'preposterous position' as housekeeper. She was to leave within the month.

Mrs Wentworth was particularly disagreeable. 'You understand, no doubt, that as a relative – and, we gather, a favourite relative – of the recent housekeeper, you are no longer welcome in this house. We wanted you to leave at once but Sir James has generously said you may stay for a further month so that you can find another position. Sir James has said he will write you a character. If you are to remain in domestic service, and there's no alternative for you, I imagine, you will no doubt wish to seek employment – no doubt as a housemaid – in a family some considerable distance from here. In the meantime we will ask Katherine to assume the duties you are supposed to carry out, and you will perform her tasks as a housemaid.'

All of this was said in the most wounding and contemptuous tone.

'Of course, should you choose to leave earlier, that will be acceptable. More than acceptable, as soon as this business is sorted out, of course. Your presence in the house is distressing to all of us. And your sister Harriet, she must go too, a month's notice also.'

'Nothing that has happened is your fault, of course,' said Emily, 'and I know that you have worked hard at Markham Thorpe. You are not in disgrace, but . . .'

She smiled at Ellen. No doubt this was intended to be winning but Ellen did not feel won over at all. Furious, rather, and she saw no reason to conceal it. She did not wait to hear any more, omitted to curtsy, turned her back on them and walked out leaving the door wide open. Ellen had done nothing wrong, in her view. They had no reason to dislike or despise her. All she had done was look after their wretched house. She felt particularly angry with James, who had sat there in silence, looking anguished. What use was anguish to her? He was very kind to the servants, more than kind in some cases, Ellen thought, but with his social equals he was weak. And how would such a man protect a wife, particularly if she came from a servant's background? And she wondered whether the sisters had any idea of their brother's interest in her.

Ellen returned to the servants' hall, where people were still lounging about. The drawing-room bell rang as soon as she arrived. She told the others that she had been dismissed, and would be leaving shortly. 'Katherine,' she said, 'you are to become housekeeper, I understand. You had better answer the bell.' But Katherine shuddered and stayed where she was. The bell rang again, more loudly and longer. Nobody moved. It rang again.

'Maybe I should go,' said Mr Wentworth's valet, and off he slouched. He was back in a moment, grinning.

'You should see them,' he said, 'such fury, they've never had a bell ignored before. Mrs Wentworth is like a tiger. You're next, Agnes, and I'm not sure they're planning to give you a bonbon.'

Off Agnes went, looking bored. She came back minutes later. 'I have been dismissed too,' she said, 'or, rather, invited to offer my resignation, which I gladly did. Though my mistress was rather kinder than Mrs Wentworth and said she was very sorry to lose me, and that I had been the best of lady's maids – which is not true, if she only knew. Three months' wages I'm offered and I shall take them.'

The bell rang again. Some of the servants laughed. Again, no one moved for quite a while. 'Well, it looks as though I am the only one who intends to stay with the family. I suppose I had better go again,' said the valet, and off he went. It was Katherine they wanted this time, it appeared. Katherine went out of the room, but if she did go to the drawing room they never knew, because they never saw her again.

Those last few days Ellen spent at Markham Thorpe were the oddest of her life.

She could not bear to leave her cousin unvisited in prison. She was curious about her, concerned for her, while angry at her behaviour. She knew she was visiting someone accused of murder, and imagined her cousin kept in some horrible place like Newgate Gaol, groaning in chains, in a cell filled with violent and diseased people. So when, one dark afternoon, she went off to Ripon, she was filled with anxieties; she only knew she had to go. Agnes would not come, nor Harriet – but they told Ellen that the visit was her duty, she being the sister closest to their cousin.

Her experience was not at all what she had feared. The prison in Ripon was newly built, a modest building in a street close to the centre of the town. When Ellen nervously rang the bell, she found there was no trouble about admittance when she told the gaoler whom she wanted to see. The other prisoners were at work elsewhere in the building and the women's wing was completely quiet. She was taken down a corridor and up a flight of stairs to a passage lined with iron doors. The gaoler opened a grille in one and without looking inside – Ellen supposed this must be an act of courtesy – said, 'A visitor for you, my lady.' He let Ellen in and left the women together, without locking the door.

It was certainly a change from the boudoir at Markham Thorpe, this narrow room with its whitewashed walls and its wooden bed and its little window secured by a grille – but at least the building was clean and new, and the gaoler who admitted Ellen was decent and polite. Even in prison Lady Markham's powerful personality had had some effect, so that a few comforts – a little carpet on the floor, an oil lamp, a rug for the bed – had been admitted. Was this a sign of respect, Ellen wondered, or had Lady Markham brought money with her? More likely the latter. She was sitting immersed in a pile of papers. She was very pleased to see Ellen, and seemed a good deal more cheerful than she had been immediately after Sir Richard's death, almost as though she were enjoying the pleasures of combat.

They talked about the charge of murder. She was quite confident it would be abandoned very soon. But she did not dwell on that – the thought must frighten her, Ellen thought. Lady Markham asked about life at the house, and was very annoyed to hear that the sisters had been dismissed.

'Foolish, they are,' she said, 'and didn't James stand up for you?'

'I don't think he can resist his sisters,' said Ellen, 'particularly now, with . . . well, with . . .'

'With me in prison, you mean? No, but I shall be out in a few days. They hate me, I suppose. A family like the Markhams, they are pleasant to you as long as you are useful, and then they discard you. What will you do, Ellen, child? Will you stay in domestic service?'

'I don't know.'

'Let me be a lesson to you, my dear. See where domestic service has led me, one step from the gallows,' and she laughed loudly. Ellen wondered whether her cheerfulness was natural. 'There are other possibilities, particularly for a pretty girl like you. What is that Agnes doing, I wonder? I always thought she had plans.'

She was silent for a while. Ellen, who knew her moods well, did not try to cajole her into conversation. She went back to the subject of the Markhams.

'They think I'm vulgar,' she said, 'but what does it mean to be vulgar? I'm harder working and cleverer than any of them, and what is more I come from a good family, just as you do. It's not a mark of God to be born to moneyed parents, it's a matter of luck. You know, Ellie, I've tried to defeat my disadvantages of birth, and I had to fight hard,' and then she seemed to recollect herself and stopped. 'I suppose that I was very harsh, that the other servants hated me?'

'The servants did find you harsh. You were very severe.'

'Well, I despised them for the most part, silly and ignorant and not an ambition in their heads. But not you, of course. I hope you don't dislike me?' she went on, as though alarmed at the idea.

'No, of course not. You have always been kind to me. I owe you a great deal.'

This did not seem to satisfy her. 'I see you as a daughter,' she said, 'my little fair-haired daughter, that's what you are, I like to think. I had such a pretty idea, I wanted you to marry James, who needed a wife – ah, that would have shown them something. Two Lady Markhams from the same family.' And she chuckled gleefully.

Though Ellen did not show any reaction to this, she knew that what she had suspected was true. And since it was true, she was determined that whatever James might offer and promise, she would never marry him; nor would she spend another night with him.

'No need to worry about money, you know,' said Lady Markham. 'There's plenty of money there. I saw how badly it was being managed. Sir Richard could not handle it, nor James, so with Sir Richard's permission I moved as much money as I could into another account so it would be ready when I could do things my own way. It's all there.' She must have thought Ellen looked dubious because she went on: 'All those bits and pieces, your dresses, for example, and your jewellery, and my knick-knacks, I paid for those myself. I'm quite a wealthy woman, you know. It's always helpful to be wealthy, even in a place like this,' and she looked around complacently at the furnishing of her cell. 'They are very good to me. They bring me everything I need, and I never see the other women at all.'

After a long while (her cousin tried to detain her) Ellen left, promising she would visit again – though Lady Markham repeated that she did not expect to remain long in confinement. Ellen had arranged that the Markham Thorpe groom, who had brought her into Ripon on the back of his horse (he would do whatever she wanted), would meet her beside the obelisk in the market-place. She was walking rapidly along on the way there, thinking about her visit and the strangeness of Lady Markham's character and wondering why she, Ellen, did not hate her but was even fond of her, when she heard a voice calling, 'Ellen.' She knew the voice, but whose was it? She turned round – and there, crossing the street towards her, was a young man with fair hair, smiling uncertainly, seeming anxious to speak to her.

It was Harry, bigger and more confident. They spoke of this and that, they examined each other secretly when they thought the other was not aware, they talked about how long he was staying with his mother and father in Ripon, about whether he had written to her (he had, several times) and why she had never written back. After the first shyness, all this was very pleasant. Ellen thought what a good choice she'd made all those months ago, how sensible she was – but then what did he think of her, could he forgive her, had he found a sweetheart up in County Durham? He was more interested in telling her about his work: he told her he had a good position in a large garden with a famous head gardener who took an interest in him. Whatever she did, Mrs Rundell – she who loved to arrange people's lives for them – had found him a fine opening. In a few years it seemed likely he would become a head gardener himself. He did not speak of having found a sweetheart.

'I heard about the doings at Markham Thorpe,' he said. 'That was the reason I came home for a holiday. I just came home today. I wanted to see how you were.'

'Well,' she said, 'I could be better. I've just been visiting my old cousin.'

'That old witch, why d'you want to be visiting her? She'll be hanged, won't she?'

'No,' said Ellen hotly, 'I'm sure she won't. I must meet John and go back to Markham Thorpe.'

'Why must you go back?' he wanted to know.

But she had to, and she was firm. They agreed they would meet in the garden of the house the next day, and a long time away it seemed when they said goodbye.

The atmosphere in the house became more strained than ever. It was hard to go back to answering bells and sweeping out fires in the way the servants were used to, and in particular to show respect for the family. If it had been Sir James in the house, and nobody but Sir James, the servants would have done their best, but then he would not have dismissed them so abruptly. What they could not endure was being told what to do by the sisters. Without much discussion at all, they decided they would do as little as they could – all of them except the visiting servants, who wanted to keep their jobs.

The organisation of the household collapsed. It was not their fault – it was the family's. Since Ellen was no longer housekeeper she was determined not to act as a housemaid, any more than her little sister was – at least, after Ellen had spoken to her. Katherine had gone. Lucy stayed all day in her room. The new maids did a little cleaning for a day or two and then they more or less stopped. Mrs Lyons cooked meals but in the most unenthusiastic way possible. The family tried to have dinner in the normal style one evening, and it was not a success. In the morning Mrs Wentworth had marched into the kitchen, flustered and nervous, and ordered dinner, but the dinner she ordered was not the meal that was served thirty minutes late that evening, after repeated ringings of the bell. Enormous quantities of not-quite-cooked Yorkshire puddings were borne to the dining room by the unwilling hands of Mr Wentworth's valet, followed by a large burnt joint of mutton. It seemed to amuse Mrs Lyons to make the meal as unpleasant as possible. The mutton – which returned hardly touched, large tough slices lying on the plates – was followed by a piece of Cheddar cheese so large and hard you could hardly cut it. She excelled herself with the pudding, a sponge that had failed to rise, a flat bed of yellowness covered with thick, reddish jam, which also came back almost uneaten. While the atmosphere in the servants' hall was hardly cordial, they felt a grim hilarity at seeing these mounds of horrid food. They, on the other hand, ate beef cooked to perfection, with horseradish sauce, as succulent as they had ever tasted. Nor were things better for the family in the morning: nobody called them, the breakfast that Mrs Lyons provided was indescribably horrid. After that they took their meals at the Unicorn. What was curious was that the family did not say anything about this meal, not even Mrs Wentworth. No recriminations, no complaints. The only servants they could bring themselves to speak to were their own, the visiting servants, who provided basic comforts. Otherwise it was as though the servants' hall and the drawing room were at war.

Ellen found this episode curious and revealing; it made her realise the vulnerability of people dependent on always being served. She longed to be able to escape from this prison: the house was so depressing and confining. The only thing that comforted her was meeting Harry every day. In a house full of people who suspected and disliked each other, with the family afraid of their servants and the servants despising their masters, yet afraid of them as well, the sense that some awful revelation was about to break made life hard to bear. And it was uncomfortable, and cold, and only a few fires were lit, and with thick snow you could hardly go outside for more than a few minutes. Ellen's only refuge was the housekeeper's room where she would sit, huddled under her covers, staring at the wall.

Only on the day of the funeral did the servants try harder, out of respect for Sir Richard, most of them following the hearse to the parish church behind the family and providing some reasonable dinner afterwards. It was a very small funeral, only the household. The widow, of course, was not present.

They talked to one another, of course – that is, they talked to the people they trusted, but only to them. No general conversation was possible: nobody could be confident that what they said might not be passed on to someone else in a dangerous way. Could Sir James have killed his father? People knew the two had never got on well and, after all, Sir James stood to inherit the estate, and maybe his father's marriage had been more than he could endure. Ellen never had any truck with this idea: she knew him too well. Or was it indeed Mrs Rundell – the moment she had secured the title and the right of inheritance, had she destroyed him? Ellen was never convinced of that either, but it was the view of some. Or the doctor? Or the lawyer, who spent so much time in the house? Or one of the servants? But how could it have been one of the servants? What would they have gained from Sir Richard's death? And, of course, it was possible that Sir Richard had died of natural causes brought on by rich food and much liquor and the other things he had indulged in on the day before he died.

And then it became clear who must have performed this act, or so at least they thought for a while. A few days after Christmas word came from the police in Ripon that the body of a woman had been found in the woods about four miles from the house, a wild, lonely place far from habitation. She was wearing the indoor clothes of a servant, and the gamekeeper who found her knew she must come from Markham Thorpe. It was Katherine, poor wretched Katherine, who had fled from the house taking nothing with her but a knife and had tried to cut her wrists. She had only partially succeeded so she had bled slowly to death alone, and no doubt frozen too, in the bitter cold of that dismal wood. She must have murdered Sir Richard, presumably by poison, though why they could not understand. Ellen was appalled to see how exciting some of the people in the house, men and women alike, found this tale. They told it and retold it, they savoured every detail of how she might have died, of how long her dying would have lasted, of her condition when she was found. The family would have nothing to do with the case and she was given a pauper's burial, attended only by two or three.

So if it was Katherine who had performed the act, what was the role of Lady Markham (as the servants now always referred to her, largely to annoy the Markham family)? She could hardly have colluded with Katherine, surely? Lady Markham was still in the gaol, and when Ellen went to visit her a second time it did not seem that she was agitating for release. She had been moved to the gaoler's house next door, and was reasonably comfortable. It was not quite clear to her whether she was still being held on suspicion of murder but it was likely, she thought, that the Markhams wanted her kept in prison. 'I am well enough here,' she said. 'I cannot go away, and I cannot stay at Markham Thorpe, and I would not be comfortable at the Unicorn with the whole town staring at me like geese, so I had better stay here until the truth is revealed.' To Ellen's surprise, she seemed sorry for Katherine. 'Poor fool,' she said. 'Life was too difficult for her, poor girl, but I suppose I did not help. I was not very kind to her. Will you write to her mother, Ellen, nobody else will, and send her this money?' and she gave her a purse full of coins. Was this kindness? Or was it a pretence of gentility? At any rate it was more human than the complete indifference shown by the Markham family.

Though most of the servants did their best not to serve the Markhams, they kept a watch on what was going on. Agnes, who always had a way with men particularly if they were rather older than she was, made herself very agreeable to the family lawyer, who was often at the house. She teased out of him a good deal about Sir Richard's will. The house and the estate were entailed on his son, and nobody else could inherit them. On the other hand, his widow was entitled to one-third of the income from the estate for life. Sir Richard possessed substantial funds of his own, left by his first wife, and these he had left outright to the second, with no bequests to his daughters. It appeared that the second Lady Markham would be a very wealthy woman, at the expense of the family. On the other hand, if she was found guilty, she would inherit nothing. All this information, in increasingly elaborate and inaccurate form, was circulated in the servants' hall and the stables and the gardeners' houses and, no doubt, all round the estate and Ripon as well. There was no doubt that the family would be much more prosperous without her.

Ellen and the others were obliged to stay at Markham Thorpe.

She found it hard to be in the same house as Sir James. They would meet now and again, and he would fix his eyes on her like a mournful St Bernard. She would not speak, merely curtsy to him, but for all her apparent indifference it hurt her to see him. He might have conspired to get her, but she could not stop feeling fond of him. She must be firm, she told herself, she must be stern and, if necessary, cruel: there was no reason for her to have anything more to do with this house or any of the people in it. All the same, it was not easy to follow these principles. She tried to help him as a way of assuaging those feelings, and because he looked so lost and confused, with those sisters gabbling away at him day and night. She did achieve something practical: she prevailed on little Maud to look after Sir James's rooms, to make sure his fire was lit in the morning and to take up his bathwater at night. After all, she said to herself, he is the baronet and he must be reasonably comfortable – and who knows? Maud is quite a pretty girl and he may come to take a kindly interest in her, one of these days.

As often as possible she met Harry, either in the garden of the house or in Ripon, where they took chilly walks hand in hand by the river. They talked about how she would escape soon, and how he would take her home to his parents and then they would be married. He was quite set in his ideas, she found, and liked to tell her what she should be doing – she did not altogether like this. She supposed that she had changed too, after her period of authority as housekeeper, and was not used to being given such strict instructions. But nothing really clouded their happiness.

A week or so after Christmas there was a further turn of events.

Ellen still slept in the old housekeeper's bedroom, next to the housekeeper's sitting room where she had been received when she first arrived as a housemaid, with the still room on the other side of the passage. Mrs Wentworth had told her to move upstairs to one of the maid's rooms but Ellen had stared her boldly in the face, pushing her chin up in the air as rudely as she could. This defiance so surprised her that she blenched and did not press the matter. Ellen was determined not to move to a wretched maid's bedroom. She was sleeping badly and the comfort of the room made the long, cruel nights easier.

That particular night she awoke very suddenly, as though she had heard a noise in her dreams. The room was completely dark, the fire had quite gone out, and she pressed the repeater by her bed. It was three o'clock. It was so cold she could feel the frost on her cheeks. For a moment she wondered why she had woken, and enjoyed the warmth of the feather bed. Since she heard nothing more, she almost fell back to sleep. But as she was dozing off she again heard the noise that had woken her. It was a scratching sound in the passage outside. Not rats, not a cat, not the wind, but something that must be human.

She climbed out of bed, nervous but determined. The cold struck her like a fist. She felt in the dark for a match to light the candle, then remembered she should not let herself be seen or heard. She crept towards the door and put her head against it. She heard a door closing, a key turning in a lock. It must be the door of the still room. It occurred to her, in a jarring moment of terror, that it might be someone coming to kill her.

She pulled open her door, as cautiously as she could, but it made a creaking sound. The passage was dark, but just as she began to open the door she glimpsed a light. It was hastily extinguished. She was very frightened. She hesitated, not wanting to advance or retreat. As she did so, she heard footsteps, very faint, and had the impression of a figure slipping past her in the pitch black. It was a very light figure, she thought, a woman or possibly a boy.

She wondered whether to pursue it, but soon gave up the idea. In the dark and the cold and with no idea of where the person had gone, other than towards the servants' side – which was a rabbit warren on the brightest day – she could not bring herself to go further. She slipped back into her room, locked the door, and went back to bed, though not to sleep.

As soon as it was light, she unlocked her door and looked out into the passage. No sign of anything. She could not unlock the door of the still room since the house keys had been taken from her when she was dismissed and, in any case, the still-room key had always been her cousin's. But someone else, it was clear, had a key to the still room and was willing to use it. Lucy? Mrs Wentworth?

The police inspector was back at the house that morning, as he was most mornings. Ellen asked to see him, and told him what had happened. He pursed his lips, thought for a while and went off.

Two days later he returned, and asked Ellen to assemble all the indoor servants in the Great Hall at twelve noon. She remarked that she had no authority in the house now, but he told her that this was an order. Accordingly they all came together at noon, a dozen or so, including the visiting servants. They could hear the stable clock chiming the hour although the clocks in the house had stopped because nobody had wound them. There were the Wentworths and the Dykeses and Sir James, lined up in their black clothes on a row of chairs by the fireplace, like a line of crows on a winter branch. There was no fire and the Great Hall felt like the Arctic Pole: it was a cruel day outside, snowing once again, the light quite dead. They sat down on the benches on either side of the long table. Miss Fisher sat on her own in a corner, looking out of the window, humming and talking to herself.

The inspector spoke. He said he was still unable to piece together the events of Christmas Eve, but that he had several clues. He talked for quite a while, in a soothing voice, explaining his fears that the murder might have been performed by a person entering the house in the middle of the night. Nobody shifted while he spoke. Then, abruptly, in a loud, accusing voice that made them all feel they must be guilty, he said, 'Someone went into the still room three nights ago, at three o'clock. Who was it?' Silence. 'Who was it?' More silence. They stared at him, not moving. 'I will not let you go,' he said, 'until I know the truth.' He knocked on the table, and as he did so the three doors to the hall were opened, and at each door stood a constable.

Before they knew what was happening, a woman's voice was speaking. It was Lucy.

'It was me,' she said. 'I went into the still room. I like to go there, I spent so much of my life working there, I like to go there from time to time and make sure it is all in order.' She stared at the ground as she said all this.

'Why did you go there at three in the morning?' he asked.

'I can't go during the day, can I, sir? Someone would see me, and ask what I was doing. No one knows that I kept a key to the still room when I ceased to be still-room maid. I can only go there at night.'

'Did you take anything out of the still room?'

'Oh, no, sir, nothing at all.'

'Did you take anything there, and leave it?'

Hesitation from Lucy.

'Did you not leave a jar there, at the back of the cupboard? A black jar with a silver top, which I am informed is the property of the former housekeeper?'

Lucy looked wildly around the room, as though seeking advice, but did not speak.

'Is it not true that this jar was previously used by Mrs Rundell to contain a tincture, which she applied to her eyes? A tincture that could be used for another purpose? Tincture of bella donna? Lucy Herring, it is my belief that you stole the bella donna from the still room, with the intention of poisoning Sir Richard, and that three nights ago you placed the jar back in the cupboard so that no one would find it around the house. Is that true?'

'I took it, yes,' said Lucy, 'and I put the bella donna in the teapot.' She spoke in a little frightened voice, like a child. Her body had changed in a few moments. Always small, now she had shrivelled into a tiny, twisted person. Then she began to cry.

The inspector looked pleased. He had, he must have thought, solved the problem. But not for long. From the corner came a loud, cackling laugh. 'You silly man, you silly inspector,' cried a voice, a mad voice, from the corner of the room, 'you don't understand at all. Lucy put the poison into the tea, but it was my idea, not hers.'

Miss Fisher stood up. This was not the Miss Fisher they had known. This was a wild person. Her wig had slipped off her head and she was quite bald. She trembled like a tree in a gale, and clutched at her black skirts.

'You don't understand,' she said, 'none of us wanted to kill Sir Richard — why would we want to do that? That was not bella donna for a gentleman, it was bella donna for a beautiful lady. It was Rundell we wanted to kill. We thought our dose of bella donna would stop her eyes sparkling, would make them dim. But she gave her tea to Sir Richard, and the whole house came tumbling down.'

Postscript

Miss Fisher was found guilty of the crime of murder, but was judged to be of unsound mind. She was sent to an asylum where she spent the rest of her long life.

Lucy was found guilty of murder, but the court agreed that she had been led astray by the governess. She was given a twenty-year sentence, and died in prison soon after.

Lady Markham was released immediately from gaol. After concluding a good deal of business with the Markham family, to their mutual advantage, she moved to Cheltenham, where she became an important figure in local society. She married a retired colonel and proved a model wife, except that she insisted on retaining her title.

Sir James recovered from these events and lived decently as a country gentleman. He married a clergyman's daughter, and had several children. His sisters would visit him from time to time, but not very often, particularly not Mrs Wentworth.

Agnes made a good life for herself, in her own terms. She was happy with the three gentlemen she lived with, one after the other, and she made them happy too. They each remained her protector until their death, when one after another they left her a respectable sum of money. She was never mentioned again by the Braithwaite parents but Ellen would see her quite often. She never told her husband that she did this.

As for Ellen, she left Markham Thorpe as soon as she could, and married Harry. His parents were not pleased at all, nor were hers, but the young people were both determined, and ignored their elders. They had a child, a boy, born surprisingly soon, only seven months after the marriage. He was christened William James, and was the first and last child they had. Harry turned out to be not quite what Ellen had thought he would be. As she discovered, he was self-confident to the point of being domineering, and she found after a while that she did not care for this. What was more, he was more interested in his gardening and his career than in her. She had her compensations or, rather, she created them for herself. After a while they spent less time together, and while he stayed on the large country estates where he worked as a prized head gardener, she lived mostly in London. She wrote novels and books about history, publishing one almost every year, and had quite a fine reputation as a writer.

Though she always liked to be informed by her friends in Yorkshire of what was happening at Markham Thorpe, she never went back there. She always kept a photograph of the house in her sitting room, in spite of her husband's protests. And when Sir James Markham died, many years after the events in this story, she sent a wreath to the funeral, with the inscription 'From E. and W.J.' on the card. Nobody in the Markham family ever knew from whom it came.